2.50

W9-BZO-532

Praise for Richard S. Wheeler and the Skye's West Series

"A master storyteller whose heart is obviously in the West."
—*Library Journal*

"Skye is the Horatio Hornblower of the Rockies!"
—*Rocky Mountain News*

"Wheeler is among the top living writers of Westerns—if not the best."
—*Kirkus Reviews*

"Wheeler deftly balances the violence and cruelty of frontier life with the love and tenderness of a husband and wife caught between cultures."
—*Publishers Weekly* on *The Fire Arrow*

"Let's face it, it's always nice to spend time with Barnaby. Recommended most heartily to anyone who likes a good, old-fashioned Western yarn."
—*Booklist* on *The Fire Arrow*

"Wheeler's Skye is a much more well-rounded character than one usually finds in Western literature. He is intelligent, erudite, compassionate, and self-aware. The thirteenth entry in the series is one of the most satisfying."
—*Booklist* on *The Deliverance*

BY RICHARD S. WHEELER
FROM TOM DOHERTY ASSOCIATES

North Star

A Barnaby Skye Novel

RICHARD S. WHEELER

A Tom Doherty Associates Book
New York

NORTH STAR: A BARNABY SKYE NOVEL

Copyright © 2009 by Richard S. Wheeler

A Forge Book
Published by Tom Doherty Associates, LLC
175 Fifth Avenue
New York, NY 10010

www.tor-forge.com

Forge® is a registered trademark of Tom Doherty Associates, LLC.

ISBN 978-0-7653-5583-6

First Edition: February 2009
First Mass Market Edition: January 2010

Printed in the United States of America

0 9 8 7 6 5 4 3 2 1

For Sue, my North Star

North Star

prologue

J awbone was stumbling now and then, but Mister Skye didn't mind. The ugly old horse still had a great heart and was as eager as he always had been. Skye was hunting high in the Birdsong Mountains this November day, and on the trail of two elk whose hoof prints unwound in the rain-dampened earth.

Except for a dusting of snow on the craggy peaks, there was little sign of impending winter. The snow and cold of the uplands had not yet driven the elk and deer down the long shoulders to warmer and safer habitat. A sharp wind cut into Skye's leathers, chilling him, but he had endured harsh winds and rain and snow and cold for half a century, and he could endure this wind too. But it made his bones ache.

Skye led an empty packhorse with a sawbuck saddle on it. If he killed an elk, he could carry most of it back to his wives and his lodge far below by quartering it and loading some of it on both horses. If that happened he would walk. He wouldn't mind that, either, because he would be bringing good meat to Victoria and Mary, his two Indian wives, and there would be some to give to the elders and the widows in the Kicked-in-the-Bellies winter encampment on Sweet Grass Creek.

He rode easily, his old mountain rifle cradled in his arm, ready to use. He knew the two elk were not far ahead, in this sheltered upland valley. Most of the timber was well below.

He didn't see the bear until it was too late. The giant, humpbacked grizzly had been denning, clawing its way into a steep hillside to prepare for its hibernation, but now it backed out of the hole, swung around, eyed Skye and his horses with small pig eyes, and didn't hesitate. It lumbered down, amazingly fast for so big an animal, an odd hiss slipping from its mouth, and Skye suddenly had no time at all. Skye swung the octagon barrel of his rifle around, but the bear rose up on its hind legs, even as Jawbone screeched and sidled away and the packhorse broke free and fled.

The blow knocked Skye clear out of his saddle, and another caught Jawbone and raked red furrows along the old horse's withers. Jawbone reeled sideways, stumbled, and then fell on Skye, who had landed on his shoulder. Skye yanked his rifle around, pointed, and fired. The rifle bucked, slammed into his ruined chest, but it caught the huge brown grizzly in the shoulder, plowing a red furrow into the caramel-colored hair.

The grizzly paused, snapped at the wound on his shoulder, where blood was swiftly rising into the hair, and then whined. It paused and licked its wound, mewling and crying like a child, sobbing and licking. It sat on its hind legs, upright, furiously working at its wound, unable to slow the blood or subdue its pain, its sobbing eerie and sad.

Skye watched from the ground. Jawbone had clambered off of him and stood, head down, shaking with his own pain.

Cruel red lines gouged his flesh. Skye's own shoulder ached, and he bled from a few places. He had no wind in him, and his arms didn't work, and he had trouble breathing. He couldn't lift his rifle even if he needed it again. He would need to make his old body work, or he would perish here. He would need to return seven or eight miles to the Crow camp, and he would need to do it without help, for there was none.

The bear, still whimpering, limped toward its almost completed den and pushed into the hillside. Skye knew it wouldn't come out until spring. Skye lay helplessly on the grade, staring at the blue heavens, which had mare's tails corduroying it now. The weather would change soon, maybe for good. He tried to inventory his body. He had a few scratches but those six-inch, lethal claws had only scraped him. They smarted but weren't bleeding. Wind eddied into the slashes left in his leather hunting coat. His pain made him faint, but he was used to pain. A half a century in the North American wilds had brought him more than his share of pain, but also inured him to it. But he could not lift his arms, or twist his body, or get himself to his feet.

He knew that time would help. He eyed Jawbone, who stood with legs locked, head low, going through his own torment. The blood on Jawbone's withers had stopped flowing and was coagulating in the cold. He couldn't see the packhorse, but it wouldn't be far away. Time, little by little, restored some control of his limbs to him, and he rolled onto his side. It was then that he saw his bearclaw necklace lying in the grass. It had been given to him when he was young, a sacred symbol among his Absaroka People of his bear medicine. His brothers were the grizzly bears, and during the whole half century he had never shot a grizzly, nor had one ever attacked him, until now. Maybe his bear medicine had finally failed. This ornery old grizzly male had come at him, and he had shot it. And now the medicine bond between Skye and the bears had been shattered. Skye gathered the remnants of the necklace. The giant gray claws had been separated by blue trade beads, and the whole ensemble had never failed to win admiration and respect among those who examined it. He picked up the beads and claws that had scattered when the necklace was torn from his chest, and these he tenderly folded into his coat pocket.

That was oddly disturbing to him. It was an ending, a shattering of an ancient bond that had made the grizzly bears his brothers and sisters, his spirit helpers in time of need. He lay quietly another while, but the wind was picking up, and he knew he would either get up now or not ever get up. He found his rifle and used it for a crutch, slowly pulling himself to his feet. He stared around the serene upland valley, its grasses brown now, its aspen bare-limbed, the gray rock and tawny earth naked to the elements. He saw his packhorse grazing downslope, dragging its lead line, undamaged.

Jawbone limped close and gently pressed his muzzle into Skye's chest. They were a pair, and they had survived yet again.

It would be a long walk back to the winter camp, but Skye knew he would make it, would have to make it. There would be no elk roasting over the fire this night.

one

One bitter dawn in 1870, Barnaby Skye realized he had not lived in a house for fifty-two years. He was thirteen years old when a press gang snatched him off the cobbled streets of East End, in London, and he found himself a powder monkey in the Royal Navy. For seven cruel years he had lived in the bowels of frigates, and after that, in the wilds of North America. But never again in a place with a kitchen and hearth and bedroom and parlor.

He wrapped his blanket tight about him against the brutal cold, crawled out the door of his buffalo-hide lodge, and slowly made his way over trampled snow to the red willow bushes, where he might find relief. More and more, as he aged, he needed to get up in the night. No matter that he was inured to discomfort after a lifetime spent out-of-doors. It was getting harder and harder to live in this fashion, among his wife Victoria's Kicked-in-the-Bellies clan of the Absaroka People, drifting through the seasons to wherever the buffalo ran or the berries ripened. Twice a night now, sometimes more, he stepped into cold, or heat, or rain, or snow, or wind. He had no choice.

He stumbled once as his moccasin plunged into a soft patch, but finally reached the willow brush away from the lodges, where he waited and waited for the slow stream to begin and comfort to return to his belly. He was sixty-five, and feeling it. The changes in his body had come on cat feet, and he had missed or ignored them, until now. The cold stung his cheeks and bit his ears, no matter that a dense gray beard now covered his weathered face. By the time he was done, he was cold.

A deep silence pervaded the winter camp of the Crows on Sweet Grass Creek. Dawn was simply a rose streak to the southeast, the beginning of another brief day. No one stirred. A few frosted ponies stood desolately, tethered close to the lodges, their breaths cloudy. Most of the lodge fires had died, and in this last hour before the camp stirred, the people lay buried in buffalo robes in skin tents that did little to turn the hard fist of winter.

Skye headed back to his own lodge, one of twenty-three here, and to his women, Victoria of the Absarokas and Mary of the Shoshones, who were used to his night-stirring and ignored it. But as he returned to his home, which was nothing but a thin buffalo hide that walled the bitter cold from those who lived within, a long-suppressed idea arose in his mind.

He needed a home. A real white man's home, with a hearth and stove, with beds and chairs and tables and windows and doors and escape from murderous winds and blistering heat and vicious deluges. He didn't want to live Indian style anymore. Victoria's people, the Absarokas, lived in lodges that they moved from time to time, and took their old and sick with them until the day came when the old and sick could be moved no more. And then the old ones were usually left to die, propped up under a tree with a little food and water. Sometimes they were left to die alone, in weakness and pain and a terrible cold infiltrating their bodies, because there was no other way.

Skye had watched the Crows leave old Indians behind. These were fathers and mothers, grandmothers and grandfathers, uncles and aunts. People he knew. Usually that was the choice of the old ones, who knew death was coming and accepted it. They asked to be taken apart and their wish was always granted. They wished to sing their death songs and be left behind, given to the sun and the wind and the spirits. It was something that the old themselves requested when the time was right and they were ready. Winter was more merciful to them than summer because they did not linger. Sometimes, though, when the village was in peril of death or disease or catastrophe, the old and sick were simply abandoned because there was no other way. There might not be horses or travois to carry them. So they were left on the spirit road, left to begin their long walk on the star-strewn trails of the heavens. Skye understood all of that, and yet he could not reconcile himself to it.

Now, in the middle of a bitter night, he hoped he might grow old and die in a house. As much as he had adapted to Victoria's ways, there was still the Englishman in him. And now the Englishman was hurting.

He pulled aside the flap with fingers already numb and stepped into the thick gloom. Above, in the smoke hole, ice-chip stars still were visible. A layer of frost coated the inside of the lodge cover, as well as the liner. It had been formed from human breath. His wives didn't stir. It was almost as bitter within as outside. He found his bed, two thick robes on the ground to protect against the terrible cold rising from it, and another he pulled over himself. But he scarcely warmed even after waiting for the thin heat to build in his bed.

He had ignored the rheumatism for years, but now he could not. Most of him hurt most of the time. He wasn't sure that rheumatism was the proper word, but it was the only word he knew for pain that radiated across his back, pierced his arms and legs, annoyed his joints, and often made his wrists and hands hurt so much it was hard even to chop wood. Whatever it was, it had sneaked into his life almost without his knowing it, and now he could not ignore it anymore. He wasn't so old, but his hard life had taken a toll. In the Royal Navy he had sometimes been colder and more miserable than he ever had been in North America. And here in the American West, he had waded icy rivers, been caught in blizzards, been soaked by cruel rains, and spent many a sleepless night shivering in wet clothes that could not be dried. And now he hurt night and day.

The heavy robes did little to comfort him. He lay impatiently, waiting for the day to begin. His wives would build up the fire and hope that the downdraft of wintry air wouldn't dampen the flames and fill the lodge with acrid smoke. He looked about him, suddenly dissatisfied with this thin layer of buffalo hide keeping the elements at bay. He wanted a house. He had never had one of his own in all of his years, and now he wanted a comfortable, solid, safe, spacious home, ten times larger than the largest lodge of the Absarokas, planted firmly in his own soil, surrounded by gardens and livestock and fields of grain and pastures.

He felt guilty. For decades Skye's home had been with Victoria's people, and sometimes with Mary's Shoshone people. Wherever they drifted, he drifted with them, as much at

home on the plains or foothills or mountains as they were.
Home was wherever they were, not just a white man's building on white men's land, surrounded by white men's neighbors. For the Crows and Shoshones, home was where the
land offered meat and roots, lodgepoles, handsome mountains, rushing creeks, soaring eagles, and safety. They had
never divided up the land, surveyed it, sold off pieces. It was
all one to them. And it had been all one to Skye, too, for all
these seasons.

But this bitter January morning, he knew he needed a
home. He wondered how Victoria would feel about it, and
how Mary would. They were traditional Indians, and home
was wherever they happened to be. If Skye were to settle
somewhere, how would Victoria feel about leaving her people? Home, for her, was being among her people: her clan
brothers and sisters, the women who shared her day scraping
hides or gathering roots or making moccasins. Home for her
was a migrating neighborhood, not a place.

He peered at her, resting still and quiet and oblivious. She
had slowed too. He had caught her straightening up after
scraping a hide, caught the stoic look on her face that told him
she ached in her shoulders and her back. She worked ceaselessly, as did Mary; there was no surcease from toil for a tribal
woman. Even the very old women sat quietly working with
awls or needles, making what needed to be made. Maybe Victoria, Many Quill Woman to her own people, might welcome
a comfortable log home, as long as it was close to her own
band. He would ask her after the day opened.

Mary, twenty years younger, was by nature more accepting, and Skye sensed that she would slip into a new mode of
life well enough. But a certain sadness clung to her, and she
seemed to pass through her days without the fire and joy that

had drawn Skye to her when she was a beautiful Shoshone girl called Blue Dawn, a granddaughter of Sacajawea. Ever since Skye had sent their son, Dirk, east to be schooled, Mary had settled deep inside of herself, living within her own private world. Skye had often agonized about it, but there was nothing he could do. His son was gone.

Skye lay in his robes, wondering how he might get a house. He had no money and none of the skills that might earn him some. He was the son of a London export merchant, and ill-equipped to plow and harrow and plant. The beaver were trapped out; game was steadily vanishing, killed by the white men. The buffalo were doomed, though Skye hoped the herds might prosper for another twenty or thirty years. But a man who hoped to build a home would need a way to sustain himself. Raise horses? They'd be stolen by the first raiding party. Raise cattle? Better, perhaps. Some cattle, horses, a garden, poultry, some grain fields, maybe these would support a man with a house.

Skye lay quietly, staring out the smoke hole, watching the gray light brighten. If he were young, he might manage. A young man full of energy could build his own house of log or rock or sawn wood, and mortar together a hearth and chimney. He could fell the logs and bark them and drag them to the house behind a stout horse, and notch them and jack them into place, one by one. He could split shakes and shingle the roof. He could raise the outbuildings, fence pastures and paddocks, sink a well, cobble together a homestead, plow the virgin earth and plant grain fields and gardens, scythe hay and fork it to a barn loft, feed it out to his horses and cattle in the winter, and somehow get along. But he was old now. Just when he needed a home, his strength had fled him.

Then he discovered Victoria, lying on her side, staring at him.

And as if by some mysterious communication, Mary yawned, sat up, and swiftly tugged a soft, thick robe about her, even over her jet hair. Their breaths steamed. Not even a lodge with an inner lining could stop the cold this morning.

"You have something to say," Victoria said.

She always read his mind. Skye sat up, clamped his ancient black top hat over his locks, and tried to warm himself.

"I do," he said. "After we are warm and have eaten."

"You are leaving us," Victoria persisted.

It had been her nightmare all these decades. Someday the white man would grow tired of living the way her people lived, and walk away. How many times, over four decades, had she leaped to that? How often had he tried to assure her, only to run into dark flowers of fear.

"No," he said. He would say more when he was ready.

She threw off her robe. She was already in her doeskin dress. She wore it all winter, but in the summer she dressed as brightly as a flock of butterflies.

This time he watched her closely, and saw that rising from the bed of robes took determination. Not that she was old or feeble. Not that he was old. But no mortal steps into subzero air without determination and courage. The very sight of her struggling to wrap a blanket around her, and make for the bushes, hardened his resolve.

Only Mary didn't seem to mind the numbing cold. She slipped out of her robes, eyed him shyly—he always marveled at her shyness, even after many years of marriage—and plunged outside with little more than a thin summer blanket carelessly over her shoulders.

He thought to start a fire, even though Victoria would

scold him. It was not men's work, she would snap, but she would be secretly pleased that he was thinking of her comfort. He made himself collect some of the kindling outside of their lodge, and with his skinning knife shaved bits of it, and added a pinch of gunpowder from his horned flask. He would not wrestle with flint and steel this morning, not with some trading post lucifers at hand. He struck one, watched the powder flare, and watched the tiny flame lick the kindling and catch. By the time the women returned from the brush, there would be a thin warmth in Mister Skye's lodge, and the nine-foot circle of his home would begin to welcome life.

two

There wasn't much to eat. For two moons the village hunters had been stymied by cold so terrible that no one could leave the lodges. It was bad enough to look after the frostbitten, starving horses. No, this was a time to huddle around fires, sing songs, play the stick game, and endure.

Mary set a kettle of snow to heating, and added pemmican and some prairie turnips, to make a breakfast stew. The lodge warmed a bit. The frost coating the lodge liner melted and dripped onto Skye and his women. The fire gathered muscle and drove heat outward and smoke upward.

No one spoke. But they all knew this was a portentous moment, and that this day Mister Skye would say a thing that would affect their lives. He was always Mister Skye. Friends and family addressed him that way because he required it. When he had arrived in the New World, fleeing the crown's minions, he chose to give himself that title. He would be Mister Skye, and not just Skye, and so it had been for decades. Others laughed at him, thought it was pretentious, but he was always *Mister*, and if you wanted any sort of commerce with him, you would address him as he required.

With a good stout fire going, the lodge warmed, except underfoot, where the cold rose straight through the robes lying on the clay. The thin warmth helped, but both Skye and Victoria clothed themselves in red Hudson's Bay blankets even so. Mary ladled out the stew; it might not be a king's feast, but it would fill them. When they were done with the morning food, she silently gathered the bowls and horn spoons and wiped them clean.

They were waiting, he knew.

But he was stumble-tongued, as usual, and hardly knew where to begin.

"I want a home," he said. "For all of us."

"Is this not a home?" Victoria asked.

"A comfortable home," Skye said.

"Is this not a good lodge?" she persisted.

"I'm getting old," he said.

"Well, so am I, dammit. And so is she."

Skye ran bony fingers through his matted gray hair. He wore a trimmed beard now. His hands were stained to the color of walnuts by a life out-of-doors. He gazed at Victoria, who was dark and suspicious and already angry. Mary, with little gray in her glossy jet hair, waited patiently, her obsidian eyes masking her thoughts.

This was already brewing into a domestic fight.

"I don't mean away from your people," he said to Victoria. "Somewhere close by."

This resulted in a terrible silence.

"I have a great need—I'll call it a hunger—for a house. A refuge against wind and rain and snow and cold and a hot sun."

He knew that these women considered their lodge to be just such a refuge, and often it was. Some periods of the year, a lodge was a marvel of comfort. But in the blistering heat of summer, and the howl of winter, it could be miserable.

"It is harder and harder for me to live like this," he said. "I need chairs to sit in, a warm bed to sleep in. I need to stand up. I want walls that keep out the wind. Walls and a roof to keep out the cold and the heat and the rain and keep me warm. I would like a hearth, and a cast-iron stove, and maybe an oven. I would like to sleep off of the ground, so my legs and arms don't ache."

He saw not the slightest response in either of his wives.

"I am not as patient as your people," he said. "My own people, the English and the Americans, live in houses when they can. Log ones, or wooden frame ones such as we've seen in the mining towns. Glass in the windows. Roofs of shakes that carry the rain away. I'm hurting a bit and this would help me. I'm not planning on leaving this earth anytime soon. I want to be with you. I'd like to grow old in a little comfort. Maybe with our pastures and a garden and a woods where we can get fuel. A few cattle, a few sheep, some chickens to feed us. I'd like to build a shelter for Jawbone, now that he's hurting, and give him his own meadow, and lots to eat."

The silence returned and clung there.

"Where would this be?" Victoria asked.

"Near your people," he said. "Here we are, near the Birdsong Mountains. I would like to build my home over in the next valley, the Shields River, where everything is at hand, and everywhere the eye gazes, there is glory."

White men were calling the jagged and isolated mountains just to the west of this winter camp the Crazy Mountains, but Skye much preferred the Crow name, the Birdsong

Mountains. What could be a more beautiful name for an iso-lated range of sharp peaks?

"But we would live there alone," she said.

"We would have many Absaroka visitors, and maybe we could care for your clan brothers and sisters and children, and they could care for us. Maybe they could help us build this place, and we could have them stay with us and take care of things."

Something dissolved in Victoria's spirit. Skye knew that if she could have some of her people around her, she would be pleased. Home for her was not a lodge, it was a village.

"Sonofabitch," she said. "I'm going to have a big house. Biggest goddamn house anywhere. Big enough for my whole clan."

It dawned on Skye that if he built a house, it would have to hold thirty or forty of Victoria's relatives. But that was fine with him. There was a way to do this. He would ask his Crow friends for help, and together they could erect a house and the outbuildings, and then farm or ranch with him.

"I have always wanted to live in a house," said Mary. "A white man's house is a place of great medicine."

"And it would be a place for some of your Shoshone peo-ple too," he said.

She smiled so sadly that he felt stricken. Anything that reminded her of her Shoshone people also reminded her that she had seen very little of them as the winters and summers rolled by. Skye and his wives had lived among the Crows.

"This is women's work," Victoria said. "We will build the wooden lodge."

"It's men's work, and hard. We have to fell the trees, bark the logs, notch them, use a drawknife to flatten the top and bottom sides, split shakes, make a puncheon floor . . ."

"What is this floor?"

"Logs carefully split down the middle which will make a floor, curved sides down, flat sides up."

"Dirt ain't good enough for you?"

Skye was tired of clay; tired of walking on it, tired of the bugs crawling out of it, tired of mud and grass. "We can do better," he said. "If the right kind of rock is around, we can use flagstones for a floor. Wood is more comfortable."

A house. Nothing but a dream now, in the middle of deep cold and near starvation.

The more Skye talked to his wives, the less he hurt. It was as if the promise of comfort was sweeping away all the rheumatism in his body. He was aware that his women were studying him, receiving unspoken knowledge from his conduct. Let them study him. The more this great vision filled his imagination, the younger he felt. By the time he began building his house, he would be a young man again.

"I am thinking about the Shields River valley, just north of the Yellowstone," he said. That was a lush broad valley west of them, near the great bend of the Yellowstone. There would be running water, meadows for grazing stock, ample pine and cottonwood and willow and aspen.

"That is a good place," Victoria said. "The People visit there every summer. Magpie always makes great noises when we are there."

The magpie was Victoria's spirit helper, and she received occult wisdom from her communing with the insolent and raucous black and white bird.

The Shields stretched northward from where it debouched into the Yellowstone, through open country with the Birdsong Mountains rising to the east, and a great range white men were calling the Bridgers rising to the west. Skye had passed through that country many times. Some places might offer grander vistas, but no place offered so much of what the earth could provide.

And there was something else:

"The Americans are talking about giving the Crows a homeland south of the Yellowstone," he said.

"We got a homeland!" Victoria said. "What the hell is this?"

Skye dreaded what he had to say. "They say they want to settle your people on the land south of the river."

"How do you know this?"

Skye wasn't sure where he had heard it. Long ago he had concluded he could do little about the Americans flooding through Crow country en route to mining camps. For a few years they came up the Bozeman Trail, until the great Sioux chief Red Cloud stopped them, defeated the United States Army, and forced the Yanks to abandon the trail. Skye had made some money guiding wagon trains over that trail, through some of the most dangerous country in the West, but then the traffic stopped, and so had his income. So once again he lived as the Crows did, migrating from place to place, following the buffalo, defending their land against the Siksika and the Lakota. But someone, somewhere, told him the United States government had plans for the Crows, and they would be confined to a reserve. It was, he thought, the finest piece of land on the continent, and teeming with game, so there was solace in it. But it all heralded great change for Victoria's people, and for himself.

The Shields River country he would call home would be just north of the proposed reservation. That ought to suit Victoria, and it ought to suit the Yanks. They surely wouldn't boot him off the land he settled. Or would they?

"I don't know it," he said. "But the place I have in mind wouldn't be on that land."

"They make invisible lines, and say this is mine and that is yours," Mary said.

The world was changing so fast that Skye barely understood it himself; his Indian wives would have even more trouble with the future.

"First warm weather, we'll go and start," he said.

"Leave the People?"

"Find a place. I may need to ride into Bozeman City for tools."

"You gonna build this big damn house yourself?"

Skye considered the ache in his limbs and the way he got out of breath these days. "I'll need help," he said. "I can't do it alone. And Dirk's gone away."

Mary's wan smile appeared again, concealing her sadness.

"You're too damn old to chop down trees," Victoria said. "I'll maybe get the whole Kicked-in-the-Bellies to come do this."

"Maybe I should talk—"

"You leave this to me," she said.

Skye felt warm enough now to begin his day. He pulled a fur cap over his head, wrapped himself in a greatcoat made of buffalo hide, and pushed through the flap into the bitter air.

Jawbone stared at him. The old gray stallion was frosted from front to rear. Icicles dangled from his frozen lips, and from his belly and mane and tail.

Skye walked to his great medicine horse, fed it some cottonwood bark Victoria had cut, and leaned into Jawbone's withers.

"You and I are going to live out our days in comfort," he said.

The old horse stood mutely, alarming Skye. He noticed yesterday's meal lying untouched on the trampled snow.

Jawbone hadn't greeting him this morning, as he usually did.

Skye stared at the ugly gray, and Jawbone stared back, and everything was wrong.

three

It was what did not happen this cold morning that worried Skye the most. Every dawn, for as long as Skye could remember, Jawbone had greeted him by butting his head into Skye's chest. It was a ritual. Jawbone would butt him, and Skye would yell at the horse, and Jawbone would butt him again just to let him know who was boss. That was their communion. But not this gray dawn.

Skye ran his gloved hand under the old stallion's mane. Something was terribly wrong. He studied Jawbone, realizing that the horse's long winter coat concealed the great hollows along his spine. The horse was starving and cold and listless.

He remembered how Jawbone had come to him seventeen years earlier, an ugly little colt that didn't behave the way horses behave, finding ways to be obnoxious. But in some mysterious way, Skye knew even then that this mustang that had appeared out of a wintry nowhere and he were mysteriously connected, and that they would share a life. For years, Jawbone had been a feared and admired sentinel, one-horse army, and protector of Skye and his family. He had also become a legend among all the plains tribes; even the enemies of the Crows hallowed and dreaded Jawbone. The horse annoyed white men so much that several had tried to kill him, but Skye had growled them off. Other white men had simply laughed: never had they seen a horse so misshapen and degenerate, with such a stupid look in his eyes.

Now the horse stood quietly, its head lowered, its back to the wind. As usual, it had posted itself near Skye's lodge. But the green cottonwood bark that Skye used to sustain Jawbone lay untouched in a scatter on the glazed snow.

Jawbone's teeth were no good anymore. Seventeen years of ripping up sandy prairie grass and masticating rough bark and chewing on dirt had worn them down so that the incisors didn't cut and the molars didn't grind. The tools in his jaws were worthless. It was a common malady in old horses, and why they slowly starved to death. Skye pulled his gloves off and grasped Jawbone's head. Usually the old horse would have snarled, but this time he just stood and let Skye run his finger between the horse's lips. He probed the incisors and found them blunt and rounded. The molars were flat and worn. What teeth were left were almost useless. Jawbone was dying, not from disease but from hunger.

In settled places there were some remedies. In Skye's own England an old horse could be fed warm sweet mash that could sustain an animal with bad teeth. But a good mash required rolled grains and molasses. There was nothing like that in this winter camp of the Crow people. There wasn't even any prairie grass. Only the bark, painfully harvested each day.

Skye felt the clawing of anguish.

Jawbone was not very old, and had more good years in

him. He was a little lame, but eager and ornery as ever. Skye didn't ride him much anymore. It was enough to have Jawbone with him, guarding the family, enjoying the life they had fashioned. Jawbone was as much a part of his family as his wives.

Skye ran his gnarled hands over the animal, discovering shocking hollows under the coat, feeling the corduroy of ribs. Jawbone stood stolidly, and that in itself alarmed him. Jawbone was not usually stolid about anything.

"You and I are old, mate," Skye said.

He ducked into his lodge and found the women staring at him. They had heard him.

"I need a blanket for Jawbone," he said.

Wordlessly the women set to work. But there wasn't much to work with. Victoria found a large piece of buffalo hide that had been in the lodge cover until it grew too soft, and had saved it for moccasins. This would make some belly bands. There ought to be a breast band too. A blanket could be sewn to them. It would take a day.

Skye watched them cut the leather, cut thong, and fashion a blanket there in the confines of that small lodge. He kept the fire going, and tried to be helpful, but they ignored him.

"I'll build a barn. I'll build a stall for Jawbone. I'll get some grain and molasses from Bozeman City," he said. "He'll be warm and he'll have some sweet feed. I'll keep him going just as long as I can."

He caught Victoria staring coldly at him. The Crows would let a horse die, because death was a part of life and because it was good for old creatures to die. This was his white man's instinct, keeping the old medicine horse alive.

All that wintry day the women made the horse blanket, using their awls on the leather and lacing the straps to the blanket. Late in the afternoon when the cold was thickening and the twilight was vanishing, they finished. They nodded to Skye. Quietly he collected the blanket and carried it into the bitter twilight, and found the horse standing nearby, its head low, its legs locked. Victoria braved the cold, and between them, they threw the white and blue blanket over the old horse and tied the belly bands. It worked well enough. The blanket hung over Jawbone's back, covered his withers, and tumbled over Jawbone's hollowed croup. The chest band would keep it from sliding backward.

Jawbone lifted his head. Surely the horse would begin to feel some warmth now, a thin life-preserving warmth. Surely this great-hearted horse would survive the winter now, and never face a brutal winter like this one again.

It was growing dark. The winter night stole over them and drove them into their small lodge, and then Jawbone was outside alone. Skye glanced about the village, and saw not a soul out-of-doors. Smoke rose reluctantly from the lodges, and then lowered under the weight of heavy air. He felt almost as cold as Jawbone, and hurried in. There was not much firewood, but it was too dark to get some.

No one spoke. The women drew their robes tight and lay quietly in the dusk, and when the fire threatened to go out, Skye added a few grudging sticks of cottonwood limb. Tomorrow, no matter what the weather, he would need to cut a generous supply.

Skye could not sleep that night. None of them had eaten, and none wanted to eat. Skye and Mary and Victoria lay wrapped in blankets wrapped in robes, and still the cold pierced to them, through the lodge cover, through the layered robes that protected them from Father Winter this subzero night. He knew as he lay in the darkness that the women were awake too. If he had said something, they would have responded.

He heartened himself. He thought of that blanket warming Jawbone, good wool holding the heat in, protecting the vital areas, lungs and heart. Jawbone would be all right. Tomorrow he would try to grind up the cottonwood bark into tiny bits, the sort that Jawbone could swallow without grinding the bark with his useless old teeth. Tomorrow would be better. They had given Jawbone a lease on life.

It proved to be the longest and coldest night in Skye's memory. Outside, there was only the silence. He itched to go out there, help the horse. He thought to bring the horse into the lodge, but the lodge was too small and the door hole too low. He dreaded the sound of a thump, the sound of Jawbone giving up and caving in. It was too black to find the bushes that night, so Skye did what he had to, just outside of the lodge. He did not see the horse.

Sometime in the small hours an understanding came to Skye, and he stared bleakly into the utter dark. He saw no stars up in the smoke hole, only unremitting blackness. There was Jawbone beside him, his flesh warm to the touch, his lop-eared gaze upon Skye, his muscles rippling, his mocking joy at the very business of being alive. There was Jawbone, waging his war against rival mustang stallions, stealing their mares, dancing his victory dance on every ridge. There was Jawbone, his hooves murderous when white men collected around him.

"Stay away from him," Skye warned.

"Does he kick?" they asked.

"No, he kills," Skye said.

The gawkers had stayed away.

Dawn came reluctantly, and as soon as Skye could see, he

threw aside his robes, wrapped his capote around him, and plunged into the obscure light. He didn't see Jawbone. The horse was not at his usual post a few dozen yards from the lodge. Where had Jawbone gone? He peered into the murk, discovering nothing. Impatiently he circled the lodge, feeling the snow squeak under him. He hunted for Jawbone, dreading to discover some dark lump sprawled on the white snow, and could not find him. Maybe the cottonwoods, then? Had the horse blanket revived Jawbone's appetite? Was the medicine horse off in the thickets, gnawing at twigs, wolfing dead leaves and stalks and bark? Was Jawbone simply drinking from the steaming creek?

He could not know. It would be an hour before enough light would collect for him to find Jawbone. He squinted into the gloom, knowing he must wait, and that he must gather wood and stir the fire and blow on coals until the tinder caught, and warm the lodge and comfort his wives.

He slid into the lodge, more by instinct than by vision.

"He is gone," Victoria said.

"He's not there," he said. "I think he's in the woods."

"He is dead," she said.

"No, he's warmed up and the blanket is helping him."

She turned her back to him, which was always her way of saying that he wasn't listening to her.

After a while it was light enough. A grudging fire was warming the lodge. Its smoke wasn't rising, and they coughed now and then. It was time to find the horse. He pulled his capote over him, pulled the hood over his gray hair, and stepped into the deep silence of predawn. Now he could see. The woods were a dark blur. The village lay quiet in the menacing cold. The air stung Skye's cheeks and burrowed into his moccasins and sliced at his legs.

He saw no living thing. The horse would be deep in the snow-drifted woods. It was a little warmer there than in the open. Skye hiked into the silent web of cottonwoods and willows, the skeletal branches patching his vision. But he saw not a glimpse of Jawbone. He did not see any of the village horses here, but he didn't expect to. He wandered helplessly among the copses of trees, but Jawbone was not present.

Now at last the village was stirring. Old people, huddled deep in blankets and robes, were heading toward the willow brush. The sky blued, and then the rising sun caught the tops of the cottonwood trees, making them glow. But he did not discover Jawbone, and felt an odd and haunting worry.

Jawbone was gone.

Then Skye knew. The great horse wanted to do his dying alone. This was the stallion's final gift. Skye would never see the husk of the great horse after life had fled.

Skye understood. He lifted his arms toward the distant bluff and acknowledged what he knew, and then turned slowly to the lodge. But not before the people of the village caught it all, knew that Jawbone was no longer among them, and knew that Skye and Victoria and Mary had lost a mighty friend. They watched, all of them bathed in morning light.

He stood at the lodge door, watching the sun illumine the ragged foothills, and then slid inside.

"Goddamn," said Victoria, and threw her arms around Skye, and wept into his capote.

four

$\mathcal{E}$ ven before the April sun had pummeled the snow into the earth, Skye knew what he must do. He would find a good way to grow old. Jawbone's wintry death had made it urgent. Jawbone, far from old, was gone. What might Skye's fate be?

He was suddenly aware of things he had ignored. His vision was changing, and he could hardly focus on things close at hand. His long-distance vision wasn't as bad, but it was changing too. He could still hunt. He could defend himself—for a while more. He felt well enough, except for the rheumatism that afflicted his very bones.

Most of those he knew in the mountains were dead. Joe Meek had headed for the Oregon country to farm in a placid valley. Gabe Bridger was ready to settle on a Missouri farm and spend his days enjoying life on his front porch. Others, like William Bent and Tom Fitzpatrick, had become Indian agents for the American government, struggling to help tribes cope with the onslaught of white men. For all of those men of the mountains, the United States was home, and most of them had headed back East.

But not Skye. The United States was not his home. British Canada was not his home. There was no home to go to, no village or farm waiting for him, no relatives or friends or family. His only home, over a long life, had been Victoria's people, and wherever they drifted, so did his hearth and kith and kin. And yet there was a home, a place where his heart sang and his spirit was at ease, and that was the Yellowstone country. Somehow, in the midst of all his wandering across the American West, he had come to love the stately river of the north.

Maybe home would be the valley of the Yellowstone, a place still rich with game, filled with rushing creeks, pine forests, and breeze-tossed meadows. It was all the heartland of the Crow people. Montana was being settled west to east, the mining camps in the western mountains little islands of European life, while the plains, where Skye lived, remained a vast hinterland of untouched, unplowed, unknown country. That is how he wanted it. Maybe there would be a home for him after all.

One late April day he proposed to Victoria and Mary that they head west to look for a place to settle. The very idea, settling down, seemed odd to him, but he spoke it.

"No, dammit, you go alone, Skye," Victoria said.

That was unheard of. Through all of their years together, Skye had traveled with his women.

"You go now," she said crossly. "This is something you got to do."

"But it would be your home . . ."

"I'm in my home."

"Go, Mr. Skye," Mary said softly. "You go make a place for us. We will make a home with you. I have no other lodge in my heart."

Skye knew there would be no arguing with them. He knew from the sharp tone of Victoria's voice that their decision had been made and it would not be revoked. They wanted him to find a place where he might grow old in comfort. And they believed he had to make these choices without consulting them.

It wrought an odd sadness in him. He peered at his determined ladies, who sat in their warm lodge, and felt himself being torn from them. It was out in the open now: he, the European, could not possibly live to happy old age in their Crow or Shoshone fashion. Skye's roots and their roots were too different to bridge this last great gulf in their lives. He had lost his medicine horse this winter, and now his wives were building a wall between them and him.

This wasn't going well. He was saying to them that their ways weren't good enough for him. Long ago, Mary had hoped that when her and Skye's son, North Star, grew to manhood he would welcome his aged parents and Victoria into his lodge, and would care for them when they grew feeble. But that dream had shattered when Skye had sent his son away to be educated. Now there were no sons or daughters who could care for Skye and his women.

He left the next morning riding an ugly ewe-necked gray mare. He was partial to ugly horses, the sort that white men laughed at and Indians put in their cook pots. But she was good and faithful and had heart. He tugged behind him a mule laden with buffalo tongue and pemmican, cookware and blankets and robes, a duck-cloth sheet for shelter, and his fine Sharps rifle.

He wasn't going far. The Yellowstone country he hoped to call home stretched west forty or fifty miles from upper Sweet Grass Creek, where his Crow band had wintered. He would hunt for the mystical place he saw in his mind's eye. It would be a good place, well watered, sheltered from the north winds, with handsome views of the mountains, plenty of pine and cottonwood, rich with game. Maybe there would be a place on this earth to call home, a place for a homeless man.

His women stood sternly outside his lodge, seeing him off, never smiling, somehow understanding the gravity of all this. Nearby, his Crow friends and villagers watched silently. He had said his good-byes to Broken Head and Sleeps In Rain, two of the headmen, and now he hurried the mare across the soft earth of spring, leaving the prints of his two animals behind him. Then he topped the ridge west of Sweet Grass Creek, and paused to look back. But his wives had vanished and the others had returned to their daily tasks. Victoria and Mary would give him no excuse to change his mind and return to the comfort of the lodge.

Soon Skye felt alone as he made his solitary way across a snow-patched prairie divide and into the Yellowstone Valley, where snow and earth mottled the landscape. The birds of summer had not arrived to trill their songs, and Skye rode through a powerful silence unbroken even by breezes. Or was he only getting deaf?

Uneasily he surveyed this corrugated land at the base of the Birdsong Mountains, and saw no sign of life. This was Indian country. Few, if any, white men ventured into it now, two years after the great Sioux war chief Red Cloud had banished the Yank army from this homeland of the plains tribes. The Yank army had lost that war, and didn't much talk about it.

Skye didn't mind. Red Cloud's gift to the Crows was to permit them to live their traditional life a little while more.

Skye tugged his soft elk-hide coat tight against the cold, which penetrated to his flesh wherever it could worm its way past his armor. Victoria and Mary had fashioned the coat and quilled it and added a hood, and made gauntlets to go with it, and given it to him for warmth and comfort. He wore their moccasins on his feet and their leggings on his legs. These days he wore a flannel shirt and long johns gotten from the traders, but in all else his wives had outfitted him.

Away from the Crows, his caution sharpened. He was alone, an easy mark for anyone or any group or any animal, such as a rogue grizzly. But on this sublimely peaceful day he saw only some ravens gossiping on a distant branch. Did old ravens fly as well as young ones? What happened to a raven that could fly no longer? Ravens were smart birds. How did they die? Were they smart enough to choose death? Skye found himself entertaining questions that had never filled his mind before.

The pack mule came along willingly, carrying all Skye might need to survive in this lonely land. The odd thing was, Skye wasn't certain why he was making this journey. What exactly was he seeking? What did he need that the Crows or the Shoshones could not provide him? It was worth thinking about as he traveled.

Well, there were a few things. He wanted fields and pastures that would yield a living from gardens, grains, and livestock. He hoped to shelter himself behind a wall of thick logs, or rock, or adobe. A roof. A door that would stop arrows. He yearned for comfort: a real bed, with a real mattress to ease the pain in his aching bones. But that was only a part of it. He had, he knew, a white man's urge to sink roots deep and true, to take up land as a possession, a holding. That flew against the visions of his wives' peoples, who never dreamed of holdings, and considered the breast of mother earth to be beyond possession.

He rode across open country, most of it the giant shoulders of the snowy mountains north and west. As the day waned he started to search for a secluded place only a few miles from the Yellowstone River where he intended to camp. It would be almost invisible now, with only a few spidery branches to reveal it and he wasn't sure he could find it. This was monotonous country before it greened, and the brown reaches were deceptive. Far across the Yellowstone Valley lay foothills, and the great chain of the Rockies, running east and west here. He topped a ridge and could make out the distant Yellowstone Valley, which was veiled in haze. But he continued to hunt for the place, and just before dusk he dropped down a slope and saw his oasis, just as he had remembered it. He hurried the ewe-necked mare to the intimate valley, and paused at the water's edge. There were several algae-lined pools and a faint smell of sulphur released when the hot water reached the air. He took hasty care of the mare, put her in a cottonwood grove where she could gnaw on green bark, and returned to his campsite. He collected dry wood for a fire, and started it burning, using a lucifer instead of flint and steel.

He tested the waters with his hand, found a pool to his liking, as hot as he could stand, and then pulled away his leather clothing and his ancient union suit, until he was bare, and then stepped gingerly into the purling hot water and slid slowly into it, until he was immersed to his nose, and thinking this was an old man's heaven. He toasted himself, paddling occasionally, letting his limbs float free, letting the water redden his flesh, until he could no longer stand the heat and he had to clamber out on some cold rocks. He found a small pool farther down, milder now, and slid into it, letting the tepid water cool him. Then he crawled out and dried himself at his fire. For this little while, he actually lived without pain, but by morning he would be hurting again. That's what old age was all about. He wished there was a hot spring where he intended to make a home. But from the Great Bend of the Yellowstone there were several hot springs not far away.

He camped that night under a south-facing bluff back from the springs. For much of this chill spring night, the sun-warmed bluff would spread its heat over him, and he would take his ease. He lay quiet under his blankets, knowing why he was looking for a place to settle. It was simple: he wanted a comfortable place to grow old. He would like to sit in a rocking chair on a veranda and watch sunsets, or feel the night-chill creep toward his door. There wasn't anything more to it. And yet there was. A true home was more than shelter and more than comfort. It was rooted in family and friends and neighbors.

He knew perfectly well where he was going. There were a dozen likely places along the Yellowstone River, but only one filled his mind. He would find a place somewhere near the great bend of the river, where he could see the craggy Birdsong Mountains aglow in the sunrise, and watch the sun plunge behind the Bridger Mountains at dusk. He would look out of his front door at the majestic Absaroka Mountains, somewhere near where the river punched through them in a narrow canyon. He would look out his back windows toward the westernmost edge of the plains, or the Shields River valley. He mused, as he lay in the quiet, that this whole trip, presuming to hunt for a place to live, was a sham. He already knew.

But knowing the general area, and selecting a specific spot, were two different things entirely. He would hunt for a place where majestic cottonwoods lined the creeks, where there was good pasture grass, where a man could put in a garden, where cold springs would make delicious drinking in summers and keep food in a spring house during hot times. He would find a place that could not be surprised, where a man would have a few moments to reach safety. He would find a place where his eyes would feast on the world, and his flesh would rejoice, and his nostrils would suck in the scents of wild roses.

The next two days he made his solitary way up the Yellowstone River, seeing no one at all. Sometimes he left pony tracks in decaying snow. At other times he took his horse through mud. His passage would be easy to follow, and for that reason he paused now and then to study the land behind him, sometimes watching from a forested spur of mountain. But he saw no sign of human life, and his journey began to take on the quality of a trip across the Atlantic in a rowboat.

But he didn't mind. He rode carefully, knowing there would be no help if he got into trouble, broke a bone, took sick, or got caught in a cruel spring snowstorm. He had lived over six decades, much of it in wilderness, by being careful when he was alone, and strangely, by loving this land so deeply that he was nurtured and sheltered and fed by it. In some places the placid Yellowstone ran between yellow bluffs; in other places it ran through cloistered bottomlands guarded by rolling prairie. In other places along towering gray cliffs that hid the snow-clad Rocky Mountains to the south. That day he shot a yearling buck, apologizing to it for taking its life. The meat was good, and the weather cold enough so he could carry the meat with him for days.

Then at last, after circumventing one impassable gorge, he drifted into the country that he intended to be his home the rest of his life. The great bend of the Yellowstone lay only a few miles ahead. And even before he reached it, he felt at home.

five

kye hurt. Instead of sitting his horse and absorbing the area that would be his home, he slid painfully off and eased to the stony turf, knowing that the minute he alighted sharp pain would shoot up his legs. He had ridden horses all his life, but now it was all he could manage to sit a horse for an hour. The hurt would drive upward from his knees to his loins to his hip and back, and then he would have to dismount and walk awhile until the pain lessened.

Now he eased to the grass and felt his moccasins touch earth. He was used to pain. He had bullet wounds, knife wounds, a nose pulped by brawling early in his life, giant scars and scratches, and more recently the pain of all his years, lancing his bones and settling in every joint.

This would be the place of his old age, and he wondered why. Of all the ranges and prairies and hills and deserts he had roamed over a lifetime in the American West, why had he come to this place? He couldn't say. It was beautiful, but there were many vistas across this country that were more so.

It was not a lush land, and would not afford much of a living. He stood on a brushy and uneven flat that had once been riverbed. One would not plow here because the blade would strike the river cobbles that lay just below.

Off to the south was a steep notch in the slopes, where the Yellowstone had washed through the mountains, and beyond that a broad valley flanked by snowy ranges. The trappers and men of the mountains had often camped here, and that was how he first became acquainted with it. Sometimes they had wintered here, built their miserable huts against the wind, harvested game, cut firewood, and then gambled and storied away the cold days and nights. Skye had been among them. He knew this place and it was just as real to him as the pain lacing his bones.

The wind here was incessant and cold, and now it slipped through his leathers and chilled him. He would need a good stout house to turn the wind, and a good stove to heat it enough to ease the pain in his joints. He wondered why he would build a home in a place notorious for its bitter winds, and had no answer. There were winter days here when the wind was so cruel that no man would venture out.

He eyed the sky, finding scattered frying-pan clouds with black bottoms skidding low over the ridges. They might snow on him. The setting sun silvered the edges of these galloping clouds, turning the sky into a kaleidoscope. He put a hand on the withers of his horse and felt it tremble.

The silent wilderness absorbed his gaze. The brooding mountains caught the last light, and now the river flat settled into obscure shadow. This place was incalculably old. For as long as the stars rose and fell, this place had nurtured life and welcomed death. These mountains rose and fell. This river had scooped away rock and cut a gorge. This was a place of mystery, the sort of place that made Europeans huddle closer to their hearth fires and listen for the unknown and unknowable just beyond the pale light.

He headed for the thick riverside brush, knowing he could find shelter there, and soon found a good gravelly flat surrounded by willows and cottonwoods, a place hidden from prying eyes, where he could light a fire that would never be seen. Why did he still keep his guard up? It was ancient habit. From silent places came silent arrows.

He unsaddled, and turned the horse and mule loose on brown and matted grass. They would gnaw a few twigs as well as last summer's grass and do well enough to sustain life. He chose a gravelly ridge, once a sandbar in the river, that would shed snow or rain. Falling water here would not pool, but would filter into the thick gravel beds beneath him.

He collected an abundant supply of deadwood and heaped it nearby. The more he moved, the better he felt. Just doing chores drove the pain away. It never left him entirely, but he could drive it back until it lurked beyond the fires, with yellow wolf eyes, waiting to pounce on him again when he pulled his robes over him.

He checked his Sharps rifle and set it next to his bedroll.

He heard an animal stirring. At dusk deer came to water, but it might be something else, so he waited. But nothing loomed out of the quietness, so he turned to his supper, a pemmican broth that would warm and comfort him.

The sole noise was that of his own making. Nearby, a latticework of naked limbs raked the stars, and little air stirred. The limbs looked like jail bars, keeping his spirit pinned to earth and preventing him from knowing all things. Earth was home, but also prison. He used lucifers now; strikers and flints were too much work and too chancy. He shaved a dry stick, built a tiny fire, added twigs, and soon had a hot little blaze, just right for his cook pot. He had learned to feed himself with only a copper cook pot, his knife, and an iron spoon, and that was all he had with him. He dipped the pot into the Yellowstone River, and set the cold water to heating, along with some jerky and pemmican and some rose hips he had harvested along the way. He wouldn't need much. His appetite had faded over the years, and now he was indifferent to food.

He lowered himself quietly to the dry gravel, a good place to be during the muddy season when sometimes there was no dry bed ground to be found.

Was this home? Had he come all the way over here only to find that home is not a place, but a collection of memories and loved ones? He could not answer it. Did anyone on earth possess a real home, a sanctuary that put all the clawing pain in one's bosom at ease? Was the only true home death itself?

He lay on his back, watching for meteors in a sky patched with clouds, but he absorbed only the silence. He could not sleep, and even the usual drowsiness that signaled sleep did not approach him. Had he come here for nothing? He had imagined a home right about where the Shields River tumbled into the Yellowstone, and now that he was here and this was real, he couldn't imagine why he had come. It was naught but a foolish fancy.

The fire reduced itself to orange coals. The night was cold but he had often endured worse. His kit departed from Indian ways in one respect: he slept inside a blanket that was inside of a good duck-cloth bag that turned water and dew and wind, and captured heat, and opened easily along one side. His wives preferred the old ways, a buffalo robe or a trade blanket.

Restlessly he arose, impatient with himself, and stretched.
A chill penetrated his leathers and reached his soft woolen
shirt. There was only a sliver moon, and this night was very
black. But he could see even so. He knew this place so well
that everything was stamped upon his mind, every skyline
and peak. Starlight glinted in the mysterious river purling by
twenty yards distant. He was not afraid.

Moving about spared him pain. He hurt most after deep
sleep, when his whole body ached and his muscles refused to
obey. It was only by working his muscles in the morning that
he drove the pain out of them. It was as if the pain were like
some poison that needed constant flushing.

His horse and mule stared at him, aware of something
different in the shifting quiet of the night. He began walking
along the river until he found himself on open rolling
meadow devoid of river rock. The going was easier, but still
he walked deliberately, a pace at a time, because his only
lantern was the stars and a sliver of moon behind him. Across
the river a snowy pyramid of a peak caught an odd glint out
of the heavens. South of the river the meadows quickly gave
way to black forests and foothills, and finally the vaulting
mountains of the Absaroka Range.

He was standing on home.

He saw this place better in the void of night than by day,
and the contours of the land were ingrained in his soul. A few
miles to the east the view was just as handsome, but there were
rattlesnakes. Here they were rare. Here were smooth grassy
meadows and the majesty of nature from every prospect.

The land was very old, but not virgin. Trails came through
this very country, followed by barefoot and moccasined people, and those with shoes and boots. There were the prints of
shod and unshod horses and mules, the split hooves of the

bovines, the ruts of wagons and carts, the furrows of travois, the prints of dogs. From here a road led over the western mountains to the distant mining towns. Trails ran north to the Missouri, and south to the headwaters of the Yellowstone, at a place Victoria's people called the roof of the world. In this land one could find flint arrowheads, and some made from obsidian collected from cliffs to the south. One could find old arrows, and great stone spear points, knife blades and buttons, horseshoes, bits of worn harness.

Skye liked that. He was a sociable man who enjoyed people and welcomed them to his hearth. He would not build a home in some remote place never visited by mortals. A night zephyr caught him, and drove cold into his clothing, so he retreated in the depths of night to his camp, flawlessly heading to the right shadow and the right gravel bar where his gear lay undisturbed.

This time he fell asleep swiftly, and didn't awake until sunlight pried his eyes open. Someone was staring at him. He quietly surveyed the empty gravel bar and the surrounding meadow, and discovered a bullock there, watching him. It was an ugly beast, splotchy brown and white, all skin and bones except for a huge set of horns that spanned six feet or more and arced forward into murderous weapons.

But not a bullock. Probably an abandoned ox. Worn-out oxen were scattered all along the old Bozeman Trail, cut loose when they were too weak to drag wagons anymore. Some died, some survived. The Indians left them alone, preferring buffalo to the stringy meat of the oxen. Still, it was odd to see a domestic animal here. Skye contemplated the animal as he lay in his bedroll. The ox neither approached nor ran, but stood there, guarding the ground.

Skye wondered whether to shoot and eat the beast, and

decided against it. A rested ox in good flesh was worth a lot of money. He rose slowly, fighting back the usual pain, while the ox watched, and then the ox trotted into the brush and hid. There was something tantalizing in all this, and Skye forgot how much he hurt.

six

Skye brewed some tea. It was a habit that rose from his very bones, and many mornings he cared for nothing more. He let the leaves steep in his pot, and then let the pot cool so he could drink from it.

The day quickened, and the low sun prized the flanks of the dark mountains south and west, sometimes burnishing the ridges until they shone like new pennies. But the sunlight was a cheat and the day didn't warm. Skye felt heavy air rolling out of Canada. He pulled his blanket about him to allay pain, and knew all over again why he needed a sheltering home.

The tea stirred his pulse, and he was ready to introduce himself to his land. He hiked slowly east until he came again to the ground that spoke to him in the night, and stood upon it. He felt some ancient stirring that could have no name, as if the earth beneath his moccasins were speaking. Maybe gravity was heavier here, making him feel heavier, connecting him to the soil below him. He saw a great meadow sloping toward the river bottoms. Behind him the land convulsed upward into grassy hills.

He ached for Victoria. She had medicine powers, and once in a while she warned him away from a campsite or some other place. He wanted her to stand beside him, and tell him what the spirits were whispering to her, and whether this would be a place of joy or danger or heartache. But she had begged off. Building a house was white man's stuff, and she wanted no part of it.

So Barnaby Skye would settle for his own wisdom this time. He noticed a shallow draw and walked to it, finding chokecherries and willow brush, and in the bottom, a thin trickle, not a foot wide. He hiked upslope and discovered a spring rising from an outcrop. He cupped his hands and lifted the water to his lips, and found it cold and sweet. The spring flowed from a vertical fault in gray rock, a good sign that it was not seasonal and perfidious. Its water could be diverted into a home, and it could cool a springhouse as well, and water livestock in a pasture, and water gardens and apple trees.

Ample wood was at hand. The meadows here were more in the nature of parks, surrounded by mixed stands of aspen, cottonwood, fir, and pine. Wood for hearth and stove; wood for timbers and planks and window frames and lintels. Copses sprang up from the meadows, especially where there was a bit more moisture in the soil. And just beyond the valley, fir and pine blackened the slopes.

It was a good and bountiful land, maybe not for a plowman but for a man who needed pasture and garden. Still . . . it was a long way from this open and virgin world to a functioning home. He had with him one small camp axe. He could no longer count on the toil of his body, his own sweat and blood and muscle, to build a house. He drifted across the parks, wrapped tightly in his blanket against the metallic air, wondering where houses came from and how he could conjure a good solid one here.

A bit closer to the river, he knew, would be good rounded cobbles just below the thin topsoil, cobbles to lift out of their ancient beds, placed on sledges and dragged to the building site. Cobbles to be mortared into foundations and walls. He studied the woodlands, looking for stands of lodgepole pine, the preferred tree for log buildings because the logs were arrow-true and easy to work. But there were no lodgepole pines anywhere near. Only a little crooked jackpine, good enough for firewood but an anguish to builders.

The nearest sawmill was in Bozeman City, over Jim Bridger's pass, in the Gallatin Valley. He could buy sawn timbers and planks there if he had some money. He could have them hauled here, if he had some money. He could buy kegs of nails and window glass or even pre-made framed windows there, if he had some money.

He eyed the sod. He could build a sod house here. He still could dig each piece of sod with a spade without help, and set it into his walls without help. He could cut poles for a roof and put thick sod on the poles for a roof. That much he could do, even at his age and with his bounty of pain. Then he could live inside his dirt house, avoid the leaks when it rained, and chase away bugs and snakes and rodents and worms. He sighed, unhappily.

He saw flatiron clouds sliding along the northern horizon, and knew where the cold wind was coming from. Before the day was done there would be a spring storm here, and he ought to look to shelter. He turned his back to the heavy air and walked to his campsite, deep in the bottoms, where the trees subdued the wind a little and a man could find small comforts.

The temperature was plummeting even though it was midday. Rain slapped him. He peered upward and saw nothing but clear sky, and yet rain drove into him like ten-penny nails. The dark outliers still rode far north, deepening the mystery. There was no time to marvel at nature's perversities, so he hurried for shelter. He had lived in nature half a century, and knew what to look for.

In this case it was an ancient cottonwood lording over a large grove. He collected his bedroll, dragged his packs to the top of the gravel bar where water would not pool under them, and then he hurried into the grove, while bullets of cold rain smacked his leather shirt and trickled down his neck. The mammoth tree spread naked branches over a wide patch of earth, but that wasn't the shelter he wanted. He studied the massive roots and found a hollow between them on the lee side, just wide enough for him to sit in. He wrapped his blankets about him, and then the duck-cloth bag, and lowered himself into the hollow. The roots rose beside him like stout walls, scraping his duck cloth, and then he pulled the cloth over his head and the ice picks falling out of the sky stopped pricking him. He settled in, noting the sweep of white rain across the parks and brown meadows. The mountains across the river vanished in fog, which soon white-blinded him to the rest of the world.

He had endured all this many times, and he would endure it again. A thin heat collected in his blankets. Water sprayed off his canvas, and rarely caught his face. He could no longer see sky; fog obscured it. He could not read the weather, and he knew this could last ten minutes or ten hours or ten days. He discovered sleet mixed in the rain, and knew the temperature had dropped. There would come a time when he was so stiff he had to stand, a time when he might need to drain himself, and when that time came, his haven would be violated, and he would return to water pooled where he sat.

The horse and mule stood with heads lowered, rumps to the wind. Their backs slick and black. A bit of slush frosted the packs on the gravel, and more was collecting here and there on dried grass.

In spite of his wraps, Skye felt cold. And worse, he was hurting again. He was breathing misty cold air, and his chest hurt too. He had weathered a thousand storms over half a century, but this was different because he hurt. As the minutes progressed to hours, his limbs ached, his back hurt, and his neck radiated so much pain that he found himself rotating his head this way and that, trying to ease the outrage of his body. A man of his years needed shelter, and he could never return to the outdoor life he had weathered for decades.

He thought he might build the foundation of river cobbles and mortar, and then add logs and a thick floor, and raise a hearth and fireplace and chimney of cobbles and mortar, and pile the logs up into walls, thick and airtight and sealed, and then raise a roof over all of that, a roof with shakes to drain the rain away and support the heavy loads of snow that would settle on them. He would add some store-bought windows, and a stout door, and a good iron stove to cook on and supplement the hearth fire. He would give Victoria and Mary rooms of their own, and partition off his own, but the rest of the house would be a great commons for them.

He would put a roofed porch along the front where a man might sit quietly and watch the future. He would build a massive outhouse in the back, where a man could sit without feeling the cold wind, and below the spring he would build a spring house to cool vegetables and preserve meat. In the bedrooms he would fashion sturdy beds wrought from poles and leather, and add stuffed cotton mattresses that could blot up a man's hurts and keep him warm and off the cold ground. Getting off the ground was the main thing. Even in a warm house, the cold of the ground in these northern places rose upward and numbed feet and made calves ache and stole warmth from each room. That was the trouble with lodges. The Crows had comfortable lodges that drew the smoke away and caught the fire-warmth, but the cold from the frozen earth stole upward, through layer upon layer of buffalo robes, and one never slept on warm ground in winter. Only on ground that made bones ache and old people draw deep into themselves.

After Skye had sat immobilized until he hurt all over, he stood, drew his covering about him, and walked through sleet and fog down to the river, where the silver waters flashed by. Slush worked through his moccasins and numbed his feet. He walked, feeling the cold muscle of his body begin to work, to drive away the pain that seemed to build up when his muscles weren't working.

So Skye walked. It was better than sitting tight. It was an old person's remedy. Old people drove away stiffness by walking. He could not see the heavens well enough to know when this storm might abate, but he would walk it out, walk until the cloud and fog lifted. He was not a good walker, his body compact and stout rather than lanky and lean, but walking would be his salvation now, and there was always this: walking took a person somewhere, and opened new prospects.

So Skye settled his soaked top hat on his locks and walked along the Yellowstone River, following game trails through brush. Walking felt better than sitting. He cold-footed his way through muck and slush, driven by some compulsion he didn't understand, to walk or die. He walked awkwardly, wrapped in his bedroll and duck cloth, but he never stopped walking. He had the sensation that walking meant life and stopping meant death, but he dismissed it. He might be old but he wasn't sick. He didn't know how far he was from his horse and mule and packs but that didn't matter either.

A stirring in the brush gave him pause. There had been only the deep quiet of the wilds, but now something stirred, and it was large, snapping twigs and piercing through brush. A grizzly, perhaps. Skye regretted that he had left his Sharps with the packs, and carried nothing but a belt knife.

The ox saw Skye at the same instant that Skye limned the ox. The startled animal lowered its giant horns, threw his head to either side, those deadly horns arcing one way and another. Then it snorted and charged. Skye had never been assaulted by a wild ox, and saw no way to escape. Brush hemmed him. The murderous horns cut a wide swath. Then it was too late. The left horn, swinging like an axe handle, caught Skye's leg and lifted him high into the fog and he felt himself tumbling back to earth, landing hard in slush and muck and brush, while the beast thumped by, its hooves missing Skye's writhing form by inches. Pain lanced him, white-hot pain shooting up from his leg, pain such as old age never knew. Then Skye drifted in and out of the world.

seven

*B*right stars glinted above. Firelight wavered and danced. Skye lay on his back, buried deep under blankets that warmed him well. Lightning bolts shot up his left leg and thundered through the rest of him, but the night sky was clear.

He groaned. Immediately a man loomed above him. Skye focused carefully. This one wore a slouch hat and a heavy coat. Another man joined him.

"You come back to us?" the man said.

Skye nodded.

"Lucky we were close. Heard you howling and come look."

"Who?" asked Skye.

"Jim Broadus, that's me, and Amos Glendive. We're teamsters."

"Didn't know anyone was around," Skye said.

"You got thrown by one of them ox," Broadus said.

"Your oxen?"

"Wild ox. That's why we're here. We haul for the Bar

Diamond outfit. They need oxen. Lots of 'em gone native around here along the old trail. They got wore out and ditched by folks. We got three span this time."

"Including the one got you, we think," Glendive said.

The memory was coming back now. That cruel horn hooking under his leg, lifting him, tossing him like a rag doll, and then the crash. He came down in a fury of pain, and howled, and then the fog rolled in.

A new bolt of pain laced Skye's leg and he groaned.

"Your leg's busted up some. Your knee ain't never gonna be the same, mister . . . mister . . ."

"Skye. Mister Skye."

"We got her splinted up, Skye, but that's all a man can do around here."

"I'd be dead," Skye said. "You saved me."

Broadus smiled slightly. "I reckon so. Leastwise, it'd be a long crawl to wherever you were heading."

Skye wrestled with pain a moment and stared about him. This was a good camp. A freight wagon slouched nearby.

"We'll take you to Bozeman City. That's where we're a-going."

"I can ride."

Glendive just shook his head, and Skye abandoned that.

"Your leg, it's some messed-up," Broadus said. "We didn't know how to splint it right, but she's tied up tight, anyway."

Skye knew the Bar Diamond Freight Company. Mostly they hauled goods from Fort Benton, on the Missouri River, down into the mining camps of western Montana. Big outfit. Always needing oxen, more oxen, more mules.

"Old man Baker sent us over here. He needs stock, and there's free stuff floating around here."

Skye craned his head, peering into the dark.

"It's all here, Skye. We moved your camp here. Your nags and all. You were going light."

Skye nodded.

"You hurting more than much?" Broadus said.

Skye nodded.

"It's gonna be a hard wagon ride tomorra. But we can carry you."

"I guess it's in store for me," Skye said. He was starting to fade again.

"You up to some broth?" one of them asked.

Skye nodded. Within moments, they were spooning some beefy broth into him, warming his innards. But he couldn't even swallow without his leg hurting him. He gave up after a few sips, and slid a hand down to the leg, discovered a tight-tied splint holding the leg rigid. He brought his fingers up looking for blood on them and found none.

"I'd say in some ways it could've been worse," Broadus said.

Skye nodded, a sea of brooding pain spreading through him again.

"Take a horse. It's yours," Skye whispered.

"No. You'd do it for us if need be."

"At least I can thank you."

"That ox, the one got you, he's under yoke now. Them wild ones remember. Whole trick is to get them into a yoke, and then they quiet right down, remembering old times. We got our ways," Glendive said. "Old man Baker, he's got forty, fifty oxen this way off the Bozeman Road. Baker sends us over here now and then to fetch him some more."

"Wouldn't mind if you ate him for breakfast," Skye said.

"You need anything, Skye?"

"You could amputate," Skye said.

They laughed uneasily. "We're here if you need us. You rest now."

Then Skye was alone with the stars and the pain.

He didn't sleep much. The throbbing in his leg never lessened. But as soon as dawn broke, Broadus and Glendive were stirring, and then bringing him some steaming coffee. Skye downed it gratefully.

"We're heading out. We got three yoke, and that's all anyone thought we'd get. We'll put you in the wagon," Broadus said. "I imagine it ain't going to be comfortable, but it's all we can do."

They lifted Skye to his feet, and he clung to their shoulders as they helped him into the wagon bed and wrapped blankets around him while he trembled. The teamsters broke camp, added Skye's few possessions to the heap in the wagon, collected Skye's horses, and started toward Bozeman City. Every lurch of the wagon shot pain through Skye.

After a while, they stopped and checked on him.

"You all right?" Broadus asked.

Skye wasn't, but he nodded at the teamster.

Soon they were off again, the teamsters walking beside the oxen as they dragged the wagon upslope. Skye thought they might make Bozeman City by nightfall.

The day went much too slowly. He felt a helplessness he had rarely experienced before. He'd been gravely wounded several times, and managed to heal up and keep on going. Now he had a broken leg. Just what had snapped or shattered he didn't know, except that pain radiated from his left knee toward his ankle and toward his hip. Victoria and Mary were far away. Someone would have to care for him.

He put such speculation aside. He was alive, miraculously discovered soon after the trouble with the ox, and now he was safe in good hands. He tried to rest, but pain kept him wide awake.

It was just after sundown when the Bar Diamond teamsters halted.

Broadus loomed over him in the dusk. "We're at Fort Ellis. There's no sawbones in Bozeman City, but we thought there might be one at the post here. You want us to find out?"

"That would be good, Mister Broadus."

"Or we can take you into town somewheres. Livery barn, maybe. Those haylofts make good beds."

"I'd like a doctor, sir."

"I'll send Amos in to talk to someone."

Skye watched the teamster vanish among the stained log buildings of the post, and eventually he returned with an officer, who looked Skye over.

"Colonel Blossom here. You're the man, eh?" he said. "Know you. You're the old squaw man living with the Crows."

Skye nodded.

"Trouble is, our surgeon's cashiered. Clyde Coffin was a damned drunk and I sent him packing last week. We're waiting for a new man. Point is, there's no one here can set your bones."

"Anyone in Bozeman City?"

Blossom shook his head. "Not as I know of. Virginia City, maybe."

"I seem to be out of luck," Skye said. "I don't know what to do."

Blossom pondered it. "There's a thing or two I can do. I've got a lot of crutches around, and I can give you some. How tall are you?"

"Five feet some. I've shrunk."

Blossom nodded to his orderly, who trotted into the post.

"Well, Skye, if I can help further, call on me," Blossom said. "Have to go now."

Skye nodded. "I'll get along," he said. "You've helped me, and I'm indebted."

"No, old fella, from what I've heard, the army owes you a thing or two."

The colonel hastened back to the post. In time, the orderly appeared with some wooden crutches.

"Try these, Skye."

Skye slipped the crutches under his shoulders and stood. They would do. He could cradle his arms in them, take weight off the broken leg. That was a start.

Broadus and Glendive looked eager to get into town, so Skye clambered back into the wagon for the final half mile. The wagon yard was east of town on the edge of the military reservation.

"I don't know what to do with you, Skye," Broadus said.

"Could you take me to a livery barn?" Skye asked. "I don't know where else to go."

They could. At the freight yard the teamsters corralled a deliveryman named Glad Muggins, who harnessed a spring wagon and helped Skye into it. He added Skye's gear and tied Skye's ponies on, and drove into town.

Muggins climbed to the seat and slapped the lines over the dray horse, and the wagon creaked westward. The horse fell into a quiet walk and Skye watched the April clouds hurry past. April was a rainy month. Luckily it wasn't raining now. Beyond the freight yard the Bridger Mountains rose high, still choked with snow.

"Now where do you want to go?" Muggins asked.

"Is there a livery barn?"

"Kangaroo. North of Main Street some."

"Take me there."

Skye didn't have a dime to his name but livery barns were the usual refuge of the desperate. There might be a bunk in a hay pile, and he had a packhorse to trade for a few weeks of chow and horse feed. He thought it would be a month before he could put weight on that leg.

Somehow he had survived. They would not find his bleached bones out on the trail. Maybe he could find someone who would reach the Crows, and let Victoria and Mary know where he was. A livery barn was the right place to find travelers.

Bozeman City was strung along a miry street that nearly coagulated traffic. A few boardwalks over the wetter spots provided the only passage for pedestrians. Rills from the surrounding mountains laced the ramshackle town. False-front frame stores, some whitewashed, lined the street, and a few grimy residences south of the grubby road completed this outpost of civilization. Skye pushed himself up on his elbows to see what might be seen. He scarcely spotted a woman. The place had functioned as a farming and ranching town supplying gold camps to the west with grains and meat. It was also becoming a crossroads, the market town of the vast green valley it dominated.

Muggins turned up a side street, at least it might have been a street, and headed for a weathered board-and-batten structure several hundred yards north. A white-lettered front proclaimed it to be the Clyde Kangaroo Livery, Stock Sold & Bought.

Muggins swung the wagon around and stopped. A chin-whiskered gent in bib overalls, armed with a pitchfork, burst out of the barn alley, and boiled down on the wagon.

"What's the company unloading on me this time, eh?"

"Mister Kangaroo, this here's a man with a busted leg, looking for a place to stay."

Kangaroo reached the wagon and peered at Skye. "I get stuck with every vagrant comes through here, and none earns me a dime," he said.

Skye found himself staring upward at a skinny gent almost devoid of chin, with bulgy eyes. A venerable slouch hat capped some dark hair.

"I'm Barnaby Skye, sir. I broke a leg. I'll trade a horse for some accommodations."

"Trade a horse, will you? You call those items horses? They look like injun ponies to me."

"You have it right, sir," Skye said. "I'll trade one for a month in your hayloft, plus feed for myself and the other horse. Take your pick."

"A month of chow and feed, you say? You suffer delusions, like most owners of nags. You want to sit in my outhouse and shit away three squares for a month, and pay me with that? That thing?" He waggled a gnarly finger at the packhorse.

Skye saw no reason to respond. He lay quietly while Kangaroo circled the packhorse, lifted feet, examined hooves, pried open the mouth, studied teeth, ran a hand over withers looking for fistulas.

"You a talker?" he asked.

"What do you mean?"

"I can't stand talkers boring me half to death. I got work to do. If you're a listener, we'll handshake it. Me, I always need listeners. I'm here alone. I'm a born talker. You come here, you gotta listen and don't talk back, and I'll put you up. Maybe I'll take that lousy packhorse, maybe I won't."

"It's a deal," Skye said.

eight

The town crier, Blue Tail Feather, announced that the People would begin their spring exodus to summer grounds on the Big Horn River. Many Quill Woman, Victoria, was a little deaf, and required that Mary repeat the word from the council of elders.

"We go to the Big Horn Valley now. Summer is here," Mary said in English. "The omens are good. The elders have spoken."

The Big Horn Valley was a good place to be during the warm seasons. There were deer and elk and antelope, and bear up in the Big Horn Mountains, although not many buffalo. It was a protected valley, not easy to reach, and mostly the enemies of the People just left them alone there. Out on the plains, to the other side of the sacred mountains, things were different. The Lakota were still stirred up after driving the Americans away, and now they patrolled that country and lorded over it and pounced on anyone entering it. There were many more Lakota than there were of Victoria's people, the Absaroka.

Victoria stood stiffly. The winter had taken a toll on her, and her body ached. More and more she depended on Mary to do the chores, gather wood for the small lodge fire, gather roots, butcher meat kindly brought to them by the camp's hunters. Sometimes all Victoria wanted to do was sit in a white man's rocking chair and rock and see all things. She wouldn't admit it though.

Mary returned to her toil. She was scraping the underside of an elk hide that had been given to her, cleaning off bits of fat and decaying flesh. And that was only the beginning of what must be done to turn it into soft, fine leather.

Victoria eyed Skye's younger wife, and saw no change. Mary was caught in sadness, but Skye scarcely knew it because Mary always flashed her brightest smiles at him and hid what was slowly eroding her life away.

It had begun years earlier when the boy was just past seven winters, and growing into a good stout son. That was when Skye arranged with Colonel Bullock, his agent and friend at Fort Laramie, to take the boy, Dirk, or North Star, to a place called Missouri, for an education offered by the black-robes. Victoria wondered about educations. Why must the boy be taken away? Couldn't Skye teach Dirk all the things that white men called an education? But Skye had only said he wanted his son to have every chance to make something of himself, and he needed to learn to read and write and do his arithmetic.

One fall, when Colonel Bullock was quitting his post, he took Dirk away with him, and that was when Mary changed, and hid the change from Skye. After that, Mary had no child to care for, and Victoria didn't either, and a great sadness hung over Skye's lodge. But it was the way of women to hide all that, and there were good moments because Skye was a man who brought happiness and good humor to his wives, and sometimes they laughed and had good times and met all sorts of people. Except that Skye never saw Mary shivering in the dark some nights outside of the lodge, all alone. There had been no more children. Who could say why? More children would have gladdened Mary's heart and Victoria's too. The barrenness was a mystery beyond knowing.

Victoria watched Mary scrape, noting the quiet resignation, the long lines on her still-young face, and the refuge Mary took in ceaseless toil. Mary worked compulsively now, never taking any time to gossip or sit with other women or play the stick game or tell stories. It was always work, work, work, for Mary, and Skye only saw Mary's big smiles.

It was Victoria's privilege, as Skye's senior wife, to make the decisions, and now she did. She settled beside the younger wife and joined in the scraping, feeling the familiar tug of the flint-edged scraper as it fleshed the hide.

"We will go find our man," she said. "Maybe he needs us."

Mary nodded.

Victoria scraped the elk hide some more, until her back hurt, and then she stood.

"I will tell them," she said.

She straightened her winter skirt, this one of softest doeskin, and headed for the lodge of the village headman, greeting many wives along the path. The Absaroka headman now was Gout Belly, and so boyish that Victoria marveled. The headmen were all scarcely weaned in these times, she thought.

She didn't need to scratch at the lodge door, because Gout Belly was enjoying his morning nap on a light-skinned buffalo robe, letting Father Sun caress his caramel flesh.

"Why, Grandmother," he said, rising, because Victoria held a position of great honor in the village, and was known for her medicine as well as her advanced years. And it was no dishonor to be married to Mister Skye, either, though she thought it might be sometimes.

"It is a warm day, good chief Gout Belly, and I have come to slap flies away from you while you enjoy the sun."

"I imagine you have something to tell me, then. There are no flies as yet, so man and horse still await their bites."

"We will be going to Mister Skye," she said.

He considered it. "Then the village will be the worse without you."

"We will go with you to as far as the Yellowstone Valley tomorrow. Then you will go east, but we will travel up the river."

"Grandmother, there will be no man to protect you and the Shoshone woman."

"Who says we want to be protected, eh?" She grinned wickedly at Gout Belly.

"Then may a dozen Siksika catch you," he said, referring to the Blackfeet, mortal enemies of the People.

"I will turn them all into boys," she said, enjoying the banter.

He smiled. There were stories about Victoria, Many Quill Woman, told around many an Absaroka campfire deep in the night, to the sound of owls hooting.

The next dawn the Kicked-in-the-Bellies band of the Absaroka Nation slowly assembled into a column. Mary and Victoria pulled the willow sticks from the lodge cover and let it sag to earth, and then folded it and carried it to the travois. Then they undid the lodgepoles and hung them in bundles from a packsaddle. They had put their possessions into Skye's canvas panniers, and soon were ready.

At midmorning the procession wound away from the campsite where they had wintered. The place stank of waste and was shorn of firewood and was grazed down to the clay of the meadows. The Kicked-in-the-Bellies headed down Sweet Grass Creek. When they reached the valley of the Yellowstone, it was time for Victoria and Mary to leave the Absaroka People, and head west.

They watched the band until it was only a small dark line on the eastern horizon and then there was only silence and loneliness. Victoria nodded to Mary. It was time for them to head upriver. Mary sat inertly on her pony. When they were younger, she was often in the lead, eager to go wherever there was to go. Her face was still young and smooth, not like Victoria's seamed coppery face that had seen so many winters. Mary was still young, but now she was acting old and weary.

They rode their ponies over a faint trail that descended pine-dotted hills into the valley of the Yellowstone. Riding a pony wasn't so easy anymore for Victoria. The sharp bony vertebrae of the horse seemed to slice Victoria in two. That was one thing about age. Everything hurt, even things that once were pleasant and joyous. But Victoria sternly set aside her hurts and focused instead on the ride, on safety, on taking themselves, hour by hour, to Mister Skye.

They reached the riverbank during a spring squall, and continued westward along a worn trail, while wrapped in good blankets. That cold night they raised the lodge and found warmth and peace within.

It was only then that she realized Mary had barely spoken all day. Mary had not resisted anything, balked at anything, shown discomfort at anything, but neither had she laughed or chattered or exclaimed, for instance, when a flock of geese rose en masse. There was only that silence, and a haunted look in Mary's face. It had taken Victoria a while to discover it.

She watched Mary collect wood and silently build a small fire, silently fill a kettle and set it to boil, silently stare into the hazy twilight, her mind some vast distance from this place and this company. It was as if Mary weren't even present; that she had left Victoria in another world. Victoria kept her peace, said nothing, and watched closely.

Perhaps it was only a mood.

But as Victoria lay in her robes that early spring night, she realized that this silence had been present in Mary a long time. Present even when Skye was there, before he said he wanted a house. Mary had not visited with people in the village much. Winter times are merry times, when the People gamble, play games, flirt, and, above all, tell bawdy stories to while away the short days and bitter nights. But Mary had taken to staying in the lodge, and was often asleep, caught in her robes, when Skye or Victoria returned from a good night of storytelling and gossip.

Victoria lay in her blanket, shocked at herself for missing this change in Skye's Shoshone woman. She sensed that Mary of the Shoshone was so desolate that she scarcely cared about tomorrow. It was worse than sadness. Mary had been sad for several winters. No, this was something darker. And with another rush of understanding, she knew that there would be no happiness in Mary until the boy, North Star, would be returned to her. And that would never happen. The boy was far away, learning how to live as a white man.

nine

A cold gray dawn filtered through the smoke hole of the little lodge. Victoria knew what she must do. She arose quietly, padded into the frosty dawn, washed her face at the river, and then composed the words she would say to Mary.

When she pierced the door flap, Mary was sitting up, looking as listless this morning as she had in the twilight.

"Go to the river and wash. Then come back and heed my words," Victoria said.

Mary wrapped her blanket about her and vanished into the cold April dawn. Victoria waited, hunting for the words she still needed.

It was time for Mary to return to her people. Over a long life, Victoria had watched captive women slowly wither away, lonely and lost, wives of tribesmen whose tongue they did not know, treated harshly by senior wives, little better than slaves. There was nothing left for them, and sometimes they walked into a bitter winter's night never to return. She knew of Absaroka women taken by Siksika or Lakota warriors, women who never saw their own people again and simply died at an early age from the worst of all sickness, the disease of despair. Victoria had seen the reverse too, captive women taken by Absarokas in war, who spent the rest of their days in listless servitude right there in Absaroka villages. They died young and unmourned. It wasn't always like that. Some women did well in other tribes and lived happily. But some didn't.

Mary, or Blue Dawn, had never been a prisoner, but had married Skye freely long ago and the marriage brimmed with promise. But ever since her sole child, North Star, was sent away to a white man's school, Mary had slid farther and farther into solitude, which she had concealed with bright smiles. Victoria felt certain about the course she would take. Mary would go home to her people. If it angered Skye, Victoria would bear his anger. But Mary must leave, and this was a good moment for it, when everything was about to change. Maybe, among her brothers and their wives, life might return to Blue Dawn. Maybe not. But even as Victoria reasoned it out, she felt a hardening of her will.

At last Mary slipped into the lodge and sat down, awaiting whatever might come.

"I want you to go away from me. Go to your people. Take the lodge. I don't need it."

"But, Grandmother . . ." Mary said, using the term of greatest respect.

"Blue Dawn," Victoria replied, using the Shoshone name, "I want you to visit your people. Your brother, The Runner, will be pleased to see you."

"But, Grandmother, I am the younger wife of Mister Skye."

"It is my command," Victoria said roughly.

Blue Dawn slid into her silences again.

"Ahead is a crossing place, shallow and gravelly. And

when you're across, start downriver and turn off where the trail goes to the Big Horn Valley. You know it well. And when it reaches the Shoshone River, you will be in your people's land again. Go!"

"Yes, Grandmother, if you say it."

"You will take the lodge. I cannot raise it alone."

Mary started to protest. It was true. It was beyond Victoria's powers now to lift the heavy lodge cover and pin it in place with willow sticks.

"The lodge will tell all who see it that you are Mister Skye's woman."

"It will say that. All the people know that lodge."

"There is a desert crossing, long and hard, before you reach the Shoshone River. Water your ponies well, and do not forget to take water for yourself."

"Yes, Grandmother."

"And honor the Shoshone people with my regards."

"I will tell them."

"And because you will be alone, go with great care."

"The spirits will guide me, Grandmother."

"We will know where you are and someday we will come for you. Now let us be off. The crossing is not far ahead."

For the first time in many days, Mary smiled.

They broke camp swiftly and loaded the ponies. Mary would have three, two for the lodge and her saddle pony. Victoria would have only her quiet old mare. She would have her blankets, a piece of canvas, a sack with some provisions, her bow and quiver, and her small rifle. It would be fine.

Two hours later they reached the crossing, and Victoria watched Mary lead her horses across a gravelly bar and negotiate the deeper channel on the far side, without trouble in this time of lowest water, just ahead of the spring flood. Then they stood a moment on opposite banks of the great river the white men called the Yellowstone. Mary lifted one brown hand high, and Victoria replied. Then Skye's younger wife mounted, settled her skirts, and rode downriver, the pack-horses just behind her.

Victoria watched her go, knowing it was a good decision. A time with her people would lift Blue Dawn's heart. Skye would approve. The low sun slanted toward the stream, raising sparkles wherever its rays touched the water. Mary's trip would take an entire moon or so, and there would be danger in every step. She would follow the Yellowstone until it had flowed past the mightiest of all mountain ranges, the Beartooths, and then she would turn south and pass between the Beartooths and the Pryor Mountains, and then cross a terrible desert, and at last she would arrive in the lands cherished by her people, but she still would have many days of travel after that.

Victoria eyed the trail westward with apprehension, not because of danger but because she felt her years and everything was harder to do. It was harder to stay warm, harder to find food, harder to find shelter. Harder to fend off wild animals. She felt an odd sadness, but pushed it aside. She would not surrender to sadness.

All alone now, she braved a brisk west wind and walked her pony along a well-worn riverside trail. Her task was to find Skye. She had been his woman when they were young; she would be his woman now, until death separated them. She would be his woman until she was helpless; or maybe he would be her man until he was helpless. She didn't need much care. She ate little more these days than a sparrow would. The only darkness she saw at all in great age was the lack of comfort. Neither she nor Skye could find much comfort these times. Their backs hurt, or their muscles, or they were too hot or cold, or their feet ached, or their food disagreed with them.

"Sonofabitch!" she said to the wind. "I want some whiskey."

Spirits still killed the pain. But they rarely had any and couldn't afford to buy any from the white men. With a few jugs of whiskey, old age wouldn't be so hard. She'd once heard an old white man call it painkiller, and now she knew why.

She loved whiskey sometimes, but not always. It took her senses away, and it was cruel too. There were other things she learned of long ago, when she received the healing wisdom of her people, good things that did no harm and brought spirit and body together. Now that she was old and hurt much of the time, these things had taken new meaning in her mind. She wanted to be whole, to make spirit and body one again, and not at war. There was one herb she carried with her for that. She prized the peppermint leaf above all else, and often made a tea of it. Deep in her kit, she had some. Just a little. Maybe she would find more. The peppermint, as white men called it, grew along riverbanks. This was a good tea, gathered and used by women. So was willow bark tea, which subdued pain and blessed the lower back, where pain gathered in old men and old women. She had some of both, and this night she would brew a little tea, and maybe that would give her strength and sustain life another day.

There were other herbs known to the Absaroka People, and not a summer went by that she failed to learn more, for the quest for medicinal herbs was a passion with her people. There were herbs for every malady of the human body. Herbs to stop nosebleeds, reduce swelling, teas to quiet an unruly stomach, herbs to calm the spirit, herbs to bring visions to those seeking them. Teas and herbs that brought comfort to the very old. She hoped to share these things with Skye in the days ahead, when their bodies troubled them more and more. Was she not a medicine woman of the People, with great powers?

But this night, alone in the great valley of the Yellowstone, she would find a place to brew peppermint and sip it and welcome the air spirits and the earth spirits to come watch over her through the cold night. Her entire kitchen consisted of one small copper pot and a knife. It was enough.

She rode quietly up the Yellowstone River. The waters of this river tumbled out of the Roof of the World and raced eastward toward the Big River. The water was icy and teeming with trout, but no Absaroka would stoop to eating fish. She despised fish, and thought that eating fish was the reason white men and women were sick all the time. But the water was icy and sweet, and sometimes she paused at the gravelly bank just to sip some.

She saw no one. Ever since the Lakota had stopped white men from using John Bozeman's trail two years earlier, the road had grown weeds and fallen into silence. Now it was rapidly disappearing as rain and snow smoothed the ruts and grass hid the campgrounds. Was this the end of white men? Had the Lakota driven them away forever? Foolish question. It was just a small time of quietness before the noise of the white men started again.

It was a good road for wagons but she felt no need to follow it. Her pony took her anywhere she wished, and not just along a trail calculated to let wagons pass over the land. So she watched eagles hunt, and hawks patrol, and listened to ravens comment about every passing thing. Her spirit helper, the white and black magpie, flitted here and there. All her life, Victoria and magpies knew each other and helped each other. Now she saw half a dozen of them making a ruckus about something, so she strung her bow and nocked an arrow, drawn from the quiver at her back, and rode ahead, not knowing what she might see.

It proved to be a black bear out of her winter den, probably ornery, hunting for food just when nature provided little. A newborn cub appeared from a hidden place in the river brush, already knowing how to hide itself at his mother's command. Victoria gave the mother bear wide berth, something her nervous pony seemed to appreciate. Let them live and grow. She honored bears as her sisters.

Later she came across a pregnant antelope, restlessly circling a sunny valley, looking for a safe place to birth. Victoria lowered her bow. Let the mother live; let the newborn suck on her teat, find life, and enjoy the spring breezes. The older Victoria got, the more something in her resisted taking female life. It did not matter why. This is how she felt, so this is how she would conduct herself. But she would kill and eat any brother male sonofabitch.

That night she brewed willow bark tea to drive away the pains of her body, and then rested, sitting against sun-warmed sandstone, her robe around her. If she didn't eat, what did it matter? What she wanted of life now was escape from the pain in her bones.

The next day was much the same, but she knew she was getting close to Skye. She entered a narrows where the river had punched through some gray and brown rock, and here the trail took her across wind-scraped slopes until she could descend again. She passed by some mule deer at sunset, and kept on because the great bend of the river was not far, only an hour or so more and she could be with Skye this evening, and maybe hold him and make jokes with him, and rub his back if he hurt, which he always did.

But when she reached the great bend in the early dark, she found no one there. It was as quiet as if no noisy white man had ever been there. She saw no cook fire. She hunted for his campsite and found nothing new; some very old and lonely-looking. She knew he was careful in danger, and might have moved his camp away from the river and into the foothills, or maybe up the Shields River to avoid someone or something. So she searched all the places she knew he would choose, and found no sign of him, and as dusk closed she puzzled where he might be.

But this was a large place, and he could be anywhere. The night thickened, and the last alpen glow vanished from the giant shoulders high above, and she could no longer see.

She built a noisy white men's fire, sending sparks high into the night, knowing he would see it and scout it out. Then she withdrew from the flames and shrouded herself in darkness some distance away, and waited. Surely her man would come, understand, and begin a search that would reunite them.

The cold settled around her, and the night grew still and dark. She undid the halters of her ponies and let them graze freely, and settled in her robes, and waited patiently for dawn and the stories it might tell her.

ten

The moment Mary crossed the Yellowstone and stood on the far shore, a river apart from Victoria, she knew herself as Blue Dawn, the Shoshone. Mary had vanished from mind. That was unexpected. Now she was Blue Dawn, en route to visit her people, maybe stay in the lodge of her brother, The Runner, until she was called to Skye's lodge at some unknown time.

But there was more. She had become a different person, too, just by crossing that river. For many years, she had been Skye's woman, Skye's younger wife, and had made no decisions of her own. Whatever Skye and Victoria did, her fate was to go with them, believe what they believed, love what they loved, befriend whomever they befriended. Now, suddenly, Victoria had given Mary her liberty, a time apart from the Skye household among the Crows.

Those had been happy times at first, time when she brought North Star into the world and loved the child and nurtured him and the three of them all raised the boy, and life was sweet. Those times glowed in her mind. She had a son, she was the woman of the greatly honored Mister Skye, and she had marveled at all the new things that came to her, things that might never have brightened her if she had become the woman of one of her people. No other child came to them, though she hoped more would. It was a mystery.

Then Skye changed everything. He wanted the boy to be schooled in white men's mysteries. Her son was taken far away, where the Big River met the Father of Waters. And that's when the sadness seeped into her life, and she learned to smile at Skye and laugh when he and Victoria laughed, and did her tasks faithfully and with many smiles. But it was not good. Who could say whether she would ever see this flesh of her flesh again? She loved the sturdy boy, and when he was taken away he was torn too, because he was too young to be ripped from his mother, and he looked desperately at her, that one last desperate look, when Colonel Bullock drove away in a buggy carrying her son with him.

The letters came once in a while, addressed to her in a child's hand, and Skye read them to her whenever they stopped at Fort Laramie, where the letters collected. And she wrote her boy, or rather had Skye make the marks on paper that signified what she said, and she sent her letters to St. Louis.

And so the years passed, and all that while Mary smiled at Skye and Victoria while her heart grew heavier and the days grew longer, until she thought she could not bear another hour of another day. But she hid it all. Now she stood on the far bank, seeing Victoria wave to her, and already she was changed. For the first time since she had reached womanhood, Blue Dawn had no master or mistress saying what must be thought or done or hoped for.

The sense of it was huge, so huge that she could not

fathom what was happening inside of her. When Victoria had proposed that she spend time with her people, she had not dreamed that she would become another person, someone new and old at once. She knew at once who this new and old self was: she was North Star's mother now, and not Skye's younger wife. She watched Victoria collect her horse and ride slowly west, upriver, and vanish. Blue Dawn sorrowed. She loved Victoria. She loved Skye. But now some inner force was rushing through her, and she knew her first task was to cache the lodge. She didn't want it. She looked for cliffs hemming the south bank of the river, and saw none. Better to cache something like that high in a cliff, where it would stay dry and undiscovered, than in any low place.

She traveled east until she found a decayed cliff with some hollows in it, well above the river. It would do. She unloaded the lodgepoles and the lodge cover and pushed them to the rear of a dry shelf where they would escape most weather. And then she hung the rest of her kit on the pack frame of one pony, and retreated. At the base, she studied the place for a landmark, found one—an odd column of striated rock—and knew she would remember how to reclaim the lodge someday.

Now, riding one pony and leading two others, she headed south through a lonely land on a chill spring day. She knew the way. She would find a home with her brother, The Runner, and renew her life. But not right away. Not for a while. Not for many moons. That insight startled her, just as everything else had startled her the moment she was separated from the iron rule of Victoria. Day after day she rode through a chill spring, alone and unnoticed, quietly following the Yellowstone as it hurried east, marveling at the change within her.

For the first time in her life, she was free. She marveled at it. She was alone. It was strange, something she felt more in her chest than in her head. Skye had made all the family decisions. Victoria had not been a bossy senior wife but had expected Mary to join her in whatever needed doing, whether it was collecting firewood or sewing moccasins. When it came to raising the boy, Victoria and Mary were both mothers. And now Mary traveled with no one beside her, the hollow land spreading away from her in all directions. It brought an almost unbearable ache to her bosom. She could turn her ponies and go west if she chose, or east, or north, or south. She could stop if she chose, start if she chose, ascend the nearest peak if she chose. It made her giddy at first, but then it made her hurt.

The vision of North Star, far away in a white man's school, made her ache inside, ache as she never had ached except for the day when he was taken from her. She wanted just to see him. This hunger arose in her breasts and womb, not her mind. She had a maternal hunger she could not drive out of her, a hunger that rode the crest of her sudden liberty, a hunger that formed visions of the eight-year-old boy in her mind, where the images burned and smoldered and built into a flood of anguish. The sun rose in the east each morning, rose where North Star must be.

St. Louis was a long way off. It lay in some mysterious place far across prairie country, and then across hilly country, and finally at the throat of the rivers. Once she had heard that it would take two moons to walk there. She could scarcely imagine it. The white men had built a railroad for their steam wagons, but she didn't know whether it would take her to St. Louis. She did know that the steamboats would take her there, down the Big River, but she had no money for that. And she didn't know whether they would permit a woman of the People to travel there alone. White men had strange rules, and she had never fathomed them or where they came from or why they existed.

The farther she rode, the more determined she became. Should she find her people first, and tell her brother where she was going to go? Should she find the Absarokas and tell them? That might be good, but it would not be her way. She had settled on a way, and now she would follow it, no matter where it might lead her.

Would she even recognize her son? Of course she would. Now he would have fifteen winters. She would know him on sight. And he would know her. She hardly dared imagine what might happen then; whether they could spend time together, renew the ties of kinship, of mothers and sons together. Since she didn't know, she set that aside. She only knew that she would follow the path to this place called St. Louis, and she would find her son, and then the future would take care of itself.

She knew how to go there, more or less. She needed to reach the Big Road, the one that went past Fort Laramie, where she and Skye had been many times. The Big Road would not have many travelers on it now that the steam wagons were going on the iron rails. That would be good. Her ponies could graze.

She wasn't sure how to reach the Big Road from the Big Horn Valley, though. If she could find the trail she had traveled many times with Skye, she would be all right. But she didn't need a road. Her pony would take her almost anywhere. White men needed roads, but Shoshones needed only a keen eye.

She traveled quietly, not thinking about anything. Once

she spotted a group of white men on mules on the north side of the Yellowstone. She feared them more than warriors from other tribes. These were probably miners. They had spread across the land, wanting to tear up the earth and rock. There was no telling what was in their minds, or what they would do with a lone Indian woman.

But they did not see her. That was because she traveled lightly across the breast of the earth, blending in to rock and clay and brush, moving slowly, as a grazing animal might move, so that she didn't stir up the ravens and magpies, and no crows scolded her. It took many days before she reached the turnoff and headed south, leaving the Yellowstone behind her. But it was all as she remembered it. She was not lost.

The great basin of the Big Horn ran north and south, and was guarded by snowy peaks to the east, and to the west barren, gloomy hills that slowly rose to high country, and the great backbone of the world, still wrapped in blinding white. It was spring in the basin, but winter above, and sometimes the winds reminded her that Father Cold had not departed and was waiting to bite her cheeks.

She stayed well away from the Big Horn River, wondering whether she might run into Victoria's people, the Kicked-in-the-Bellies band, making their summer home on lush pasture along the great stream. Her trip to St. Louis would be a secret from all the people. They were all her friends and would welcome her with smiles and much honor, but they might also ask too many questions and she was not in a mood to answer them. So she ghosted south, clinging to the barren foothills, where there was little game. She did not suffer for food, for she could make a meal of almost anything, and now tender buds filled her cook pot, and little new roots, and fresh-laid eggs stolen from nests. She did spend time at all this, but did not hunger and was content.

One night she weathered a sleet storm and bitter winds, but she turned her sleep-canvas into a poncho, and rode her pony while inside of her little tent, and kept Father Cold at bay.

The next morning frost lay thick upon the land, and every stem of grass was whitened, but that did not stop her ponies from grazing it.

She thought she knew where the Absaroka People were summering and gave that place a wide berth so that no tribal elders would stay her or ask where she was going. She did not feel that she was doing anything wrong; only that she had chosen a Way, and she intended to walk the Way, and it was not anyone else's business where she walked, or why.

But if she avoided contact with the Absaroka, she dreaded even more an accidental meeting with her own band, where she might find herself the guest of her brother The Runner, a great headman among them, and then she might be required to tell them where she was going. Then she would be forced to divulge her secret. In truth, she would be less free with her clan, and they might not honor the Way she had chosen for herself. But they were mostly likely on the Wind River, far south, with the Owl Creek Mountains lying between this valley and that one. That was their true home, except when they went hunting for the shaggies. She would not go that way. There was a creek named after Mister Skye's friend Jim Bridger that would take her across the eastern mountains to the Big Road.

She drifted south, and her ponies fattened as they walked, nipping at the tender spring grasses that now were pushing exuberantly toward the heavens. She chose a path that took her across the foothills of the Big Horn Mountains, a path that was not easy because it was up and down, but a path that let her follow her Way. Her resolve hardened in her. She had wavered for many suns, wondering what her man, Mister Skye, might think. He might not like her new Way, but she couldn't help that.

Several times, while she sat quietly on her pony on a pine-dotted slope, she saw horsemen far below, small dots moving in a hurried way. She could not tell who they were. She could not even say whether they were one of the People or white men.

One day, in the middle of what white men called May, she found the road up Bridger's creek and took it. This was a wagon road, but not much used anymore, and now the ancient ruts were filled with grass, and places where the white men had carved into slopes or built little bridges were washing away. She had been on it several times with Skye and Victoria; it would take her to the Big Road and Fort Laramie.

It was also a twisty, hilly road and that was what bought her trouble. She rounded a shoulder one moment, and there before her was a cavalry patrol, ten bluecoats, all mounted, with several packmules behind.

Within moments they swarmed around her, eyeing her from under their duck-billed hats. Their leader, a one-bar-on-the-shoulder, motioned her to halt.

"You speekee white?" he asked.

She thought better of replying, and slowly shook her head. It was safer to say and do nothing. One never knew about blue-belly soldiers.

He tried a few hand signs he had picked up somewhere, signs that read, Who are you? What tribe? Where are you going? She smiled and shook her head.

They were eyeing her ponies and the little that she was carrying, mostly her bedroll and a small kit of personal things.

"I guess we'd better take you with us," the officer said after a few moments of impasse. "Can't rightly say what a lone squaw's doing around here."

eleven

$\mathcal{M}$ary wondered whether it had been a mistake, hiding her English from them. Now they wanted to take her somewhere, make a prisoner of her.

She chose to speak in Shoshone, telling them that she was Blue Dawn, of the Eastern Shoshone people of Washakie, and she was going to Fort Laramie now.

"I think that's Shoshone," said a three-stripe sergeant tanned to the color of cedar bark.

He eyed her, and made the wavy line in sign language that signified her people.

She nodded slightly.

"Squaw's a Shoshone, all right, but that ain't what they usually wear," the sergeant said.

"Can you talk it?" the one-bar-on-the-shoulder asked.

"Not enough to say anything to her. I can listen it a little."

"Try telling her she can't leave the reservation. Washakie's got himself a home over on the Wind River, and now they got to stay there."

Mary bridled at that. What was this? Making her people stay on the river?

The seamed old sergeant tried a little sign language, a few Shoshone words, and a few English just to salt the talk a little.

"See here, little lady," he said, his hands making signs. "You got to go back now. You got a nice place, and you got to get a paper from the agent to leave."

She refused to acknowledge what she was hearing and seeing, but sat sternly on her pony. How could this be? Were the People prisoners now?

She didn't want to know any more. She would ask Skye about it.

"I don't see she's doing any harm here," the sergeant said.

"Search the panniers," the one-bar said.

Mary slumped deep into her saddle, pushing back an anger that boiled through her.

A one-stripe got off his pony and opened the pannier, poking around at her kettle and flint and steel and bag of pemmican. Then he lifted up the packet of letters, the ones from North Star that came to Fort Laramie, the ones Skye patiently read to her, over and over.

"She's got some letters, looks like," the one-stripe said, and handed them to the one-bar-on-the-shoulder.

"Sent to a Barnaby Skye, care of the post sutler, Fort Laramie. Never heard of him."

"I have," the sergeant said. "Old squaw man. Thought he was dead long ago. He was a mountain man before he settled in with the Crows."

"Still alive, looks like," the one-bar said. "Postmarked this March."

"She's just checking the fort for Skye's mail," the three-stripe sergeant said. "Probably some slut of Skye's, sent down to get the news."

Mary reddened.

The one-bar turned to her. "Fort Laramie?" he asked, slowly enunciating La-ra-me.

She nodded.

"Well, no harm in it. Now if you were a buck, we'd march you back to your reservation."

He returned the packet to the one-stripe, who put it back in her pannier and closed it.

"Free to go," he said to her. "I imagine you understood some of this, if you're tied up with the squaw man."

Mary didn't acknowledge it.

The patrol formed into twos and headed toward the Big Horn Basin. She suppressed a tremor and urged her ponies south. She needed to think about this insult. And about this penning of the People.

The whole world looked different now, as if the sun had decided to travel from west to east, or as if Father Winter decided to be warm and Brother Summer decided to freeze the toes of the People. How could this be? The Absarokas had talked of it, but she hadn't paid much attention. Skye didn't talk of it at all, which told her much.

Whose land did she now walk upon? She walked over the breast of the earth, and it was the privilege of all to walk upon all the earth. What were the soldiers doing? Looking for hunters or war parties, to send them back to their new prisons? And how was all this arranged? Who agreed to it?

She remembered that two summers earlier there had been a great gathering at Fort Laramie, in which the white fathers had proposed homes for the several tribes. And her chief, Washakie, had agreed to it. He was their friend. But did this now mean that the People were prisoners, unlike white people, who could go anywhere they chose?

Was this what her son, North Star, was learning in this school in St. Louis? What of him, half of one blood and half of another? If they looked at him as Mister Skye's son, he could go anywhere and live anywhere. If they looked at him as her boy, they would make him stay on the Wind River Reservation, and not leave without permission. He would have to stay inside of some invisible lines, best known by the white men who drew them. Was this right? Was that why Skye had sent him to the school, so that he would be free?

The encounter with the bluecoats had changed everything, but she didn't quite know how. She would sort it out as she traveled. She hurried along the road—the white man's road—that would take her over the mountains. Whose mountains now? Did these white men own the sun and stars and moon too? Did they claim the rivers and lakes? Was all the fish and game theirs now? Were the blessed buffalo and elk and deer and coyotes theirs now, except when they crossed a homeland of a tribe?

The land looked just the same as she had remembered it. The rushing creek, just beginning to swell with snowmelt, raced beside her. The cliffs that hemmed the creek and its valley were ancient beyond measure, gray rock that no man could ever own. The pines that scattered themselves in the watercourses of this dry land belonged to no one. As she gained altitude the cold grew intense, and soon she was in rotting snow, which wearied the ponies. She wrapped the bright cream blanket with red stripes—a white man's blanket—tight about her as her pony slopped through slush.

Did the slush belong to white men? Did the grass her

ponies ate belong to white men? Did white men have the right to graze their ponies on the homelands of the tribes? Did the white men own all things in the earth and water and high above?

Late that day she reached the summit, and walked her ponies through soggy snow, dirtied by dust and the passage of animals. Now she could see the prints of the shod hooves of the soldiers, caught in cold shadow where they would remain until Father Sun caught them.

Dusk caught her well down the southerly flanks, on a grassy flat that had warmed all day in the tender spring sun. She scouted for a place to make a camp; the whole world was wet and there was nowhere to lie down without an icy soaking. She turned toward distant cliffs, knowing those would be her sole comfort. She easily found a hollow under an overhang, and knew it would do as well as anything. She was well off the trail, but that was good. She had no protection at all except for a few knives, one sheathed at her waist, the others in her kitchen gear.

The hollow had lion scat in it, and not at all ancient, either. A mother had nursed her cubs here. Mary didn't know how she knew that, but she did. Women found safe places and made homes of them.

She turned the ponies out on the grass. They were docile, and would graze deep into the night, unless a wolf or a lion prowled. She would forgo a fire this night, and instead settled in the back of the hollow, wrapped tightly in her blanket. She felt comfortable in this woman's place.

She had rarely seen a white woman. The men had pushed into these lands, gangs and pairs and columns of them, leaving their women behind. Even Skye had come alone, without a woman, long ago. Now it was men, not women, who were drawing an invisible line upon the breast of the earth, and making her people stay on one side of it. Would a woman do anything like that? Men were mysterious, and the cause of all change. She knew it was not her office to do those things, draw boundaries, make war, make the earth different. Her office was to gather food and feed the men, and to bring her boy to manhood.

Maybe when she got to this place called St. Louis, she would see lots of white women, and not just the handful who westered with their men. She could talk to women. She could share knowledge. She knew the best ways to gather roots and seeds and cook them. She knew the best ways to make elk-skin clothing for Mister Skye. She made the best moccasins, better than Victoria's moccasins, and they lasted longer too.

She knew it would be easier for her to go to this faraway place because she was a woman. A Shoshone man might find trouble with every step. White people didn't like Indian men and were suspicious of them, and thought they would steal or kill. So it was good to be a woman going to the place Skye called St. Louis.

The night passed peacefully. She had dozed eventually, and had seen many night-visitors who had stopped at the hollow to see who was there. She sensed the mother lion had come and gone while she slept, and had left her alone.

In the dawn she discerned her three ponies grazing peacefully. Patches of fog hid the world. She felt good, had enjoyed a bone-dry night, and now it was time to ghost through the mist, ever downhill to the river the white men called the North Platte.

When she reached the Big Road days later she found it empty, and the reason was plain. It was so wet that wagons could not roll over it without miring. She saw awful ruts dug by iron wheels, and ox-prints deep in the muck, where weary animals had struggled to drag the gumbo-bound wagons. It was too early for the great migration of white people, and those who had tried it this time of year were undoubtedly regretting it.

The muck was hard even on her ponies, but she was not bound to the road, and found easier passage off to the side, away from the mire. She was in no hurry, either, and let her ponies fatten on the tender grasses joyously reaching for the sun.

When she did come across white men, they were usually with pack animals rather than wagons. They always looked her over with curiosity, but she never let on that she understood what they were saying. Sometimes their comments about savages or filthy squaws made her burn. Whenever they stopped to converse with her, she spoke only Shoshone and smiled quietly. It was good. One cheerful company of bearded prospectors even gave her a sack of flour as a gift, just because they felt like it.

"Lifts the heart to see a right pretty lady," one said.

She nodded, and acknowledged the gift with a bright smile.

By the time she reached Fort Laramie she had resolved not to stop there. Skye's friend Colonel Bullock was no longer operating the store. She didn't know a soul, and had no money or credit to buy anything. And she didn't need anything anyway, but some bright ribbons would have given her joy.

She was observed. All who passed the post were carefully observed and counted by the army. But she was a woman, after all, and what did it matter? So she walked her ponies past the flapping red, white, and blue flag, and the blue regimental flag, and the blue-bellies who were lounging on the shaded veranda of the store, and the others working at the stables or chopping firewood. There was scarcely an immigrant wagon parked there, but in this month of May, as they called it, who could travel? It was chilly, and she smelled the pine smoke from all the fort's fires drifting through the narrows that contained the post.

And then she was free, advancing eastward toward the great quiet prairies, where only the wind made a sound.

twelve

Many Quill Woman—she used her Absaroka name more and more these winters—woke alone after a light doze. Skye was not at the bend of the Yellowstone. She padded down to the water's edge and washed her face and hands, feeling the icy water abrade her seamed flesh. There were young cattails rising from the mud of a slough nearby. Maybe she would make a breakfast of their starchy roots. But she didn't feel hungry. She often forgot to eat, just like so many of the old ones in her village.

She felt all right, except for the great weariness that comes to reside in one's body after a long life. She was used to it. But she thought she could never get used to the loss of vision, the thin yellow skim that softened everything and made the bright clean world hazy. Someday soon the only light that would reach her would be milky and the world would be white and without form.

She found her pony grazing peacefully, and bridled and saddled her. A simple hackamore and a light saddle built over a sawbuck frame sufficed. She had made a hundred of them over the years. A saddle provided a place to hang her feet and kept the pony's backbone from sawing her in two. She rolled her few things in her blankets and tied the roll on the cantle. She would not bother with breakfast.

She began a spiral circle, looking for anything she did not wish to see. Her eyes weren't good, but she would not miss what she dreaded to see. She stopped at the ashes of a campfire, dismounted, and studied the area. She could not tell how old it was. She remounted, circled wider, probed adjoining gulches, and studied the land from ridges.

He was not there. He had not died there, either, unless the relentless river had washed him away. She hunched into her saddle a moment, drawing her old coat tight against the probing May breeze, and then turned toward the mountains. Beyond them was white men's land, and the place called Bozeman City.

She ascended into winter, and the next day descended into spring, riding past Fort Ellis, built to protect white people from the wild Indians to the east. No one at that sprawling complex of log buildings noticed. She was a bony old squaw, and thus not important. She reached Bozeman City a while later, passing a wagon yard first, and then a barn, and finally a scatter of wooden buildings, some of sawn wood, some of log, some whitewashed, most of them weathering gray with the sun and rain.

No adult noticed. Who cared about a lone squaw? But finally some children collected, trotting along beside her as she sat her pony. Boys, mostly, wild little things without the manners of any Absaroka child.

"Hey, you speak English?" a blond boy yelled.

"You're goddamn right," she replied.

"Oh!"

"Hey, how come you talk that way?" a freckled kid asked.

"So white boys will shit their pants," she said.

"Boy, wait till I tell my pa about you!"

"Where you going?" asked another, this one smaller.

"I'm going to scalp everyone in town and burn it," she replied.

"How come?"

"Because I'm a warrior woman, that's why."

"You ever kill a white man?"

"You bet your ass," she said.

That subdued them a little. They trailed a little behind, and finally out of arrow range, and she steered her pony along a mucky street lined with sagging mercantiles with false fronts, most of which looked ready to burn away at the slightest excuse. The tawdry little town darkened the golden expanses of the Three Forks country beyond, and she wished it would turn itself into dust.

Now that she was in Bozeman City, she scarcely knew what to do, where to look, what to ask. She felt safe enough. Age and femaleness protected her. If she had been a young Absaroka warrior riding proudly into town, things might be different. She felt an ancient helplessness she had known all her life when it came to dealing with white men.

Was Skye here? The town wasn't so big it could hide him. She chose a saloon. She could not read its name, but she knew somehow it was a drinking place. Maybe Skye would be inside.

She slid off her pony, letting her old limbs adjust, and then drew her blanket around her. The blanket warded off the gazes of white men, so she pulled it tight, to make a barrier to their eyes. She opened the creaking door and confronted the rank odor and darkness of these places. This was lit by a small window and nothing else. A line of hairy and smelly men stood at a bar. They all stared at her. Skye was not among them.

"Hey, squaw, you're not allowed. You want a bottle, you come to the back door. And have cash. I ain't bartering," the barkeep growled. He wiped his hairy hands across his grubby apron.

"Goddamn outhouses smell better than here," she said, and walked out.

There was no place for native people in this new world, she thought. Maybe Skye was right, sending the boy to be made into a white man. Maybe her people were dying out, never to return. Maybe she was the last generation of the Absaroka.

She looked for his ponies. She tried a clapboard mercantile, where the suspicious clerk, wearing a black sleeve garter and chin whiskers, followed her every step through the dry goods, obviously determined to prevent imminent theft.

"Shit on you," she said pleasantly at the door, which jangled as she left.

She probed a grocery, wandering past cracker barrels and pickle jars, again followed by a slit-eyed boy who carried a rolling pin as a defense against ancient redskins.

"Go to hell," she said.

She peered into the window of a saddlery but did not see him. She entered another saloon, but the barkeep barreled down on her, pointed toward the door, and pushed her through it. She did not have time enough to see if Skye was there, but his horse wasn't tied to the rail in front of the place. She circled around and checked the alley just in case he was lying in it.

To hell with all white men, and maybe Skye too, she thought. White men with their bread-dough faces and wiry beards and greedy eyes.

She peered into a restaurant, this one operated by a matronly woman wearing a black eye patch who frowned at her, and she did not see Skye there. Nothing but hairy white men eating away. She discovered a bank, one of those mysterious places she knew little about except that money issued from them and they took money away from others. She thought Skye might be in it, and discovered a great silence within, with two whiskered men locked into cages eyeing her. But no one said a word. They stared at her; she grinned at them.

"Goddamn," she said.

"May we help you, madam?" yellow whiskers asked.

"I want money. I think I'll be a rich sonofabitch," she said. "Build us a goddamn house."

"You will want to talk to our mortgage department," orange whiskers said. "And he's out foreclosing on a ranch."

She didn't know what that was, but it sounded bad. But she liked this whiskers. He had orange hairy cheeks, but he cut off the hair at lip level. And he wore an orange bush between his lips and his nostrils. He probably didn't like the way he looks, if he did that, she thought. Skye didn't care one way or another, and had himself a big hairy beard. But this one shaved in patches, smooth here, hairy there. Maybe that said something about him. Damned if she would ever understand white men.

"Hey, my man wants to build a big house. You got money for him?" she asked.

"He could apply for a mortgage," whiskers said. "He would need to have good credit."

"What's that?"

"Assets. Something to protect our loan to him."

"Like what?"

"Oh, deeded land, a business, a mine, a herd of cattle, investments. Does the gentleman have these things?"

"Hell no," she said. "He's got a lodge, two wives, a Sharps rifle, and bear medicine. He's got a bear-claw necklace, biggest goddamn claws you ever saw. You want collateral? Bear medicine is it. No one got medicine like Skye."

He pursed his lips. "That would make it more troublesome. We need tangible assets." He paused. "What does he do?"

"He sits in the lodge all winter and makes love first one wife and then the other."

"Is he a big chief?"

"Hell yes, biggest goddamn chief ever lived. I'm his older woman, and he's got a younger one too. More wives you got, the richer you are. How about that?"

"Ah, that wouldn't be collateral," whiskers said.

"Young wife, Mary, she's still pretty."

"Ah, madam, I'm afraid—"

"Damned if I know what this collateral is, but when I find him I'll drag him in here as soon as he's sobered up and we'll get you some. He's off sucking a bottle somewhere. Then we'll figure it out. Two wives, that's good collateral, eh?"

Whiskers smiled. "You make an interesting case," he said.

"Hey, goddamn, I'll be back," she said.

She perused the rest of Bozeman City, saw no sign of him, checked the alleys behind the saloons, where he wasn't, and finally realized the sonofabitch was somewhere else. On her way out of town, she passed the livery barn, saw his nag in the pen, got off her pony under the suspicious gaze of the owner, and approached.

"Where are you hiding the sonofabitch?" she asked.

The liveryman yawned and jerked a thumb toward a hay barn. "I got him where I want him," he said. "He's got no choice. He's the worst audience I ever had. I'd like a little respect but I don't get it from him."

She tromped into shadow, was struck with the sweet, pungent smell of hay, and found Skye lying on a spread-out canvas on a plateau of soft, prickly hay. She stared. His leg was bound up. Her man had a broken leg. Maybe he fell down in a saloon.

"I thought you might find me," he said.

"Goddammit," she said. "I leave you alone for a few days and you get into trouble."

He didn't laugh. She looked into his face and saw gauntness and pain there. There was more. She saw a broken man, hemmed by age.

"Now I listen," she said. "Tell me. You get drunk or something?"

"I got thrown by an ox," he said.

"You what?"

"Thrown by an ox! Don't you hear me?" he snapped.

Wearily Skye told her what had happened at the bend of the Yellowstone, and how he was rescued by some teamsters looking for livestock, and how the very ox that had caught and thrown him with its horns was now at work dragging a freight wagon.

"Still hurt some," he said. "But I'm here, and they're feeding me. I've got a roof over me and a bed."

"Oh, Skye," she said, and knelt beside him, then clung to him.

thirteen

The man looming above Skye as he lay in the hay barn proved to be the town marshal, Magnus Cropper. Skye assumed as much, noting the man's black frock coat and the steel circlet pinned to his lapel.

"I've been looking for you," Cropper said. "Complaints is what I'm dealing with."

Behind him, Clyde Kangaroo hovered, bristling with curiosity.

Skye felt Victoria tense beside him.

"This old squaw, she's not welcome in Bozeman City, scaring white boys half to death with her foul threats."

"They deserved some scaring," she said.

"Who are you?" the marshal asked.

"Mister Skye."

"A drifter, I suppose. Squaw man, looks like."

Skye sat up and clamped his ancient top hat to his locks.

"This is my wife, Victoria, of the Absaroka People," he said. "And you, sir?"

"Cropper, Skye. The law here." He had the look of someone not expecting trouble.

"I prefer to be addressed as mister."

Cropper smiled. "Don't matter how you want to be called. You're leaving town. Vagrants and tramps and foul-mouthed squaws, they ain't welcome. We're a proper town."

"He's a border man," Kangaroo said. "Been here forty, fifty years. He come to this country long before there was any Bozeman City. He led them fur brigades."

"Am I supposed to be impressed, Kangaroo?"

"He's got him a real reputation. I know all about him. He don't say nothing about himself, but I found it out. You ever heard of Jim Bridger? Well this one's twice Jim Bridger."

Cropper ignored the liveryman. "Don't matter," he said. "This pair ain't respectable white people, and that matters. And from the looks of them, they don't have a plugged nickel, so they're beggars, vagrants, and I'm shipping them out."

"I've a broken leg," Skye said.

"It matters not to me. Use a crutch."

"Goddamn savage," Victoria said.

"Public cussing, that's a misdemeanor," Cropper announced. "Taught some boys to foul their own mouths is what you did. I heard about it fast enough from a few folks. Here's your choice. You git out right now on your own, or I'll break your other knee."

"He didn't do nothing," Kangaroo said. "He's paid up for two more weeks. I traded him a month of chow for a pony."

"Then I suppose you owe him two weeks of chow," Cropper said.

"Marshal, this here man, you ask the old-timers who he is."

"He ain't welcome. We're civilized now," Cropper said.

Skye nodded to Victoria. "I can ride," he said. "My knee won't like it, but I'll deal with it."

Victoria stared bitterly at the marshal and headed for the pens where Skye's buckskin horse stood quietly, as well as her own pony.

"I tell you, Marshal, this here man is more than you think," Kangaroo said.

"What I think is that this hobo in greasy buckskins is on his way out of town."

The marshal hadn't backed down an inch. Skye looked him over. A bull of a man, with a boxer's build and stance and a lantern jaw. He seemed unarmed, but who could say?

"Any houses for sale in town?" Skye asked.

Cropper stared. "You couldn't afford an outhouse," he said.

Kangaroo vanished and Skye thought he was seeing the last of the liveryman.

"You took up with the Crows, so go back to them," Cropper said. "Go live in a skin tent."

The sheriff was somewhere in midlife, his face seamed from hard living. He was tough but his gut was bulging. He had Bozeman City in his pocket.

"Help me up," Skye said.

The marshal did so, lifting Skye by the shoulders. Skye stood on his good leg and leaned against a post.

"It ain't you bothers me, it's that foul-mouthed squaw. I don't want that kind of trash in my town. If it was just you, a white man, I wouldn't give a damn," Cropper said.

"That's a shiny badge," Skye said. "Too bad it doesn't shine."

Cropper spent some time processing that, looking for the insult, and finally snarled.

"Get on that nag and get out."

Victoria brought the saddled ponies up and helped Skye up. His knee howled, but there was nothing he could do about it. He tried to keep it pushed forward rather than bent, but it didn't do any good.

Then Kangaroo emerged toting a burlap sack.

"Here's two weeks' grub," he said. "Fair's fair. You didn't stay a month."

He handed it to Victoria.

It was all Skye could do to keep from fainting. The savage pain at his knee laced his leg, his thigh, his hip.

"Don't come back," Cropper said smoothly. "Next time, I'll get rough."

"A goddamn savage," Victoria said, loud enough so Cropper couldn't miss it.

"You want a night behind bars?" the marshal retorted.

They rode a well-worn trail toward the mountains.

"What's a vagrant, dammit?" Victoria asked.

"A drifter with no money or job."

"Well, hell, my whole tribe's vagrants."

"That's just about how the marshal sees you."

"But we got food and good ponies. We got houses and bows and arrows. We got everything we need."

Victoria took them east, going slowly to keep Skye from jarring his knee any more than necessary. But Skye knew he couldn't last long, and he felt sweat build in his brow. He wondered whether he'd manage one mile. But he hung on. Damned if he'd quit.

He lasted about as long as it took to reach Fort Ellis, three miles from Bozeman City, and then Victoria had to help him down. He tumbled heavily to the ground, his descent barely checked by her, and lay flat on his back. This was open

meadow, close to the post. He didn't know how he could
go on.

It didn't take long for the command to send a pair of
bluecoats to them.

"Trouble, sir?" asked a corporal.

"No, I'm just fine, and my wife's just fine, and the world's
just fine."

"Trouble, then."

Skye was too worn to respond.

"Get my man a wagon, dammit," Victoria said.

In time, Colonel Blossom appeared.

"You, is it? Something go wrong in town?"

"The city marshal decided we're vagrants."

"I insulted some boys, goddammit," Victoria said.

A faint smile bloomed in the middle of Blossom's beard.
"I'll get you settled, and we'll talk," Blossom said.

Skye nodded, too wearied by pain to say much.

They brought a spring wagon, gently lifted him into it,
and drove him into the post. Skye listened to the debate about
what to do with the civilian and his squaw, but hurt too much
to care. Eventually they cleaned out a harness room, brought
in a stuffed mattress, and settled Skye in the stables.

"Bring them a ration every mess," someone said.

Skye felt lucky, and soon felt luckier. He had a visitor.

"Mister Skye, I'm Balboa, the new post surgeon. Mind if
I have a look?"

"It can't hurt any more than it does now, sir."

The man was surprisingly gentle, and set about to replace
the splints the teamsters had used to encase Skye's leg with a
proper cast.

"I don't know for sure what's what in there, but nothing's
poking through. Your tibia's probably broken across here, but

you're too swollen up for me to tell. The fibula's broken here, where the hardness is. It's bad, and you'll limp. I'm going to give you some powders," Balboa said.

Skye nodded and downed a pill. That was the last he knew. He awakened in darkness and awakened in daylight, and the world turned over, and the pills they gave him leached the pain away, and he slept some more. Sometimes he awoke thirsty and they gave him cool water. He wasn't hungry, but the water was good. Victoria held the cup. Then they began slowing down the pills, and night and day slowed down too, until one day he awakened clearheaded and as weak as an infant.

They helped him sit up.

"It's been a while," Colonel Blossom said.

The man was sitting on a keg beside Skye's cot. Victoria sat on the rough plank floor.

"How long?"

"Five days. Your leg's not so inflamed, I understand."

Five days? Five days and nights lying in this harness room?

"I got your story from Mrs. Skye. I also talked some with Marshal Cropper, and Clyde Kangaroo, and a few others. Some of the teamsters too."

"You're going to send me back to Victoria's band, then?"

The commanding officer shrugged. "That's up to you. The story I've got from Mrs. Skye is that you're looking for a place to settle down. You'd like a hearth and a stove in the winter, and a veranda with a view in the summer."

"It got hard for me to winter with her people. They're good people, and they've taken care of us. But I need a home. I set out for the bend of the Yellowstone, that being the place with a good view every way a man looks, and that's where I ran into trouble."

"From an ox."

"Yes, an ox. Not a bear, not a catamount or a wolf, but a bloody ox. The country's full of wild oxen, abandoned along the Bozeman Trail—before the war."

"Dr. Balboa tells me you'll have a limp. The leg is pretty well locked up at the knee. That might change your plans."

Skye hated it. All his life he'd been fit. It would take a fit man to build a house. He had no money and would have to build it the hard way, the way the Yank pioneers did theirs, with an axe, a drawknife, and a stone boat.

"Not if I can help it," he said.

"I'm not here to discourage you, sir. You'll find out soon enough what you can do—and can't do."

"I'll do whatever it takes."

But Skye knew it was bravado. A log home might not be possible now, not if he intended to build it himself. Age and injury were murdering a dream. Had it come to this?

"At any rate, Mister Skye, you have the hospitality of Fort Ellis for as long as you need it." The colonel rose. "Glad you're coming along. Balboa's a good man."

Skye watched him go. He turned to Victoria, discovering that she had bedded herself on the floor of the harness room all this while, with nothing but her blankets. They had not offered a mattress to the squaw.

She sat beside him. "It's been a damned long time," she said roughly.

He felt all right, but his leg was a numb thing he couldn't move or flex even if he wanted to.

"You're looking at me," he said.

"I don't want to see your face," she replied.

"What's wrong with my face?"

"You're no good at hiding what you feel."

"I feel fine."

"Bullshit, Skye. You look like the sun will never shine again."

fourteen

*S*kye's bones healed steadily, but not the rest of him. One May day he was on a crutch the army lent him. One June day he hobbled around needing only a staff to cling to. Then the post surgeon, Balboa, cut away the plaster, and Skye discovered his leg was not going to flex at the knee anymore. The rotation at the knee didn't amount to much. Skye stared at the offending limb, and then at Victoria, and shook his head.

It was time to try riding. He managed to sit his pony, but only with the sore leg hanging free, out of the stirrup. Still, he could ride, and soon was able to go awhile on horse before the pain forced him to the ground.

He developed a new gait, one in which he furiously arced his injured leg forward and progressed with a rolling lurch. It took so much energy to walk that way that he soon wore out, and then his face was drawn and white, and his eyes turned as black as obsidian. Pain lines radiated from his mouth, and a perpetual frown furrowed his brow.

Still, he was tough. No man of the borders was ever

tougher, and Skye was learning new ways to endure. He was alive, and was flying his flags. Victoria had never heard a word of complaint. And not a word about the pain running through his body. There was just obdurate silence, quietness, and determination.

It was time to leave Fort Ellis. Victoria had dreaded the moment but the Skyes had worn out their welcome. Skye had said nothing of his plans. Whatever their future, it was locked in his mind. Victoria felt left out, isolated, and sometimes angry. It was as if he had crawled into himself and would not come out. One June day Skye thanked Colonel Blossom, and he and Victoria turned their ponies toward the mountains.

She didn't know where he intended to go. She sat easily on her pony, even though her own bones ached these days. But she was used to that. She was aging in a different manner, turning into a dry husk of a woman, and filled with an odd lightness. She didn't query him about anything. His plans would all come clear—if he had any plans. That was the terrible reality of age. The future simply vanishes. If he was heading for the Bend of the Yellowstone, and planned to stay there, she would know his plans were unchanged. He would build a house there or die trying.

She couldn't imagine it. She had watched white men build permanent houses. First they gathered rock for the foundation, dragging it from quarries on sleds they called stone boats. Then they trenched the earth with their spades and made it level. Then they mortared the rock into low walls. Then they built a framework of timbers for the floor and covered it with thick sawn wood. They felled straight pines, preferably lodgepole, barked them, skinned away the irregularities with a drawknife, notched the ends with an axe, and raised log walls with block and tackle, log by log by log. They sawed out a doorway and windows and cut lumber to frame them. They raised log rafters and laid down thick roof planks gotten from a mill, and shingled them with shakes they split off of short chunks of log. They added an iron stove or a big hearth of mortared stone, and framed rooms within. And that was just the beginning. They added doors and windows, stairs, porches and outhouses, a kitchen, a spring house, a well or piped-in spring water. They built sheds for their horses and hay. It took a lot of men to do all that, and it wasn't done quickly. And if they had livestock they would need to fence the land, and plant gardens, and build a paddock for the horses. That was one thing about white men she admired. Some of them worked ceaselessly, unlike the Absaroka men, who gambled and hunted and told stories and made war, and died, but rarely toiled at anything.

They made only a few miles that day, but the next day they topped the divide and descended a drainage that would take them to the Yellowstone. The day after that they were back in what the white men called Indian Country, though it was only twenty-odd miles from Bozeman City. Skye rode to the place where the ox had destroyed his body, and pointed. There was nothing to see. Whatever happened was locked in Skye's head, and he would not share it.

He sat on the horse, surveying the place he obviously loved, the place that had wrought dreams in him. Spring rains had greened the slopes. Puffball clouds hung on snowy peaks. The river, gorged with snowmelt, sparkled in bold sunlight.

She watched him quietly, knowing something of what was passing through his heart. He didn't move for the longest time, but she knew the exact moment of surrender. Something in him changed. He was letting go of this dream, defeated by age and wounds and a hard life. Instead of sagging into his saddle, he stiffened, sat more rigidly, clamped the old top hat tighter. It was as if, in defeat, he would fly all his flags.

"Mary's with her people?" he asked.

The question rose out of the mists.

"I told her get the hell down there."

"You had a reason."

"She ain't herself, dammit. I told her to visit her brother. Talk to all them goddamn nieces and nephews and aunts and uncles and cousins and clan. Talk Shoshone with all of them Snakes around there."

"Where's the lodge?"

"I told her to take it."

"I always liked Chief Washakie," he said.

And so it was settled.

But the Eastern Shoshone were far away, and it would take many days to reach them. He didn't want to say what both of them were thinking. Mary was younger and strong, and would help care for them.

But Victoria felt a searing pain, not only her own pain but his, for in that moment he was surrendering his dream of a homestead at this place that sang to him, a home with a great porch where he could watch the last light of the sun fall upon the vaulting mountains that formed the spine of the whole world, and gild them.

They rode quietly eastward. Both of them were thinking the same thing; she didn't know how she knew that, but she did. To reach Mary, they would have to cross the Yellowstone, which now was at flood tide, wide and cold and swift and cruel. This was the time of year when gravelly fords vanished, hidden logs careened down the river, ice floes jammed themselves into temporary dams, and the water was barely above freezing. Still, they didn't have to deal with any of that for a few weeks. They were many sleeps away from the place where they would turn south.

They struggled downriver. Skye had turned stoic. Sometimes he looked ashen, his lips compressed, the ridges of corded muscle lining his face. A June thundershower pelted them where there was no shelter, and they endured the slap of rain and the spray of hail. Afterward, they found a dry place, built a fire, stripped, and set their clothing and unrolled blankets to drying on a rustic frame. She still enjoyed the sight of Skye naked, all fishbelly white except for his face and hands and neck, and his venerable hat perched on gray locks. Nothing was quite as amusing as a naked white man. She was brown everywhere, brown and slim, with withered arms and small breasts.

A magpie had joined them, gaudy black and white, bold and raucous. She nodded. This one perched on a limb, then on the heap of driftwood she gathered, and then paraded back and forth, its lurching walk different from that of any other bird.

"Go to hell," she said to the magpie.

The bird heckled her and flapped away.

Skye cleaned the rain off his Sharps while she gathered wood to keep the smoky fire blazing. Everything that took work was now up to her. She unsaddled the ponies, haltered and picketed them on good grass. She dug into the burlap sack, extracting more flour she would turn into fry cakes. They had enough stuff from the liveryman for a few more days. June nights in the mountains were plenty cold, but with luck they would have their wet clothes dried before they were chilled.

A night fog descended just about the time when Victoria thought the clothing might be wearable, and they were glad to crawl into the slightly damp leather and pull blankets over them. Skye carefully settled his leg, and then drew the wool around it. Warmth mitigated the pain a little. Victoria studied the night sky, hoping it would not rain again. This time of year, it rained often and hard, and sometimes hailed. She wished they might have their lodge, but that was far away, and they had no ponies to carry it.

"We could go back to your people," Skye said.

"No damned good," she said. She was thinking of Skye's age and bad leg, and the way her people moved about all summer and fall, gathering, hunting, and warring. The Shoshones were more sedentary.

"Where then? Up to you," he said.

That shocked her. Up to her?

"Magpie," she said.

She would go where her spirit sister, the magpie, led her. Skye didn't respond at first. He lived in a different world, with one Creator and no spirit helpers. They had talked about this many times, and it had come down to respect. He respected her beliefs; she respected his white-man religion.

"Suits me," he said.

She didn't like it. She didn't like this deep change in him. She wanted the old Skye, bold and strong and decisive, looking after her and keeping her fed and safe and warm. She tried to imagine what life was like for him now. Always before, he could command his body. It had been injured many times but he still lorded over his body, made his legs work, ignored pain, did what needed doing, whether it was hunting or fighting or finding shelter, or protecting her from a lion or a bear. But now his body was weaker, and it hurt, and he could not tell his leg to bend and walk and carry his weight and take him across meadows to the very horizon. His life was lost in a haze of pain now. She knew pain herself, the pain that came with many winters, that crept across her shoulders and collected at the small of her back and made her legs wobbly. But there was no way to get their youth back.

Her heart ached for him. He had the harder life, from a pressed British seaman to a mountain man to a guide, to a man living with her in the fashion of her people. He's the one who had to adapt, surrender his London upbringing, make himself a new man in this world of mountains and plains she knew so well. Had it been a good life? She was shocked at her own thought. Placing his life in the past, like that. He was alive beside her. He had never complained, never even talked about the pain that wracked him. She reached across to his blanketed form and touched his arm.

Two days later they had run through the white man's food the liveryman had given them, and Skye said he would hunt. He could not walk toward game, so he would wait beside the Yellowstone for game to come to him. His Sharps was too heavy for her now, or she would hunt with it, and her strength had waned so she could no longer use her bow and arrows as she once had as a young huntress.

So he settled himself beside a fallen cottonwood, downwind of where he thought game might come to drink, and waited until twilight for game to come. He rested the heavy Sharps across the log, tried to make his bad leg comfortable, and eyed a place in the riverbank where he had seen the split hoofprints of deer. And then one did come; actually two, a doe and a newborn fawn still on her teat, a small spotted waif of a deer-child. The mother looked everywhere, her tail twitching, and then drifted toward the riverbank, across the sights of Skye's Sharps.

But he did not shoot. He could not say why, except it had to do with his age and a reverence for new life. He watched the doe drink for a few moments, and then drift into shadow, the baby a few paces away, and then vanish into brush.

"Goddammit," Victoria said. "I was afraid you'd shoot her."

fifteen

*B*lue Dawn of the Shoshone People was a curiosity to every passing wagon company. The Big Road wasn't crowded but she passed companies every little while. Most of them were entirely male, and they walked beside creaking wagons drawn by oxen. A few companies consisted of families, and these usually had wagons with the big sheets curving over the tops. Once in a while a single family traveled on its own, risking trouble but going at its own pace.

She rode beside the river the whites called the North Platte, with her two spare ponies behind her. Once in a while she shifted her high-cantle squaw saddle to another of the ponies, so that all bore her burden. The breeze-curried prairies stretched endlessly in all directions, and at some distant place they merged with the sky. Often they were rough and hilly, and in these places she feared trouble, apart from the eyes of other travelers.

She had evolved a way of dealing with these white people, and stuck with it. She never spoke English but only her own tongue, though she understood them well enough. She scarcely knew what to expect. The all-male companies sometimes eyed her in a way that worried her, their assessing gazes obvious. Other times, when westering families crowded around her, parents sharply warned their children to stay away from the filthy squaw.

"Don't you get close to her, hear me? You'll get nits."

"Hey, Ma, a wild injun! You think she'll kill us?"

"Diseased, that's what. Look at her, dark and savage, them eyes full of fever."

She pretended not to hear. It was safer. But sometimes men who knew a thing or two about sign language or Indians waylaid her.

"What tribe's you, little lady?" an ex-Confederate soldier asked. He was still in his shabby grays, but the stripes had been ripped off from his arms. He was walking beside a mule-drawn wagon with half a dozen bearded young men.

She ignored him.

"You understood me well enough, I'm thinking. Was I to guess, I'd say Snakes. You a Snake?"

She saw he knew something, and finally nodded.

"You going somewheres?"

She shook her head.

"I'd say you's going somewheres. We're inviting you to dinner, little lady."

She stared, and moved to go, touching her moccasins to her pony, but this one caught her hackamore.

"Such a rush," he said, grinning. He had watery blue eyes and a gray slouch hat, and a hairy face. She read his intentions all too well.

There wasn't much she could do with only a sheathed knife at her waist, and half a dozen of these rather young drifters eyeing her. For the moment she would stick with her silence. They caught her ponies, peered into the panniers, found the packet of letters, and read them.

"Looks like these are for some squaw man named Skye. But you ain't Crow, far as I can see," the blue-eyed one said. "You got you a man named Skye?"

She simply refused to acknowledge anything.

"You git yourself off that pony, sweetheart, and join up with us for some chow and we'll pass a jug around after she gets dark," he said. "Don't pretend you can't understand me. I read you mighty well, and I know damned well you've got every word I'm saying."

She saw how it would go. Once they started drinking, it wouldn't be long before they would have their way with her, and then maybe kill her.

"Miz Poontang, off that pony now," one said.

"I do not know that word," she replied.

He grinned. "Likely we'll teach you."

"I am on my way to St. Louis to see my son. He is in a school run by Jesuits."

"Yeah, they got a school for breeds and bastards."

"I don't know those words."

"Half-breeds, Miz Poontang, whelped by whites and colored."

"I am very happy to go see my son."

"Well, we're right happy to spend a happy night in this happy place with a happy lady."

"Please let go of the horse. I will go now."

"Get down, little lady. We're going to have us a party."

The others were igniting a fire of kindling and buffalo chips. They looked as eager as this unkempt veteran in gray, but were leaving the matter to him. There was no one else in sight. They were a mile or two from the North Platte River, where she might escape in the underbrush, but here they were in open prairie.

"Guess I'll have to help you down," he said.

"I don't know your name."

"Johnny Reb," he said.

In one fluid move, he slid an arm around her waist and lifted her down. He pushed her to the ground and held her there with a strength that surprised her.

"Got some ponies here," he said to one of the others.

That one gathered the lead lines and led them into the twilight.

"Nice party, Miz Poontang. We got a little jug we've been saving, just for this heah evening."

Once they began sampling the jug, she would be lost. The others looked uncommonly cheerful as they did their evening chores in a lingering twilight.

"My husband, Mister Skye, was with the Royal Navy. Then he was a big man with the American Fur Company. Then he was a guide."

"Husband, is it. You mean he took up with you."

"I was given by my family, the Shoshone way."

The talky one grinned. "Sho 'nuff," he said. "What did the white man pay, eh?"

"He gave the gift of blankets and horses."

"And you went off and whelped."

Why did this man talk like this? As if it was all bad or wrong or cheap? Mary thought maybe she knew.

"Colonel Bullock took my son to St. Louis when he was eight," she said. "I have been sad ever since then. Many winters have passed, and now I will see him. It is said he learns well, and knows words and numbers. I am very proud of him."

"Breed," her captor said. "Just a breed."

"Our friend Colonel Bullock watches over us."

Johnny Reb grinned. "Yank colonel, eh? That ain't the way to make friends with me, Miz Poontang."

"This man, he comes from a place called Virginia. He says it's a very good place."

"Likely story, squaw."

The company had completed its evening chores and was gathering at the fire now, an eager anticipation flushing their faces. She thought she had sealed her own death, letting them know of her connections. They could not afford to let her go, now.

She studied everything in the twilight, noting where her ponies were picketed, where her packsaddle was, where they had put her halters and hackamore. Darkness would be her friend, if she survived that long. She eyed them coldly, a deep dread in her, but one mixed with resolve. She might never see her son, but some of them would never see another sunrise. She feared it had come to that.

Why did they dismiss her so? Her race, maybe. These were those who had black slaves, or at least fought on that side. Anyone colored like her could be beaten and used. They might do both, beat her and use her before they killed her. It would all be fueled by the fiery water in that crockery jug. Maybe if they had enough of it, they would fall senseless and she could escape. But maybe they would force her to drink, hold her arms, pry open her mouth, and pour it into her. She had heard of such things.

She knew then what she would do.

"Hey, Johnny Reb. You want a party? Let's party."

He grinned at her. "We'll take our time, Miz Poontang."

"You got two jugs? Three jugs?"

"Just this one, sweetheart."

"I'd like a jug all for me."

The others were paying attention now, smiling. She wondered if they were going to eat, but no one was cooking anything. Apparently the evening's entertainment trumped hunger. But the dark was the only friend she had.

"Hey, how about some eats, all right?"

"Who needs food?" Johnny Reb asked.

"I do. You keep me here, you feed me."

"Nah, Miz Poontang, you don't need a mouthful."

"You make food. I make food."

But she heard a cork squeal out of its socket and laughter. The plug was gone from the tan jug, and now the six men were all smiles. They settled into a small circle, legs the spokes in a wheel, as the night thickened. The smoky fire threw wavering orange light on them.

"Oh, it do smell like heaven," one said.

"Want it neat, or cut?"

"What do ya take me for?" One of them lifted the jug and sipped.

"Ah!" he said, and laughed.

The jug went around. It came to her. She took a tiny sip.

"Oh, no, that ain't how it'll be, Poontang. Drink!"

She pretended. They watched hawkishly.

"You drink or we'll pour it down you, bitch."

She sipped slowly, not swallowing, and passed the jug along.

"Swallow, bitch!"

They were staring wolfishly at her now.

"Makes me sick," she said, and spit it.

"Then get sick, squaw."

But the jug had passed her by that time, and now the slugs going down male throats were longer and fiercer.

When the jug returned to her, Johnny Reb grabbed it, grabbed her, stuffed it into her lips, hurting her teeth, and poured hard. She gasped, coughed, and splattered whiskey over her heavy skirts.

"Drink!" he snarled.

He jammed the jug into her face and lifted it.

She clasped her hands around the jug to steady it, and then he let her hold the jug.

That was her moment. She lifted the jug upward, and then threw it with both hands into the smoldering fire. It shattered. The whiskey spread, and then flared in yellow flame.

"Goddamn bitch!" her captor cried, and threw her to the earth.

She rolled and sprang up, ran away from the flame, her heavy skirts slowing her progress.

He cursed, raced after her, grabbed her, and threw her down again.

She fought crazily, raking him with her fingernails, biting and writhing, but he caught her hair and yanked hard, throwing her head back with such violence that she felt something snap in her neck.

Then he was riffling her skirts, jamming them upward, his big chafed hands rough on her legs. She bit his arm, her teeth drawing salty blood, and he howled. She slammed a knee into him, catching his groin, and he howled again, his body folding. He let go of her, grabbing his crotch, and she rolled free. She didn't wait, but staggered to her feet and plunged toward the mercy of dark, stumbling over prairie until she tumbled into a shallow depression, a foot or two deep, and there she threw herself to earth and stretched tight in the lee, where the bold orange light from the whiskey-fueled fire would not probe her. She scraped air into her lungs, quieted her gasping, and then forcibly stilled her body in the shallow safety of the gully.

"Goddamn squaw," her captive yelled. "She's out there."

"Get the horses in," someone said.

"Thieving redskin'll steal 'em."

"What'd you give her the jug for, goddammit?"

"Oh, shut up, damn you."

"A tin cup. Shove the tin cup of it down her throat."

"Go to hell, Jackson."

She heard someone come close, and this time she pulled her skinning knife from its waist sheath and waited. If it was to be blood and death this night, then she would give and take, even if she was one lone woman among hard young men.

"She ain't far, and we got her nags," someone said.

"I'll kill her. Breaking that jug. Goddamn squaw."

"Who cares about the jug? I was looking for some entertainment."

"Who'd a thunk a squaw'd fight back? They just roll over."

"You think she'll give us trouble?"

"We'd best find her and shut her up for good."

"Fat chance in the dark. She's down to the river by now."

"We'll find her. Get the horses in, and if she comes for them, we've got her."

Mary listened bitterly.

sixteen

he higher the half-moon rose, the more danger she was in. The shallow trough that protected her from firelight did not protect her from the cold white glare from the sky. The fire had died, and the men had fallen into their blankets. She peeked, and was disheartened by what she saw. Her packsaddle and saddle and horse tack had been placed close to the fire, within the circle of their bedrolls. Her ponies were picketed close. The chance of collecting her things and escaping in the white of the moon didn't really exist. What's more, one man was propped up against some harness, a rifle across his lap. She could not tell whether he was dozing, but he surely was a sentry.

She felt a moment of desolation, but quieted herself. All those years with Skye and Victoria had hardened her, given her a cast of mind that refused to surrender. She slowly raised her head again and studied the scene, thanking Mother Moon for giving her light. The high-walled wagon stood nearby, its tailgate down. Its mule team, six mules in all, were picketed some distance away. A saddle horse was tied to the wagon. On

its back was a saddle. The men had a mule team plus one saddle horse, apparently kept ready to ride if trouble arose. She
had seen this sort of thing before. The saddle would not be
cinched.

She eyed her own saddle, with its bedroll, two blankets,
rolled up and tied behind the cantle. But it and the packsaddle were within a few feet of three of the men. If she tried to
lift either one, they would snare her.

She reluctantly gave up on that. They well knew she would
be back and would try, so they made themselves ready for
her. The same with her ponies. The picket pins were only a
few feet from the men. If they caught her, who could say what
they might do? These were the ones from the South, and what
did they care about people whose flesh was darker? If they
cared nothing for their black slaves, why would they care
about her, with her copper flesh?

She eyed their saddle horse, which stood, head lowered,
half asleep, one leg cocked. Would it startle if she approached?
She saw no other choices. She crawled slowly along the trough
in the earth, glad she was dark and was wearing a blue blouse
and black skirt. She absorbed the light. She reached a place
where the wagon cast a moon shadow. The horse was alert
now, and she feared it might bolt. She stood slowly in the
moon shadow, and the horse actually quieted. That was good.
She took her time, studied the sleeping men, especially the
one propped up on harness collars. Nothing changed.

She reached the horse, which turned and sniffed her. She
ran a hand under its mane, and then under the surcingle, and
found it loose, as she expected. Her fingers told her this was
the type of girth with a buckle. She slowly tightened and
buckled it. She located the reins, tied to a ring on the wagon.
She might have an escape now if this horse didn't give her

away. She ghosted around to the tailgate, which was partially lit by the moon, and studied what lay within the wagon. Something white intrigued her and she tugged at something made of heavy fabric and discovered it was a poncho. That lifted her spirits. This time of year, a poncho was more valuable than a bedroll. She felt around, her fingers clasping on a small copper pot, and then on a cotton bag of something she thought was cornmeal. Food, a little kettle, a poncho. She laid the sack and the little pot in the poncho and rolled the poncho over them. She needed something to tie her kit together, and saw the heap of harness, with its lead lines. With her skinning knife she sawed some lines free, tied her bedroll kit together, and anchored it behind the cantle of the horse.

Someone stirred and she froze. A man rose, stared, headed toward the very trough that had hidden her, urinated, and returned to his bed, while she stood stock-still. These men were not caught in deep sleep, not with a white moon pouring light over them. She feared that they would follow her even though they would have three ponies in exchange for their saddle horse.

She waited until the camp quieted again, and then sawed through the tugs, the thick leather bands that collected the harness to the wagon. She could not get to her own hackamore to saw it in two, but she could cut the rest and give them a day or two of repairing. That would teach them to respect a woman of the Eastern Shoshones. She sat down and patiently cut here and there, her knife purring and muttering its way through leather until she was sure this company would not be moving soon. Her own ponies were staring at her, which was dangerous.

It was time to go. She paused in the moonshadow of the wagon, untied the saddle horse, which finally began sawing its head nervously, and then tugged. The horse followed along after a moment's pause. She surveyed the country. If she headed straight east, she would be in sight a great distance, in this cold light. If she reached the woodlands along the Platte, she would swiftly vanish from view. She would walk north to the river, then, and hope they slept.

She took one last look at the camp. The man lying against the collars had sat up and was staring. She had apparently made enough noise to stir him out of his doze. She froze. He stood, alert, but not knowing where to look.

She had intended to lead the saddle horse away and mount it later, but now she tried to wait him out. The wagon was the one area he was not looking. He was eyeing the mules and her ponies, looking at the way their ears were cupped. Only then did he turn slowly toward the wagon. She stood in shadow, and was grateful she wore dark clothing. Still, he was not satisfied, and finally drifted toward the wagon. She knew she had only moments, so she put foot to stirrup and lifted herself onto the saddle, as the horse sidestepped nervously, unfamiliar with this rider.

He saw her then, shouted, and she kicked the horse hard. It bolted toward the river. She heard another shout, and a blast, and felt her horse react to something, even as something stung her arm. A fowling piece. The horse pitched and then settled into a hard run, but she had no trouble hanging on. It leaped the trough that had sheltered her and thundered hard toward the loose-knit cottonwoods ahead. She heard a few more cracks, rifles now, and some distant shouts, and then she fled into the moon-dappled shade of wide-spaced cottonwoods and willows, their leaves throwing darkness here and there. She reached the North Platte suddenly, pushed through thick brush, felt her horse sink in muck, remembered that this wide, shallow river sucked horses and people to their doom, and yanked the horse sharply right. It floundered a moment, gathered itself, and plunged out of the sucking sand onto firmer ground. She halted, and it stood trembling, its breathing harsh and desperate. She itched to move, but knew she was a long way from the men, and let the horse regain its composure. Then she steered the horse free of the band of brush and into the moonlit woods. She paused, looking for the men, and heard distant shouts and curses as they discovered the extent that she had immobilized them.

She thought she was free, and steered the horse quietly downriver, but then she saw that one had saddled her pony and was trotting hard toward her. The others had caught her other ponies and were obviously rigging makeshift tack.

She kept her horse at a walk, but steered him into deeper woods, until the horse was slowed by fallen limbs and brush, and then let the animal pick its way. This was noisy. The horse was snapping limbs, lurching through brush, and advertising itself. The other rider gained ground over open grassland and eventually passed her, which troubled her. Now one of the others was coming her way also, having rigged some sort of bridle for one of her ponies. Something glinted in the man's hand.

So it was not over. Still, she had shadow; the others had moonlight and open meadow. The second one rode by, and now two were downriver from her. They would wait for her. They knew she had gone into the bankside band of willows and cottonwoods, where she would be slowed. They had sprung a trap that might not catch her in its jaws until daylight. Still, she had shadow. She slowed her horse and let it pick its way quietly. Through the leaves she saw the two riders far ahead of her, still out on the open meadow.

She thought she must say good-bye to her boy, The Star That Never Moves, fifteen winters of age, and say good-bye to Skye, and to Victoria, his older wife, and then say good-bye to life, for these men with guns would end it. They were in a rage, and they were good horsemen, probably former cavalrymen, and they would know how to run her down.

It was best to give her horse a free rein, so she did. This horse had a bit in its mouth, and was easy to guide, but she stopped guiding it entirely. She touched her moccasins to its flanks. It veered a little and drifted along a narrow trail where it made no noise at all, maybe a trail used by deer or elk, or even the great brown bear, but a trail even so, and she let the horse go where it would, even when the trail turned toward the wide, shallow, treacherous river that white men called a mile wide and an inch deep.

The trail ended at water's edge, but not far out lay a large island, mostly covered with brush, but with a few gauzy trees. She slid off her horse, untied her moccasins, lifted her skirts, and stepped in, probing one step at a time for quicksand. But she was walking on gravel, and slowly made her way out, tugging the horse behind her. The water never reached her knees. But she was wading under an open sky, where the moonglow made her visible to anyone on any shore. Still she continued, step by step, and then slowly climbed onto the island and led the horse through thickets and onto a grassy patch well hidden from both shores.

It would do. She quietly unsaddled the horse and let it graze.

Mosquitoes hummed, but she had a partial remedy. She untied the poncho and slid it over her black braids, and swiftly felt its protective comfort. She undid her braids and let her hair fall loose.

"Ah sure don't know where that little bitch got," someone said.

She peered discreetly at the near shore, but saw no one.

"Find her. She got mah horse and saddle, goddammit."

"We got three of hers."

"Never no mind that. I don't much care how many ponies
and saddles and what-all; I just ain't of a mind to let some
redskin git away with this."

"Looks like she did."

She could see them now, back from the water's edge,
studying the shoreline. She hoped her new horse wouldn't
whinny. After some peering around, they gave up and crashed
their way through the belt of trees and she heard no more.

For them, it was the principle of the thing. Three horses,
a packsaddle and riding saddle, and a pile of gear weren't a
good trade for what she got because she was a Shoshone, because they intended to use and kill her and keep everything
she had, and keep their own stock too.

She turned quietly back to the center of her island, her
small refuge in a moon-whited river. She wondered if she
would recognize her half-white son if ever she found him in
this place called St. Louis, or whether she would like or trust
him if she did find him.

seventeen

Victoria heard the cattle first, a great lowing and bawling just around a bend, and didn't know what to make of it. Then riders appeared, white men with broad felt hats, dressed in a fashion she had never seen, with leather chaps and neck scarves. She stopped at once. These men were well armed, and she wished to be careful. Skye pulled up and watched as the herd, which numbered many hundreds of long-horned cattle, bawled and bleated its way west, guided by numerous riders who walked quietly ahead, behind, and on the flanks of the herd.

Two of them rode toward the Skyes, who waited quietly in the broad valley of the Yellowstone. The riders were wary, with carbines across their knees, but the Skyes gave them no reason to be alarmed.

Eventually the pair, both bearded young men in broad-brimmed hats with creased crowns, reined up before the Skyes. Victoria didn't like the looks of them.

"Howdy," said one.

"Good afternoon, sir," said Skye.

"You injuns?"

"I'm Barnaby Skye, sir, and this is my wife Victoria."

"Injuns, then. What tribe?"

Victoria wondered how these white men could mistake Skye for one of the native people. He was weathered to a chestnut color but hadn't the face or bones of her people.

"I am Mister Skye, sir, from London, and this is my wife of many years, of the Absaroka People." There was an edge in his voice.

"Just checking. We like to know who we're dealin' with."

"So it appears. And who are you?"

"Harbinger's the last name, Slocum's the first. Texas born and bred."

"Your men, they're Texans?"

"What else?"

"You're running true to form," Skye said. "And where are you headed with all those animals?"

"The big bend of the Yellowstone, Skye. That's good country. This heah's the second herd; I ramrod for Nelson Story. He brought the first bunch up in 'sixty-six, right through the injun wars, and pastured it in the Gallatin Valley."

"It's Mister Skye, sir. I prefer to be addressed in that fashion."

"It don't make no never mind to me, Mister Skye. I'll call you whatever you want. We'll have you just sit heah until them cattle trail by, so you don't booger them."

The herd was drawing close now, with a slobbering wide-horned multicolored bull leading the whole parade. Other of these Texans were drawing close as well.

"In fact, Mrs. Skye and I were thinking of settling on the bend of the Yellowstone, sir. Maybe we'll be neighbors."

"No, Mister Skye, we ain't gonna be neighbors. Nelson Story's done took it, all that country."

"By what right?"

"By the law of armed force is how. Any questions?"

"By land-office claim?"

"I don't suppose it matters none to a Londoner. But no, we'll take the land and keep it. We got there fust. There ain't no land office within hundreds of miles, but we don't need one. There's land, lots of land. There's twenty-four of us, all Texas men, and that's all we need to hold it. That was enough to get us past the goddamn Sioux. They didn't want no fight with Texans with repeater carbines. The redskins ain't so strong, anyway. Degenerates, ain't gonna be around much longer."

"The army found them invincible, sir."

"Yank army. Rebs would've walked through them savages. We drove these here animals a thousand miles, and we're going to sell beef to the mining towns."

"On the Bozeman Trail? The closed trail?"

"The same. Not one sonofabitching white man on it. Good grass all the way."

"And no Sioux?"

"None as wanted to test our repeaters."

"You came without army protection, then?"

"Now, Skye, why would Texicans want protection from a Yank army? Know what we saw? Lot of ash, where them Yankee forts got burned down by Red Cloud."

"You are brave men," Skye said.

The herd flowed by them now, and several more Texans drifted by, curious about the Skyes but staying close to the skinny red, brindle, black, gray, and multicolored cattle that seemed to be all rib and no meat.

"And what's your business, Skye?"

Skye stared long and hard. "Just passing through," he said softly.

"It figgers. I knew it when I saw you. A squaw man, looks like. Well, we got some ambition heah. We got white-man plans, and we're going to make our way."

Victoria listened with growing irritation. "Sonsofbitches," she said.

Harbinger grinned, revealing gapped teeth. "This heah squaw talks my language," he said.

The cattle flowed by endlessly, strangely disturbing Victoria. These were white men's meat animal and intended to replace the buffalo that had fed and clothed and sheltered her people for as long as her people could remember. Hundreds of cattle, more than she could count, slobbering, skinny, wild of eye, mean-spirited. She found herself hating these animals, which had none of the courage and dignity of her brothers the buffalo.

More riders passed, eyeing them curiously but continuing to flank the herd. Men in red shirts, gray shirts, tan shirts. Men without women, young and bearded and bristling with weapons, six-guns at their waists, carbines in sheaths or on hand, looking ready to shoot anything that moved.

And now they were simply taking away the land, claiming it for themselves, and holding it by force. She marveled. She marveled that they could tell Skye to settle elsewhere, to go away, because they would not let him settle there, in the place he had dreamed of for many years.

Long ago, Skye would have put up a fight. But now, he sat his pony, his lame leg dangling out of the stirrup, his eyes sunken and his hair gray, and she knew there was no fight in him, at least not that kind of fight.

"We'll be seeing you, Mister Harbinger," Skye said.

"I don't suppose so," the man replied, and turned toward his herd. "Nice to pass the time with you all."

Skye and Victoria watched the last of the riders, the drag, trot by. The air and the ground quieted. But no bird flew or sang.

"There was enough land for everyone once," Skye said.

Victoria slid into a crabby mood. She didn't know what to say. These things unsettled her. Everything was changing, and too damn fast. Nothing but a faint dust in the air remained of the herd, that and a few green cow flops that sat moistly in the peaceful light. She hated the sight of the cow pies, hated them for what they meant. Cow pies instead of buffalo chips. Great herds of stupid animals, surrounded by men with guns, taking away land for their own use.

"Let's get the hell out of here," she said.

They resumed their ride downstream, but somehow the world seemed violated. It wasn't just the cow flops lying moist everywhere. It was something else, more subtle, as if nature had retreated and now this was simply ranching country. Victoria couldn't quite fathom why the very land had changed, but it had.

They camped at one of the favorite places of her people, where the Stillwater River tumbled out of the mountains and emptied into the Yellowstone. Now the river was flush with snowmelt, and it proved difficult for the horses to negotiate, with water hammering at their bellies. But in time they reached the east bank, picketed their ponies, built a fire, and cooked antelope steaks. June rains threatened, but the Skyes had no lodge and the best they could do, if showers started, would be to burrow into the woods.

That's when three large ox-drawn wagons arrived, each

the property of a westering family. In minutes the area was chock-full of people, including women and children. They didn't see the Skyes at first, and began the many twilight tasks that occupied any wagon company. They unyoked the oxen, picketed horses, collected wood, started water boiling, spread bedrolls, all before they discovered the Skyes, off a quarter of a mile.

Then the men of the company descended on them, most of them armed with rifles or scatter guns.

"Good evening, gents," said Skye.

The men collected around the Skyes, studying them, eyeing Victoria, noting her Indian features.

"I'm a goddamn Absaroka," she said.

"Barnaby Skye here, and you?"

"Oliver Skaggs," said one. "She safe to be around?"

"No, I'll cut your heart out in the middle of the night," Victoria said.

No one laughed.

"I'm Mister Skye's sits-beside-him wife. He got another, Mary, she's a Snake. She's a lot prettier than me, and keeps him happy."

This wrought a deeper silence.

"She's off ahead of us. Otherwise you'd get to meet the whole family."

Skye's eyes glinted at Victoria, telling her to shut up, but she wasn't in the mood for it.

"Where's your tent?" asked one of the scowling men.

"Who the hell needs one?" Victoria said.

"How do you protect yourself from prying eyes?" asked Skaggs.

"Nighttime, that's all we need. We pull off our stuff and howl at the moon and dance around nakkid."

Skye sighed. Victoria was on a tear, and she wasn't going to slow down for him.

"We have some antelope we'd be pleased to share. Shot it this morning. Would you join us?" Skye asked.

"Any more of you hidden around here?"

"Just us."

Victoria could see women and children boiling toward them, and then an odd thing happened. Several of the men swiftly corralled them and kept them perhaps fifty yards distant. She saw much gesticulating and waving of arms.

"We'll stay with our own mess," one said.

"You people heading west?" Skye asked.

"Gallatin Valley."

"You came over the Bozeman Road?"

"Oh, no, not with the Sioux there. It's closed. We came up Jim Bridger's road, and a poor road it was too. A wagon near tipped over," said Skaggs. "But there were no redskins, thank the Good Lord."

"The Gallatin Valley's a good place," Skye said. "You going to farm?"

"We're merchants and farmers. We've got seed potatoes. Got orchard stock. We've got a lumber man with a small mill. But we hear there's Indian trouble."

"Goddamn Blackfeet," said Victoria. "Scaring the hell out of everyone. Bloodthirsty bastards."

They stood about silently, absorbing that. Behind them, where the bonneted women and a dozen children of all descriptions were halted, there was a great deal of talking, and then one of the bearded men approached.

"Skye, would you mind camping somewhere else? You and your squaw's upsetting our folk. Scaring the children."

"I guess a man and wife can camp where they choose.

Free country," Skye said. "You're free to move somewhere yourself."

"I guess I shouldn't have put it as a question, Skye. We're not asking you, we're telling you."

"And if we choose to stay here?"

"Someone might get hurt, and it ain't gonna be us."

Victoria wondered if her old man would do what he might have done long ago, but he didn't. He arose slowly, balancing on his game leg, using his Sharps as a crutch.

"Did you bring some spades?" Skye asked. "Start digging our grave. We're not moving an inch. The only direction you'll move us is six feet down."

Victoria listened to the bark in his voice, and thrilled to it.

"We'll haul you off on a wagon, then," one said.

Skye ignored him and lumbered painfully toward the children clinging to their mothers a few yards distant.

"Hey, where you going?" Skaggs yelled.

"I thought to get me a little girl and boil her up."

The women shrieked.

Skye continued to limp toward the children.

Then Skaggs laughed. The other men laughed, uneasily. Some mothers looked flustered, ready to bolt.

Skye reached a woman whose son had buried his face in her skirts.

Slowly he leaned over, even as the men of the company hastened to surround him.

"Hello, young man," Skye said. "I'm Barnaby Skye. Who are you?"

The boy eyed him suspiciously.

"Your folks heading west? There's good farm land there."

The little boy tugged himself tighter to his mother.

"I was here before there were a hundred white men in the

whole western mountains. Now I live the way the Indians do, and I have an Indian wife. That's her, over there. She's a Crow, and very pretty, and I love her just the way your mother and father love each other."

"Is she a witch?" the boy asked.

"She's a medicine woman of her people. She has great powers. She's also a warrior woman, very good with a bow and arrow. Would you like to meet her?"

The question occasioned a flurry of worried glances among the adults, but then the boy nodded.

"Come along now, all of you," Skye said.

They hesitantly followed Skye as he limped back to Victoria, and let them gather around her.

"This is Many Quill Woman of the Absaroka People. I didn't know her tongue at first, so I called her Victoria, after the Queen. And she is a queen. You might call her a princess. That's a good word for her, because she was given great powers to help and heal people."

They stared at Victoria, seeing an Indian for the first time.

"Is she a real princess?" one woman asked.

"I would say so," Skye said.

Victoria felt the glint of wetness forming in her eyes.

eighteen

Barnaby Skye sliced the antelope haunch thin and used up the last of it. The company hadn't had meat on its tin mess plates for a week. Some of the women contributed boiled spuds. Skye hadn't had a potato in years, and relished every bite. The women from another wagon boiled a kettle of parched corn. With a little salt, it tasted just fine, and built a comfort in the belly.

They all eyed the Skyes, sometimes furtively, sometimes boldly. They studied Skye's top hat, this one the fourth or fifth he had owned, gotten at a trading post. It was a silk one because beaver had gone out of fashion. It sat rakishly on Skye's gray locks, and never moved, as if it had grown from his scalp.

Skye thought that Victoria had exhibited great restraint, remembering not to cuss in front of the smaller children, except for a few hells and damns, which they had already mastered from their fathers. Victoria had never quite understood tabooed words. There were none among the Absaroka People. All words were good. So over a lifetime she had derived a vast repertoire of forbidden white men's words and phrases, which she employed with great relish.

Soon the women hustled the children off to their bedrolls, which were laid out under the three wagons, and then most of the adults hastened back to the bright campfire, which the men of the company had built up to drive back the darkness. Skye never was quite comfortable with fires like that, which turned them all into targets. But he was too old and crippled to care now.

The adults drifted to the campfire as soon as chores were done, all of them eager for what was to come. This would be a night of stories, and Skye knew they intended to pump him for all he could tell them. Much to his astonishment, these westering people pulled two rocking chairs from wagons, and these were soon occupied by elder women, the dowager queens of this wagon company.

"Ah, Skye, did I hear you say you had a younger wife?" asked one of the gents named Monroe.

"I do, sir, Blue Dawn of the Shoshones. I call her Mary. She's quite a bit younger than I, sir, and a beauty."

"Ah, Skye, that's very unusual."

"Not at all. In most plains tribes, men of prominence have several wives, and the more wives, the more prominent they are. A chief might have several."

"How does the Mrs. Skye with us feel about this?" asked a graying woman, in a rush.

"Hell, I pushed and shoved for years to get my man to take one. I even made the match. The old cuss, he kept saying one was enough, but I would have liked a dozen. I'd get to boss 'em all around, because I was the first."

"A dozen wives? Surely you're making a joke!" said a lady.

"Hey, wives do all the work, see? The more wives, the less work for me. I gotta scrape a buffalo hide for weeks if I'm alone. Get a bunch of wives, and I'll scrape a hide and tan it in a day or two. I get tired of cooking. Give me a few wives, and I'm happy."

"But how . . . do you have separate teepees?"

"Hell no, we're all in there together. Me and Skye and Mary, we got one little lodge."

"One lodge! How do you manage? I mean, privacy?"

"I don't know that word," Victoria said. Skye laughed softly. Victoria knew the meaning exactly, but it was more fun doing this her way.

"It's dark in there," Skye said. He was starting to enjoy this.

"Where is she now?" someone asked.

"With her people, the Shoshones, far south of here," Skye said. "That's where we're headed."

"I would think each wife would want a lodge of her own. Just to tell the children apart," said a woman in brown gingham.

"Children, they're all the same. I got children I never had," Victoria said maliciously. "Every time I look, there's a new one."

Skye thought he heard breaths released.

"I don't suppose these were proper Christian marriages, were they?" asked a frowning young man.

"We were married according to the customs of the Crows and Snakes," Skye said. "A pleasant ceremony in which the parents give away the bride."

"Did you pay a lot?"

"A gift to the family, sir, not payment. You offer a gift. Some horses, or a rifle, or blankets. You offer the biggest gift you can, and the bride's family decides whether that'll do. When you get married, they gift you back, help you set up your household."

"Sounds like buying a woman to me." The stuffy fellow was determined to prove the moral superiority of whites.

"Oh, white women sometimes come with a dowry. Their parents are buying a husband, I suppose," Skye said.

"That's different," the fellow persisted.

"I'd like to buy a few white men," Victoria said. "I'd like half a dozen."

That stopped the talk for a stumble or two.

"Tell us about your days in the fur trade," an older man asked, obviously steering away from plural marriage. "Were you ever comfortable, living in nature?"

"Hardly ever," Skye said. "We lived in the wilds. We took our ration of rain and sleet, of heat and starving. We took arrows and sickness, broken bones and tumbles off of horses. We froze at night, hurt all day. Some Yanks, they make it sound romantic, but I assure you, sir, it rarely was pleasant. My bones hurt just thinking about wading a river in winter. There weren't a hundred comfortable days in a year."

"How many grizzly bears did you face?"

"More than I want to remember. See this?" Skye lifted up his repaired bear-claw necklace "Those are grizzly claws, and they give me my medicine."

"What's medicine?"

"Inner powers, I suppose. Other things too. Bear wisdom. Bear whispers in my ear, sometimes, so I stay away from a cave, or watch out what's on the riverbank, or I study the sky because weather's coming."

They stared at the old necklace, that Skye had restrung half a dozen times in his life, including the time last fall when he stumbled upon a denning grizzly. Those six-inch claws were formidable.

"You put a lot of balls into a grizzly? I've heard it takes ten or fifteen to kill one," a man named Peters asked.

"The grizzlies are my brothers," Skye said. "They know another bear when they see one, and leave me alone. We see each other and turn away."

"You pullin' our leg, Skye?"

"It's Mister Skye, sir. Form of address I prefer. When I was a seaman in the Royal Navy, the officers were all 'mister' or 'sir,' and the rest of us, we hardly had first and last names. When I got to the New World, to this place where ordinary men could be misters, I took to it. From then on, I was as good as any officer in the Royal Navy. Call me Mister Skye, and I'll be grateful."

"You left the navy?"

"I deserted, sir. I was pressed in, right off the streets of London at age thirteen, and it took me seven years to escape. That was at Fort Vancouver, on the Columbia River, in the twenties. I jumped ship with nothing but my clothes and a belaying pin. I've been on my own ever since. I haven't regretted my escape, not for a moment. And I don't apologize for deserting. They made me a slave and I escaped their slavery."

"Amen to that," said Skaggs.

"You fight injuns?" That question rose from a nervous young man with muttonchops.

"There's no way I could have survived, sir, without defending myself."

"Which tribes are the worst. The most ruthless?"

"Goddamn Siksika," Victoria snapped. "Blackfeet."

Several women began fanning themselves with their hats.

"The Crows and the Blackfeet have a few grudges," Skye

said. "I think the fiercest I've ever faced were the Comanches. I tangled with them once, taking some people to Santa Fe. They don't fear death and like to give pain. They are the world's most terrible torturers," he added. "We saw it, and we'll never forget it."

Victoria looked grouchy. She considered the tribes of the southern plains to be toothless.

"Cheyenne are better," she said. "Old Cheyenne women, they'll tie you to a tree and skin you alive, piece by piece."

That caused a stir.

They listened to Skye tell about that trip, and his other trips from his years as a guide, and the people he had taken into the unknown American West, the peers of England, the missionaries, the scientists, the army officers, and even a traveling medicine show once. He told about meeting Victoria and courting her, and learning about her Otter clan and family and Kicked-in-the-Bellies band. He told them about the rendezvous of the mountain men, and the artists and noblemen and adventurers who showed up at them. He told them about Jawbone, the strange fearless colt that became his horse-brother, a ferocious warrior in his own right, and a sacred animal known to all the tribes of the plains. The ugliest, strangest horse that ever lived, but also the greatest of all horses.

And before they knew it the hour had grown late, and these weary people were drifting off.

"Well, Skye, ah, Mister Skye, this has been quite an evening," Skaggs said. "We're lucky to have run into you. We've never met a mountaineer before."

"Or a medicine woman, either," Skye added.

Skaggs seemed discomfited.

Skye watched them settle. The men unrolled blankets under the wagons. The women and children crowded into wall tents. This company paused for evening prayers. Skaggs offered up the Lord's Prayer, and then they drifted to their beds.

Victoria was smiling broadly, as she always did when she had done the most mischief.

They had hardly settled in their blankets when lightning whitened the western heavens, followed by a distant roll of thunder. They both sprang up at once. They had no shelter and needed one fast. June thunderstorms could be vicious, cold and cruel, and often dumped hail on unwary people. There were a few cottonwoods around, but they offered no protection.

They had settled on an open flat at the confluence of the rivers. Behind a way, the south cliffs of the Yellowstone rose high, but these were half a mile off. They didn't hesitate. Skye caught the picketed horses and threw on the blankets and saddles and pulled hackamores over their heads. Victoria rolled up their blankets and their handful of possessions, and tied them behind the saddle cantles. Gamely, he clambered into his saddle, while she climbed aboard her pony. They reached the majestic cliff about the time the sky whitened regularly, and a drumroll of booming thunder seemed never to stop. The wind picked up, eddying cold moist air over them, with its promise of torrents. An overhang eluded them, and Skye was just surrendering to the idea of an icy drenching when Victoria steered her pony up a crevice in the cliff and under an overhang. A bright white flash of lightning informed them they would share the refuge with an angry black bear sow and cub.

There was perhaps twenty yards between the bears and the ponies. Skye halted. It was only the continuing lightning that revealed the presence of the bears.

"We're staying here," he said to the sow. "Sister, you're not going to scare us off."

She rose on her hind legs, while the cub ran behind her. Lightning caught her at her most angry, her claws extended.

"We're staying here, woman. Look after your cub," he said.

The rains swept in, a sudden rattling and clattering everywhere, and Skye was grateful for the refuge. It was even better than his lodge. The winds gusted moisture over them, but that was nothing compared to the torrent a few feet away.

Somehow, the rain settled the sow, and she returned to four legs and then drove her cub to the far edge of the overhang, another few yards distant. There she paused, just before a sheet of water, and halted. It would do.

Sister Bear would let Skye and Victoria live.

nineteen

*M*ary regretted slicing up the harness of those men. Now she was stuck on a mosquito-ridden island while they repaired it. She wore the poncho, and it helped, except around her ankles and neck and forehead. But the horse suffered, and the constant lashing of its tail did little to relieve its torment.

And across the channel of the North Platte, those former Confederates were no doubt riveting or tying their harness, unable to move until they could hook the mules to their wagon. If they had rivets they could make repairs easily; if not, they would have to bore holes in the leather and then lash the severed pieces with a thong, a slow and miserable process.

Mary bitterly endured, knowing the men were not far distant, beyond the band of riverside trees. She was fairly safe behind walls of brush and trees on her island, but the whine of mosquitoes maddened her and the horse. She finally led the miserable animal to a place where there was mud stretching into water, and patiently coated the horse with it. One handful at a time, she ran a protective coating of mud over its rump and flanks and withers and neck and chest, and then its belly and legs. The horse eyed her gratefully, she thought, and quieted. She rubbed mud over her own neck, without doing much good.

At one point the horse's ears pricked forward, and Mary feared it would whinny. She crept to the edge of the island and peered across the channel. Downstream a little, the men were watering their mules and her three ponies. She ached to have her own ponies back, but remained still. She glided back to her new horse and gently rubbed its nose, hoping to keep it from signaling the other horses. Eventually the men and the livestock left the riverbank.

Mary hunted for food, but the bird nests she found were already deserted, and she spotted no turtles. She saw whiskered catfish, loathsome creatures, and would have eaten one if she had to, but she was spared that. She found bountiful cattails, and systematically pulled them up from their swampy habitat. They had gnarled white roots that could be pulverized and boiled into a thick paste that was nourishing, though vaguely repellent. She would do what she had to. Rocks were hard to find on that island, but she finally found what she needed and mashed the white roots, and added them to a growing heap in the copper pot.

She built a small fire directly under a stand of cottonwoods that would dissipate the smoke, lighting it with the flint and striker that hung in a pouch from her belt. And then she waited for the water to soften the cattail roots into something she could stomach. Much to her surprise, this had consumed her day, and as twilight overtook her she doused the fire, let the mush cool, and then ate it with her fingers.

She would not endure another night in this mosquito-misery, and resolved to use the friendly dark to escape, no matter that those men were nearby and might discover her. As darkness settled, she brushed mud off her horse, settled the blanket pad over its back, dropped the saddle and tightened it, and bridled the horse. She rolled up her few goods in the poncho, braving the whining mosquitoes again, and tied the poncho tightly to her saddle. She was as ready as she could be. She mounted, eased the horse across the gravel bar to the south bank without discovery, and made her way downstream, worried that she would be halted at any moment. She stayed in the loose-knit woods, finding just enough light to avoid copses of trees. No one stayed her progress.

She startled a deer, which startled her, but soon she was some good distance from the men and wagon, and steered the horse out to the well-worn trail and into a starlit night. She did not pause, but rode steadily east, the Star That Never Moves always on her left. She rode past a wagon with people bedded down, and was glad her horse and their horses didn't exchange greetings.

She rode most of the night, and only when the first blue line of day stretched across the eastern skies did she look for a place to rest herself and the weary horse. She found a low knob, scarcely twenty feet above the country, and took her horse there. It was a much-used place, but there were no mosquitoes, and its contour concealed her from prying eyes.

She rested until the day was warm and velvet. She saw no one. The Big Road was used mostly by people who could not pay to take the steam trains rolling over the nearby rails.

On the south slope of the hill she discovered yucca plants, and she rejoiced. A large one dominated a dozen more.

"I will leave you, Grandfather," she said to it, but selected a sturdy one for her purposes. She had no digging stick, and would need to use her knife to cut the yucca free, which she did with great care because she did not wish to break her knife. She dug patiently until she could pull the yucca out by its roots, which were thick and long. These were her treasure. She cut off the top of the plant, but kept the roots.

She eyed her mud-streaked horse and herself, and headed down the hillock and toward the river half a mile distant. The North Platte was lined with thick forest on both sides of its slow-moving current, forests that would shield her from the world. The sun had stirred a soft breeze that carried the scent of spring flowers. She thought she smelled roses, but maybe it was lady slippers. She could not say. She passed through lush grasses joyously reaching for the heavens, and wandered through copses of willows and trees she didn't know, and finally to a riverbank where there was a soft curve of sandy shore. She scared up red-winged blackbirds, and alarmed a few crows, and then she found herself alone.

At the river she cut the roots into small chunks, then mashed these between two rocks, dropped them into her copper kettle, and added water. She manipulated the pulped pieces and soon had foaming suds filling her kettle, a rich lather to wash with.

She shed her clothing in the hushed bower, and stepped into the flowing water. She was tall and bronze and thin, and the years did not yet show in her, except for the beginnings of gray in her hair. She undid her braids, letting her rich jet hair fall free, and then knelt in the purling water and let her hair float in the stream. The water wasn't cold, as it once was tumbling out of the mountains. Here it was mild and slightly opaque, carrying a little silt on its way to the distant sea. She sudsed her hair with the lather from the yucca roots, which she called amole, and felt the lather cleanse her hair until it felt silky. Then she rinsed it in the gentle flow of the river and washed her body with the amole. She ran rough willow bark over her flesh, abrading it gently until it tingled. She knelt in the shallow water, rinsing herself and then letting the river strain through her hair one last time. She finally felt chilled, though the sun warmed her in this quiet glade.

But she was not done. She immersed her clothing, piece by piece, in the river, washed them with the yucca lather, and then twisted the water out of each piece. Then she spread her skirts and blouse on the grasses, and began the long wait for the sun to dry them.

She led the horse into the river and washed it carefully, sudsing away the mud until its coppery coat shone. It was a good horse and it stood patiently while she cleansed it. She combed its mane and tail with her fingers, plucking thorns and debris from the horse hair. She rinsed it with kettles of water, and let the horse shake water off its back with several violent convulsions of its flesh. Then she led it back to grass and picketed it once again.

She spread the poncho on the grasses and lay down upon it, letting Father Sun finish her cleansing. She loved the warmth of the sun on her tawny flesh, and for the first time in many moons she felt utterly clean. She wished for sweetgrass, so she might bathe in its smoke and might take onto her body the scent of the sacred. But she was far from the places she knew and the herbs and grasses she knew. White men called this place the territory of Nebraska, but she knew no more than that. She spent much of that day lying in the sun, screened from the Big Road by a band of forest, waiting for her clothing to dry.

There were no mosquitoes there, at least not yet. With evening, things would be different. She dressed late in the afternoon, eyed her contented horse, and decided to ride a while. Her son was calling her. In some mystic way, she could hear him within her heart, calling for her to come to this place called St. Louis, where he resided with the blackrobes called Jesuits.

She dressed in slightly damp clothes and found her way back to the Big Road, heading east once again. The road was empty, and that pleased her. It felt good to be washed and clean. The horse was well rested and set an eager pace. This night she would be that much closer to the big city, and that much closer to her son.

She passed an encampment of several wagons and could see various men at their evening chores. Some were gathered at a cook fire. She saw no women, and thought it would not be a good place to stop, so she rode onward, but then they were shouting and mounting their horses and coming after her.

"Hold up there," one yelled.

She dreaded it and kept on walking her horse.

A shot from a revolver changed her mind. She reined in the horse and waited, while half a dozen bearded white men swiftly overtook her and surrounded her.

"That's her! That's the nag!" one said.

"What is it you wish?" she asked, not concealing her knowledge of their tongue.

"Stolen horse, chestnut like this, proper shod, and taken by a squaw!"

She addressed an older one, with massive shoulders and a hard look in his eye. "This is my horse."

"No it ain't, woman. We're taking it. Feller came by yesterday, said look out for just such as you. Said 'twas his saddle and tack too."

"Did he tell you he took three of mine, and all I possessed?"

"Likely story. Squaw story, you ask me."

"Did they tell you they tried to force themselves on me, and I barely escaped? Do you approve of violating a woman?"

"I ain't here to argue that. I'm here to get that horse and send it forward. Them fellows are ten, twelve miles west and we're going to take this nag to 'em."

"Did they tell you they planned to kill me after they had used me?"

The bull-shouldered one only smiled. "You'd better fetch yourself off that nag, or we'll pull you down, and maybe you'll get used after all."

He had ahold of her rein. The others crowded close, eyeing her.

"I'm on my way to visit my son in St. Louis," she said. "He's in school there."

"Sure you are," one said. "More likely you're just findin' ways to make a nickel along the road."

"Would you speak of your own mother in that way?"

"Where'd you learn English so good, eh?"

"I am a Shoshone. My husband was born in London and has been in the fur and robe trade all his life. We live in the territory of Montana."

"Stealing horses from white men, I imagine. West's full of renegades, and more'n half are hitched up to squaws." He paused. "Off!"

She saw how it would go, and slid off. She started to untie her kit, the cornmeal and cook pot wrapped in the poncho, when he snarled at her to leave it alone.

"I wish to have what is mine."

"That fellow, Willis, he said the horse and every damned thing on it was took."

She saw half a dozen men looking for an excuse, and quietly subsided. With luck, maybe she could walk into the thickening dark with the clothing on her back.

twenty

arkness cloaked Mary. Or maybe it was the indifference of those men that really cloaked her. Once they took the horse, they didn't seem to care much. She slipped beyond the campfire light and no one stayed her. The river would be to the north, so she studied the heavens and found the Star That Never Moves, and walked that way. This was an inky night, and she scarcely knew where she was walking. She dropped into a slough, pulled her wet moccasins from the muck, and worked around it. She didn't know she had reached the wooded bottoms of the river until she ran into a limb, which knocked her flat.

She stood, waited, saw vague limbs lacing the starlit sky, and knew she was close. It was time to sit. The men wouldn't find her. She felt about, and then settled against a tree trunk and waited. It didn't take long for a slim moon to rise, and with that lantern casting its ghostly light, she made her way through a thickening forest, then canebrakes and sedges, and then a spit of sand surrounded by wavering water.

She settled there, and took stock. She was an Indian

woman alone, with no food or weapons, save for her skinning knife, no shelter, no horse, and no friends. This was country where one could run into Peoples from many tribes, or white men, or the bluecoat army, or bears or wolves or coyotes. It was also a long way from the place called St. Louis, where she would see her son, if they would let her. She wasn't sure she would be allowed to see him.

She might keep from starving if she stayed close to the river. The Oregon Trail often ran a mile or two away from the river, working in straight lines rather than following the meandering bank. But the Big Road was too perilous for a lone woman of the People, and the river offered a chance to find food. The river was full of the fish with whiskers, which she despised but maybe they would keep her alive.

She thought about turning back, making her way to Fort Laramie and then to her people, but without food or a horse that would be even harder than continuing downriver. She might perish. A woman alone might die apart, trapped or destroyed or captured or sickened. The bitter reality was that she was caught. Maybe she should sing her death songs, and lie down and let the spirit fly away. Maybe she could send a spirit messenger to Skye, the man who filled her heart with tenderness every moment she was with him, and tell him she was going to fly away to the Long Walk.

She found the sand dry and soft, and lay down for a rest, cradled in the softness of a quiet June night. She drifted off, and the night was quiet, and then light was in her face, and a man was nudging her with his boot, and she looked up into the face of a young hard stranger with angry eyes.

She clawed her way up, not wanting him to look down on her.

He was not alone. Two others stood back. The one who

had nudged her was clean-shaven, with a revolver at his waist, and he had a flair for dressing. He wore a blue shirt and black vest and a flat-crowned hat. The others were dark and had ill-kempt beards, and heavy bandoliers laden with copper cartridges. Still more lined their belts. Each carried a repeating rifle. She had never seen men so heavily armed.

"What do you suppose she's doing here?"

"Don't rightly know. No horse, no nothing. Not a kit or a bag. Just one lone squaw."

"Think she talks English?"

"Hey, you." She was being addressed by the shaven one. "You speaka da English?"

She elected to hide her knowledge. It might save her life. It also might give her a clue of her fate.

She stared blankly at him.

"Hey, Kid, she can cook. We need a cook."

"Yeah," the Kid said. "She can cook and we can figure out what to do with her."

He prodded her forward. A camp came into view, and in it were several more young men, all busy with camp chores.

"Looks like we got us a squaw," said the Kid.

"Well, hell, ain't that nice," one replied.

He addressed her. "Go make johnnycakes." He pointed. She stared. "Hey, squaw, cornmeal and grease, and water, and fry 'em up." He pantomimed.

"I will," she said.

"Ah! I thought so. Where you come from?"

"I am Shoshone, Snake, going to St. Louis to see my son. He's in school."

"Goddamn educated injun," a bearded one said.

"You with anyone?"

She debated what to say, and opted to tell her story. "I lost everything. I had my ponies and my saddles and things, but white men stole them and were going to use me and kill me. Twice this happened."

The one called Kid yawned, and motioned for her to get to work. The men were hungry. Now they collected, eyeing her as hungrily as the others. Maybe she was in even worse trouble than before. She knelt, stirred cornmeal into mush, added grease to the hot fry pan and the meal, and began forming patties with her hands.

"Thought you'd know how," the Kid said.

She started the johnnycakes frying, and hunted for a spatula to turn them. She found none.

"I would like something to eat," she said. "I have nothing."

"Why should I feed you?" the Kid asked.

"Why should I cook for you?" she retorted, and started to walk away.

"Ah! I like that. A real bitch squaw! You eat, woman. What's your handle?"

"I do not know this word."

"Name."

"My husband calls me Mary."

"Where's he?" But before she could reply, a motion from the Kid sent a couple of men out to guard the perimeter. "Around here?"

"Yellowstone River," she said.

"You want to stick with us? You get fed."

She returned to the fire, found a knife stuck in the sand, and flipped the cakes while they watched. She eyed the knife, eyed them, and slowly plunged it back into the sand. Kid did not ignore the gesture.

"Sweetheart, that knife was a little test. You don't know bad when you see bad. I'm bad. I'm badder than bad. I'd cut you to ribbons if I feel like it. All these gents are badder than you ever saw or ever will see."

She shrugged.

"I'm the Choctaw Kid," he said. "That's my business. Being bad. Ain't no sin on earth I ain't done a hundred times."

She gazed up at him, finding cruelty in his face. He was a breed himself; she could see that.

"Why did you go bad?" she asked.

"No reason except I feel like it. There's posters in every burg around here. I'm wanted by a dozen lawmen. Army wants me. Over to Fort Kearney, they have a reward for me, dead or alive."

"I don't know what bad is. Shoshones don't have bad."

"Don't hand me that. You get a killer, what do you do with him?"

"He's got to pay the family of the dead. Or else they get to kill him."

"That the law?"

"We don't have laws. Only white men have laws. We have justice. Someone hurts you, you get revenge. It all works out."

"This lady, she's got no laws!" the Choctaw Kid said.

"All right," she said, pointing to the black fry pan.

These men scooped up the cakes on their knife blades and took them off to cool. She started some more cakes while the rest watched her closely. She did not know how this would end, or whether she would ever see her son. Probably they would take her with them, and her only escape would be death in some lonely place.

The Kid ate his in a moment and waited for another.

"What do these men look like? That took your horses?" he asked.

"Bearded men, in gray, with a mule wagon."

"Saw them pass," he said. "The other bunch must be the ones around here last night."

She nodded.

"Maybe we'll kill 'em. Kill 'em real slow and long."

She averted her gaze.

"Would you like that?"

"It's not for you to do," she said.

He smiled darkly. "We do what we feel like doing. And these wouldn't be the first I've killed. And won't be the last."

"And then the army will kill you."

He shrugged. "Not many in my line of work live long."

"Then why do you do it?"

"Lady, you ask too many questions. Now git them fry cakes done. I do whatever I feel like doing, and if I feel like killing a few, I'll do it."

"What are your bloods?"

"Half and half, and it makes me crazy. Don't never trust a breed."

"I do not know Choctaw."

"Now you do. My ma, she was Chocktaw. My pa, he was Dutch. Don't never marry Dutch to any injun because it'll come bad."

She fed them a second fry pan of johnnycakes, and waited. But he signaled her to scrub out the pan and clean up. The men left her one, which she ate quietly. It tasted oddly delicious.

"What's your son?" Kid asked.

"His name is North Star in my tongue, Dirk in yours. He is a grown man now. The blackrobes have him. I want to see him. I haven't seen my boy in many winters. Maybe he will not know me."

"He'll know you. If he don't like his Snake ma, I'll kill him," the Kid said.

That shot a chill through her.

"Religion ruined everyone," he said. "Plumb ruined me. I almost was good until I got smart."

"What are you going to do?"

"Rob and ruin until I die."

She stared. He meant it. He had worked out his future, knew it wouldn't last long, and wouldn't change a particle of it.

"We're tired of this here Oregon road. We're heading for the Union Pacific next. Them rails down on the Platte, below here. We're going to cut wires and clean out trains like you never saw, until we got the whole cavalry on our ass."

"Why?"

He eyed her. "I'll tell you why. Someday you'll tell people you met the Choctaw Kid. You tell 'em and they won't believe it. You tell 'em what the Kid did. Promise me that?"

"What the Kid did?"

"The Choctaw Kid. Not any kid, the Choctaw Kid."

"If you want to be known, why not be bad in St. Louis?"

"Don't ask stupid questions," he said.

"Here, no one knows you're bad," she added. "Maybe you not bad."

He turned to the ones with the bandoliers. "Fix her up. Two horses and a kit."

"For me?"

"Mary, we're going to get ourselves two horses for every one we give you. That's what's going to happen this day."

Men headed for the picketed horses, selected two small ones, saddled and bridled a bay, collected a big buckskin, haltered the big horse and added a blanket and packsaddle, and then strapped on panniers. Into these they added a kit. Bedroll, fry pan, pot, a bag of cornmeal, another of rolled oats, and various other things she could not see.

The Kid led the bay mare to her. "Up," he said. "I'll look to your stirrups."

But the stirrups were fine. She sat, amazed.

"These here got no brand, and no one knows where they come from. But I'm gonna write out a bill, just because you're a redskin and they'll be picking on you."

He dug into a saddlebag, found a pencil and a sheet of paper, and wrote on it.

"What does it say?" she asked.

"It says I, Harry Kidder, sold you two nags. Sold to Mary of the Shoshones for consideration of twenty-five dollars of service, June twenty-five, eighteen and seventy."

"And you signed it?"

"I did. Show it to your son." He handed her the paper. She slipped it into the pannier.

It was true. There were no brands or marks on these ponies that she could see; not even an ear notch. They had come out of nowhere.

"They're not shod, and you'll want to go easy on rock."

"You are a good man," she said.

His face darkened, and she thought she had made a fatal mistake.

"Go!" he snarled.

She touched her moccasins to the flanks of the bay mare, found her responsive, and slowly made her way downriver. Behind her, the bad men watched.

twenty-one

*H*is old black top hat flew off his head even before he heard the distant crack. From ancient habit, Skye dove off his horse, feeling pain shoot through his bum leg as he landed. He snatched his old Sharps from its sheath as he went.

Victoria had done the same, and now they stood behind their ponies. The shot had come from some vast distance far ahead and to the left, probably in the bottoms of the Big Horn River. She strung her bow and nocked an arrow. The ponies sidestepped nervously. Skye peered over the neck of his, wondering what lay ahead. He saw nothing. But someone had just tried to kill him. He wished his eyes were as good as they once were but now age blurred the horizons. He checked his Sharps. It was ready.

He retrieved the top hat, which had fallen ten feet away, and found a fresh hole through it, just above his hairline. He had been an inch from death. This was his fifth hat. The first two had been beaver felt; the last three silk.

A rage built in him.

There was only silence. No crows flew, no wind whispered. They were proceeding south along the arid Big Horn River valley, on a trail laid out by Jim Bridger, the old mountain man. They had thought they were alone.

"Goddamn white men," Victoria said.

Indians wouldn't snipe at them from several hundred yards.

His leg hurt. He had landed squarely on it, and while his knee didn't capsize or break again, everything ached anew. He squinted at the silent bottoms of the distant river, ready to shoot back.

After a while they moved slowly southward, walking between their horses, and thus walking within a living fortress as they had often done in the past. Occasionally Skye studied the river bottoms, ready for anything. But they proceeded peaceably south without hindrance.

That lasted only a minute or two. A gaggle of horsemen boiled out of the brushy bottoms, heading straight for Skye and Victoria. Skye continued quietly, his bum leg paining his every step. There were six in all, skinny horsemen in slouch hats, all except one. A fat man, bulging at the belly and thighs, mounted on a thicker horse, followed along just behind. They were spread in a half circle, ready for whatever trouble they faced.

They swiftly surrounded Skye and Victoria.

"Hold up there," the fat one bawled.

Skye waited quietly. This was a tough outfit, with mean thin men sporting an unusual amount of facial hair along with revolvers and saddle carbines.

"Gents?" Skye asked.

"This here's claimed land, and we don't allow no goddamn redskins on it," the fat one said.

"I'm Barnaby Skye. And who am I addressing?"

"It don't matter none. This is my range, and you're on it, and you're going to get yoah ass off it."

"That's interesting. I didn't know there was a government land office anywhere around here," Skye said.

"It don't mattah whether they is or ain't. Yoah getting yoah red ass off. Ah'm claiming this heah Big Horn Valley, top to bottom, mountain to mountain, and that's that."

"I didn't catch your name, sir."

"It's Yardley Dogwood, but never no mind; I could be God and it won't make a bit of difference to you."

Skye had lived among the Yanks long enough to detect region in a man's voice. These were Texans, he thought. Bitter men, defeated in war, swarming out of a ruined South, reckless of life and law.

"Texans?"

"We sure as hell ain't Indians. Now you turn around and git. We don't allow any trespassing here. You git or face what you get."

"Just passing through. Visiting my wife's people."

"Did you heah me? Git out!"

"Did you bring a shovel?" Skye asked. "Dig a grave for two people passing through?"

Dogwood glared. "We don't give a damn who you are, what you are, or whether you git buried or just rot until the coyotes eat what's left of you."

"Got a few longhorns? I don't see them."

"There a-comin' and you're a-going."

"Who are you going to shoot first? My wife or me?"

"You're both going to buy the ticket, mister."

"Mister Skye, yes. That's how I prefer to be addressed. Do you prefer to be called Mister Dogwood?"

"Enough talk." He motioned to his men, who withdrew revolvers. Skye found himself staring into half a dozen muzzles. "That's how I talk, redskin."

"Born in London, sir. This is my wife Victoria, born among the Absaroka People. And who are these gentlemen?"

For an answer, Dogwood lifted his hog leg and drilled another hole through Skye's silk hat. It flew off again. Skye winced.

"You fat sonofabitch," Victoria yelled. "You miserable bastard. I own this land. You get your ass off. This land's mine. I've owned it since before you were born, fatso. My people owned it before Texas was. This is my home, and you can damned well take your fat ass out of here."

The whole lot stared at Victoria, whose drawn bow was aimed square at fatso's chest.

"Kill me, go ahead, you pile of grease. Only you get an arrow before you do."

Skye marveled. Dogwood sat, breaking the back of his nag, utterly paralyzed. One of the cowboys began easing sideways, out of Victoria's vision.

"One more step by that bastard and you croak," she said.

The cowboy stopped.

"Looks like there's a standoff, Mister Dogwood," Skye said. "Now, are you going to let us through, or do we die? We're old; we don't mind dying. You're what? Thirty?"

"Tell that squaw to put the bow down."

"Tell your cowboys to holster their guns."

Dogwood plainly didn't wish to do it.

"Did you bring a shovel, Mister Dogwood? Three graves, one for you, two for us."

"I'll tell you what you're going to do, you fat bastard,

you're going to turn around and ride away, and when you're
out of range, we're going to go ahead and cross my people's
land. And then you're going to take your cowboys and your
cows and get out of here."

Dogwood was hefting his revolver, twitchy, daring himself to shoot her.

Skye deliberately reached to the grass and plucked up his
hat, which lay between his and Victoria's horses. When he
was down, he swung his Sharps around. He put his hat back
on, and his Sharps was at his waist, pointing at fatso.

"Looks like you put another hole in my topper, Mister
Dogwood," he said.

But Yardley Dogwood was staring at the huge bore of the
Sharps, which now pointed blackly at his chest.

"I don't mind dying, but I guess you do," Skye said. "You
back off now. Turn your men around and get out of here."

Dogwood slowly, carefully, holstered his own Navy revolver and wheeled his stout gray horse. He nodded to his
men, who followed suit, and soon the horsemen were retreat-
ing toward the bottoms. No tricks. Skye didn't trust them,
and rested his Sharps across his saddle, ready for a long-
distance shot.

The horsemen were soon beyond the effective range of
their own carbines, but Skye didn't move. Not yet. He waited
until they were deep into the river bottoms, where they probably were camped in the middle of the mosquitoes awaiting
Dogwood's trail herd.

Skye was in no hurry, and stood on an aching leg for a
while more.

Victoria eased her bowstring, returned the arrow to her
quiver, but did not free the bowstring. Not yet.

"Can they do that? Take land?" she asked.

"No Yank government's here yet," Skye said. "They just claim it, and drive others off it, and call it their own."

"The goddamn government's worse than the cowboys," she said. "One of these days they'll tell my people to go to some damned place with four invisible lines around it and stay in there."

All that day they rode hard, wanting distance between themselves and fatso. The Big Horn Valley was flanked by the Big Horn Mountains on the east, and rolling arid hills on the west, and was easy to travel. Skye's leg hurt from the new insult, but he concluded nothing was damaged. They scared up some mule deer, but Skye was slow to draw his Sharps, and the deer vanished. Old age wasn't helping him keep meat in the cook pot, which was still another reason why he was feeling the need to settle somewhere and raise his own beef.

Midday heat suffocated them but Skye felt compelled to keep going, and as the day waned he knew they had traversed a long stretch of the arid valley. This arid land was going to fool fatso. Only the green bottoms along the river offered much feed for the longhorns, and most of that was brush-choked.

Along toward dusk, Victoria grew restless.

"Something ahead," she said.

"I don't hear anything."

"You're deaf as a stone, Skye."

It turned out she was right. Just about when Skye was about to call it quits for a day, they rounded a river bend and discovered a sea of cattle ahead, longhorns of all shapes and colors, brown, brindle, bluish, spotted, black, gray, bawling and milling, many of them along the riverbank. And herding them were a dozen or so men on horseback, some barely visible in the distance.

"More goddamn cowboys," Victoria said.

"Fatso's herd coming up the river."

This time they rode straight toward the camp, where a fire was blooming. They were noticed, but no one was pulling weapons or showing any signs of trouble.

But the foreman did pause and await company.

"Evening," he said, looking Skye and Victoria over.

"Evening. I'm Mister Skye, and my wife Victoria Skye. We're angling through here and thought to say hello."

"I reckon you're welcome," the lean man said. "Light and set."

Skye and Victoria gratefully slid from their ponies, picketed them, and joined the busy trail crew. The lowing of the cattle wrought a constant sound, almost a wail, as the animals watered and spread out on thin grass. Here were a dozen more of these wire-thin men, trail-worn and tired.

"Name's Higgins," the man said. "Seems to me I've heard tell of you."

"I used to guide once, and before that I led a fur brigade."

"You a friend of Bridger's?"

"Sure am, Mister Higgins. You're on his road. Old Gabe worked this out, mostly for wagons, but you've taken a herd over."

"You pass my outfit north of here?"

Skye nodded. "Maybe twenty-five miles. That's Yardley Dogwood, right?"

"They let you through?"

"It took some persuading, Mister Higgins. That fellow, he's a big target."

Skye laughed. Higgins laughed.

The foreman turned to several of his men. "Gents, this heah is a fine old man of the mountains, Mistah Skye, and his woman, Victoria. They been here before we were born. He's rassled grizzly, put bullets into Blackfeet, taken people where white men never been, and he's too tough to eat so we ain't going to roast him for dinner. They's passing through, and we're going to welcome them. We got us a quarter of a beeve to eat this heah evening, before it turns rank on us, and pretty soon now we'll be roasting the meat, soon as that fire gets hot. And you, Mistah Skye, you're going to tell us some stories."

"Some good beef for a few yarns? I imagine that's a bargain, Mister Higgins."

"Goddammit, Skye, you call me Mister one more time and you can just starve."

"Higgins, you call me Skye one more time, and I won't tell stories."

"You got any booze?" asked Victoria. "He don't tell stories good until he gets himself sauced up."

Higgins sighed. "I'd give a dozen steers for a bottle," he said. "But we're out of luck."

twenty-two

*B*lue Dawn of the Shoshone People made her way east along the Big Road. She was no longer Mary, the name Skye had given her. She was no longer the woman of a white man. She was what she had been born to be. She sat perfectly erect in her saddle, and did not slouch like white men. She sat with her head high and her back straight, and thus she told anyone who saw her that she owned the world and was a woman of the People.

But she met very few westering parties, and they paid her little heed. There was something about her that discouraged contact, and that was how she wanted it. Skye would count miles, but she never fathomed those invisible marks, and instead counted horizons. On a good day she rode past several horizons. She was now some unimaginable distance from her people and from Skye and Victoria. It was so far she had no word or concept for it; and yet the land never ended, and the only thing she observed was that the grass was thicker and taller, and there was more standing water and evidence of generous rain. But each day she was a little closer to her son.

When North Star had been old enough, Skye had taught the child the mysterious signs Skye called writing, and taught the boy to read these signs. Sometimes Skye would draw them in charcoal on the back of a piece of bark, or an old paper, and then have the solemn child learn the letters. Then Skye taught his son words. Often this was early in the morning, before the world stirred much. Sometimes Skye found a book and taught his son the meaning of each word, even as Mary listened. She often thought that she, too, could read with a little help, but he never offered to teach her. He only told her he wanted their son to have a chance at life, a chance that was taken away from him when he was young.

Skye had been a patient, cheerful teacher, who never reprimanded the boy when he could not fathom a letter or word or idea. Skye often illustrated the words, making up little stories, or telling the boy all about the place called London, with its streets and half-timbered houses and fog and thousands of people and frequent rain. So the boy had soon connected words and letters to these magic things, so different from the buffalo-hide lodge that was his real home, far from any sort of building.

She had watched this mysterious ritual proudly, watching the boy discover a word and point a finger at it, watching Skye rejoice whenever his son had made a bit of progress. North Star was a patient boy, but sometimes he got restless when Skye detained him too long in their lodge on a winter day, or outside when the weather was good. Her son wanted to run and walk, like other sons.

She only vaguely knew what this schooling was all about. Her boy would learn the magical powers of white men and be able to do the things white men did, and know what they knew. She knew this would take her son away from her, bit by bit. He would not be a Shoshone boy when he had mastered all this, but a white boy. That was a great sorrow to her, and yet she also was proud that he was learning Skye's ways.

"He needs to know these things," he told her. "If he learns these things, he can choose the sort of life he wants to live."

That seemed strange to her. Why would one choose a life? What was wrong with the life they were sharing? Did Skye have some sort of plans for the boy that she knew nothing of?

Sometimes North Star would pull out a scrap of paper and read words to her, pointing at each one. The child scarcely imagined that only one parent had these mysterious secrets hidden inside, and that she knew nothing of writing and reading. But she could at least teach him the ways of her people, and she showed him how to draw language-pictures, how to make the signs that were understood by most plains tribes, and she taught him all the words of her own tongue that she knew, and Victoria taught him the words of her Crow tongue as well, so the boy grew up trilingual, switching easily to her tongue, or Skye's, or Victoria's whenever he was addressing one of his three parents. This was a beautiful thing, for the boy had drawn close to each. He was quiet and sunny, and she had watched him proudly as he grew into a person, and left his infancy and childhood behind him. But what did Skye intend for him?

Skye had seemed driven to teach the boy his words and his writing, and it troubled Mary because it was as if Skye were investing something in the boy that she couldn't understand. All he would say was that he didn't want Dirk to be trapped in the life that Skye had lived after being put on a ship and sent into the Big Waters. It amazed her that Skye's people would snatch him away from his father and mother as a boy and put him on a boat and keep him from ever seeing them again. Surely that was a terrible violation of Skye and his parents, and it made her wonder about the English. No Shoshone boy would ever be captured and forcibly taken from his parents. It was unthinkable. These English, they had no respect for the liberty and rights of the family they had torn asunder. They must be a very hard people, she thought, to permit such a thing. Hard and cruel. She liked her people more, because each boy could choose his own path, and was not stolen from his family.

Skye was a hard man, she thought. He could have taught her to decipher the letters and words, and shape them into language. He could have taught her, the same as he taught their son. He could have taught Victoria too. But they were women, and he never thought to teach them how to put words on paper with marks. That was for white men. She didn't mind much. She liked being his woman, and gathering nuts and berries, and firewood, and mending the lodge cover, and nursing the boy, and making quilled shirts and moccasins for him. But he was hard, and more often she could not fathom what went through his head. White men's thoughts were so different from hers, and sometimes he seemed to be an utter stranger to her.

Still, it had been a happy lodge, the four of them, his late-in-life boy, she and Victoria sharing the work and Skye's arms. North Star had prospered. The Absaroka boys taunted him because he was different, but he gave back as much as he got. He was Skye's son, and that gave him an aura of mystery, for Skye was a legend among them, the strong white man who had come to live with the Crows and fight beside them.

Then one day, her happiness fell apart. North Star had lived eight winters. They were at Fort Laramie, and Skye was talking with his friend Colonel Bullock, who was the sutler. They talked for a long time, and Skye brought North Star to the colonel, and presented him, and the men all talked a long time, while she and Victoria wandered outside. She knew it had been a bad year for Skye; he could not pay the colonel what was owed. Fewer Yankees wanted guides to take them into the lands unknown to them, because now the country was known, and there were trails. And Skye went ever deeper in debt.

Then at last Skye appeared on the veranda of the post store, looking solemn. He was searching for words, trying to bring himself to say something to his wives and son, and the more Skye struggled, the deeper was the dread in Mary. He was having such trouble that even the boy caught the malaise, and stared.

Skye ran a weathered hand through his graying locks, and settled his old hat, and began.

"The colonel's retiring," he said. "He'll no longer be my agent. He's sold his inventory to a new post sutler named Harry Badger. The new man won't extend credit. I owe over two hundred seventy dollars, and we'll be unable to buy anything until that's paid." He stared glumly at Victoria. "We'll do without."

That was bad enough, but then it got worse.

"I don't want my boy to grow up without a chance at life," he said. "He needs schooling, and a trade, so he can make his way. He'll need to support a wife and family someday. He'll need to read and write and pay bills and earn his way. I just can't give him that here, with a few old books and newspapers."

Skye looked so uncomfortable that Mary took alarm.

"Colonel Bullock's leaving for the East tomorrow. He's retiring in St. Louis, and he'll be taking Dirk with him."

A sudden desolation broke through her.

"It's all arranged. The blackrobes have a school for Indian boys in St. Louis. This is Father de Smet's dream, helping native boys get an education and passing that along to their people. They'll take Dirk and give him an education. They're good people. They'll teach the boy whatever he needs, and start him on his way."

Skye had been talking about Dirk almost as if the boy weren't there, listening to every word.

"But, Papa," he said.

"How long will this be?" Mary asked. One winter, maybe. That would be forever. One winter, and then her son would come back.

"Until he's sixteen," Skye said.

It was as if she had fallen off a cliff and were tumbling down, down, down to the cruel rocks far below. Eight winters.

"But he will have no mother!" she said.

"The blackrobes will care for him. And Colonel Bullock will look in on him. There is a dormitory, a place where he'll be with other boys, safe and warm."

"Eight winters."

She felt dizzy as grief overtook her.

"Sonofabitch, Skye!" Victoria snapped.

He started to reply, and subsided into silence. He tried to draw them to him, but she went stiff and wouldn't let him touch her, and Victoria stalked off the porch. He tried to catch his son, and soothe him, but Dirk had gone pale and was sliding deep into himself. In that moment Skye's family had shattered, and it didn't seem possible that it would ever be put together again.

"I can't even pay my debts anymore," Skye said.

That made no sense at all to Mary, but sometimes white people made no sense to her. She glanced furtively at her son, as if she shouldn't be looking at him because he wasn't hers anymore, and felt something shatter inside of her.

Skye knelt before his son, and clasped the boy's shoulders in his gnarled old hands.

"It's for you, Dirk, not for me. It's to give you the chance to make something of yourself. You'll be grateful someday. You'll be lonely and homesick for a while. But then you'll be too busy to worry about that. And the blackrobes will help you grow up to be whatever you want to be."

But Dirk's face had crumpled into fear, and Mary ached at the sight.

"They took me off the streets of London and put me on a ship," Skye said. "I never saw my family again. I had to learn how to live, how to survive. It won't be so hard for you. You'll see us in a few years, and we'll all be glad. You'll be better off than we are."

But it was as if Skye were talking to the wind. There was only the terrible reality that Skye's son Dirk, and Mary's son North Star, was being torn from the lodge.

"Now, son, it's time to say good-bye to your father and your mothers."

But the boy could not manage that. He simply stared, a tear welling in each eye. Skye took him by the hand and led him to his mothers. "Son, you'll see them in a few years, and we will all be proud of you. Colonel Bullock and the Jesuit fathers are giving you something precious, something that will help you to have a good life."

But Dirk simply stood mute and miserable.

"We'll say good-bye now," Skye said, but no one did.

Finally, helplessly, Mary watched as Skye led her son to the clapboard house where Colonel Bullock resided. She watched a woman welcome the boy, and then the door closed, and so did her own life.

twenty-three

$\mathcal{S}$kye awoke with the sense that something was wrong. It was an ancient feeling, honed from a long life lived in a way unknown to most white men. It was not yet dawn, but a band of light cracked the eastern horizon. He peered quietly at the slumbering cow camp. The cook was already up and building his morning fire near a wagon with bowed canvas over it. The cattle were grazing quietly. He saw a night herder sitting his horse, unmoving.

There had been a light shower in the night, pattering down on Skye's canvas-covered bedroll and annoying his face and hair. The air this June dawn was moist and fresh and sweet. He peered into the darkness, unable to banish his malaise, but he saw nothing amiss.

The evening had been enjoyable, though not for Victoria, who had sat bitterly among those who were occupying her homeland, a valley the Absaroka People had considered their refuge. But the trail crew had sawed off some thick beefsteaks for Skye and Victoria, and after beef and beans they had peppered them with questions about this country. Victoria had subsided into silence, staring flintily at these bearded Texans, but Skye had relaxed some. These were working hands, without large ambition, unlike their employer and the men two days' travel downriver, the ones who had nearly killed him. Skye didn't hold that against this trail crew, but he knew Victoria did.

They had mostly wanted to know about the valley they would be settling; what tribes visited, what creeks ran through. This was home to the Snakes and the Crows, he had told them, employing white men's names. It was arid, caught in the rain-shadow of the great chain of mountains lying to the west. It wasn't prime buffalo country, but the river bottoms would support plenty of longhorns. He never did tell any yarns from the old days. These drovers wanted only to know about the present.

Now he peered about the slumbering camp, taking inventory, but he saw nothing amiss. Victoria still slept. He threw his bedroll off and lumbered to his feet, wrestling with his stiff and pained leg. The river brush wasn't far, and he headed there in the deep silence. Dew caught at his moccasins. Even as he relieved himself, his gaze roved because his sense of malaise wouldn't leave.

When he returned, limping painfully, he saw Victoria sitting up in her blankets.

"Something's wrong," he said.

She nodded curtly. She hadn't liked being here last night, and still didn't. She rose easily, her age affecting her less, and studied the camp. The cook busied himself, and ignored them. Their ponies were picketed on good grass.

"Go?" he asked her.

She nodded.

She would fetch the ponies. He couldn't get around much

anymore. So he shook out his bedroll and tied it tight. Then he shook hers and tied it. Then he took his over to his saddle to tie it behind the cantle, and that's when he discovered what was wrong.

His Sharps rifle was not in its sheath. Had he pulled it out, as he often did, to keep it beside him as he slept? He didn't remember that, but checked the ground where he had slumbered. No rifle lay there. He limped in widening circles. Had he left it at the campfire? He hadn't. Was it lying with Victoria's stuff? It wasn't. Her quiver and bow rested beside her Crow-made saddle. Was the light tricking him? No, the widening dawn skies were concealing nothing.

He had owned the Sharps for decades. It used an old technology now, but that didn't matter. It had been a great lifesaving weapon, a weapon that had kept him fed and safe, for as long as he could remember. Its throaty boom had aided his wife's people in their battles with the Sioux and Blackfeet. Its big bullet had dropped buffalo for her people and kept her Kicked-in-the-Bellies band fed and sheltered. With the Sharps, he had earned enough in buffalo hides and tongues to support his wives and son. The robes and hides he had brought to the traders had kept him in powder and caps and paper or cloth cartridges, had purchased pots and knives and thread and awls and calico. Long after the guiding business had faded, his Sharps had brought precious Yank dollars to keep his wives and himself alive.

Now it was missing, and he felt deprived and, in a way, naked. The Sharps was still his meal ticket and his safety. He stared at the empty sheath, willing his rifle to be there, willing it to be on the ground under his saddle, or close by. But it was gone, and without miracles, he could not replace it.

"We'll look," he said, not yet ready to make accusations.

She nodded. They separated, each drifting toward a group of slumbering drovers. She in particular had a way of gliding through unseen. No one paid attention to an old Indian woman. He watched her pause at each bedroll, pause at a pile of gear near the horses, and even stoop at one point to examine something closely. He drifted toward the cook and his fire and wagon. The cook was a cranky old gent, as disapproving of the Skyes as he disapproved of everyone else in his company.

"Looking for something of mine got misplaced," Skye said.

"Nothing gets misplaced in my kitchen," the gent said.

"I lean on it a lot," Skye said.

"No sticks around here I haven't burnt up to make coffee," the cook said, dismissing him. Skye peered in the covered wagon.

"Ain't nothing in there for you. Iffen you're hungry, you can wait like the others."

Skye had seen nothing resembling a rifle anyway.

Some of the hands were stirring now, rolling up their blankets, stretching, washing down at the river. Two night herders were riding in slowly, and Skye waited to see what was hanging from their saddles. But, in fact, neither had a saddle scabbard or a rifle on board. If they had lifted Skye's rifle, they had hidden it somewhere in this brushy river-bottom country.

Someone had it. He hadn't lost it. He didn't know how to deal with it.

Victoria slid close.

"Some sonofabitch stole it," she said. "Good at it too."

Her grudging admiration was drawn from her own culture. The Crows were some of the best camp robbers on the plains, and were masters at lifting valuables from any white party wandering through their country. Only this time the game was reversed.

Skye debated the proper course. There was no good way to deal with it. Accuse them? Threaten them? Systematically tear into their gear while they bellowed at him? No. The Sharps would not be in this camp, and would not be picked up by its new owner until the Skyes were long gone, and then it would be a source of great good humor among these drovers. But at least he'd put them on notice, one way or another. Some trail bosses ruled with an iron hand and wouldn't let a guest at their campfire be harmed.

Victoria brought the ponies in and saddled them. Skye watched her lift his saddle over the blanketed pony and draw up the cinch. The scabbard hung uselessly from the right side.

Higgins approached. "You ain't staying for a little coffee and cakes?"

Skye seized the moment. "Mister Higgins, I'm missing my Sharps rifle. It wasn't in the sheath this morning."

The foreman absorbed that for a moment. "Must be lying around here somewheres, then."

"We've looked."

Higgins studied the Skyes' campsite, as if expecting the rifle to materialize.

"You used it some as a crutch. You reckon it got left in the bushes?"

"We've looked."

"I don't recollect seeing it when you-all rode in yestiddy."

"I had it."

Higgins paused a long time, and came to some sort of conclusion. "I imagine it's around heah somewheres. I'll ask. Let me do the asking, friend."

Skye watched the foreman approach knots of men and converse with them, and watched them shake their heads. Higgins headed out to the horse herd, where other of the drovers were saddling up for the day, and once again the same questions wrought the same shake of the head in them all. Higgins must have directed them to start a search, because half a dozen yawning drovers began a broad sweep of the camp, the herd, the brush along the river, the riverbank, and the surrounding meadow.

They turned up nothing, which was what Skye expected.

Higgins ducked his head into the cook wagon and poked in there, and finally withdrew with nothing in hand. He returned to Skye and Victoria.

"It sure ain't showing up nowheres. Maybe some thieving redskin come in the night and took her off."

"In other words, it wasn't your outfit."

Higgins absorbed that a moment, and then agreed. "It sure as hell wasn't any of my boys, and if I see one toting a Sharps, I'll fix to get it to you. You going to the Shoshones on the Wind River, right?"

"Yes. They have an agent."

"Well, Mister Skye, I'm plumb sorry. It makes the Republic of Texas look bad, and that makes me feel bad."

"You tell Yardley Dogwood he owes me a new hat and a Sharps."

"I don't suppose I'll tell him that. What happened to your hat?"

"Those bullets holes are what happened to my hat."

Higgins had nothing to say after that.

"I suppose if a Sharps turns up in your outfit, Texas will be disgraced," Skye said.

"I'm afraid that would be true."

"And so would Texas and Yardley Dogwood, and each of you."

The foreman stared.

There was no point in dragging it out. Skye painfully clambered onto the buckskin pony, and Victoria lithely settled in her squaw saddle, and they rode away, feeling the stares of a dozen men on their backs.

He and Victoria rode silently for an hour, wanting to escape that place and those men, and finally a certain tension lifted and they relaxed a little.

"I am watching the death of my people," Victoria said.

"I'll get a new one somehow," he said. "Muzzleloaders are cheap."

But the thing he had shoved to the back of his mind, the bottom of his heart, and the farthest reaches of conversation welled up in him, and he could not banish it. His vision was going bad. More and more, distant things were blurred, and words on pages were blurred, and he had been hunting now for two or three years in dread of not seeing clearly what he was going to kill, and that dread had so suffused him that more often than not he had let blurred moving objects pass by, for fear that he was shooting at a friend's horse, and not the wild animal he wanted for meat. And he was more and more afflicted in his near vision too, often asking some white man to read something to him because he couldn't make out the letters and words and sentences. Nor was that all. He had acquired a slight tremor, one he hoped was not visible to Victoria and Mary, but one that weakened his aim and required him to use a bench rest as much as he could.

The terrible reality was that he was not far from having to set aside his fine old Sharps because age had caught up with him. He had intended to give it to Dirk when Dirk returned, or rather if Dirk ever returned. There was one more year of school with the Jesuits, and then Dirk would be sixteen and free to choose his life: Indian like his parents, or white. It was odd. He had driven Dirk from his mind, refused to think about the boy, loathed his decision to send his son east for schooling. But now he found himself aching for his son.

twenty-four

Victoria watched Skye ride a little ahead, unbalanced in the saddle, his stiff bad leg twisting him. He was riding with his spine straight and rigid, his shoulders thrown back, not with his usual slouch. He was riding as someone new to horses would ride, ill at ease in the saddle. She stayed a little behind him, aware that she was seeing something fraught with pain. Skye didn't ride like that.

She elected to stay back, knowing his silence meant something also. Sometimes in the past they had walked their ponies side by side, communing with each other out of ancient love.

His rifle sheath bobbed uselessly on his saddle. He ignored it. An empty flaccid sheath, a lost rifle, an old man. Wearily, for she no longer rode easily for long, she followed, letting his silence command the hours. They were two days from the Wind River Reservation of Mary's people, two days from Mary herself. Mary would pitch Skye's lodge near her brother, and her brother would be looking after her, and they would all welcome Skye and Victoria.

Ahead the treacherous Wind River canyon blocked any direct route to the land given to the Shoshones by the white fathers. Skye steered west, up a red rock canyon that would lead to a divide and down an ancient route much favored by the Shoshones themselves. And in a while they would all be together again in Skye's lodge, and Mary would look after them. More and more, Victoria was glad that Skye's small family encompassed the younger Shoshone woman. Victoria wearied easily now.

They nooned in an enchanted park encased in tumbled red rock. A clear creek ran through. The red walls were decorated with ancient stick figures, the language of people long gone. But the stories told by the figures were sometimes clear enough for anyone to read. This small avenue over the arid mountains was a sacred route, filled with mystery and holiness.

Skye eased off his pony but landed badly, gasping when his bad leg shot fire through him. Victoria watched helplessly. She led their ponies to the creek, where they nosed and swirled the water before lapping it.

Skye, afraid to settle into the verdant meadow without a crutch, chose to sit on an old cottonwood log.

Victoria washed her face in the icy water, enjoying the shock of cold that stung her skin. Then she settled in the grass near him, planning on a brief nap in the breezy shade.

"I was going to give it to Dirk," he said.

It had come out of the blue, and she puzzled a moment to connect these words to anything. But he was talking of the Sharps.

"I can't see much anymore." He stared at her. "Next year. He's supposed to come back here next year. The rifle, that's what a father gives to a son."

She marveled. She had known for a long time that his vision wasn't good, knew that when he hunted he wanted her along. Knew when he asked about things ahead, or moving animals, he was making sure. He couldn't see things close at hand, either, and had stopped studying those mysterious signs in books, stopped reading. But never until now had he confessed to it, and somehow he had even been able to hunt well enough. He knew from the way animals moved what they were, knew the stolid walk of the buffalo, the bounce of a running deer, the race of antelopes.

Now, for the first time, he was acknowledging it. And for the first time in many winters, he had spoken of his son, as if the boy were back from the dead.

"Will he come here?" she asked.

"I don't know. Eight years of schooling. Who knows?"

"Next year, he is free?"

Skye lifted his hat and stared into the red-rock high country. "I don't know that he'll want to see us. He's been away a long time, and he's got a good schooling now. He's used to the city. He wouldn't like it here. Stuck with an old man who hasn't seen the inside of a school for half a century."

She marveled. He had not talked about Dirk for years on end, and sometimes she thought the boy was dead, and Skye wouldn't mention his name, the way the Native people didn't name the dead. But now, suddenly, sitting on this cottonwood log beside a clear creek, he was talking about a boy who was ripped away and scarcely heard from again, except for a perfunctory letter waiting each spring at Fort Laramie saying he was well and learning his lessons.

"This school. Is it like a white man's prison?" she asked.

"I haven't ever seen it," he said. "But there's a dormitory for younger boys, another for older boys, a dining hall, some classrooms, and a church and rectory."

She hardly knew what all that was about. "The black-robes?" she asked.

"Jesuits. Society of Jesus. You've met Father de Smet on his travels."

She had liked Father de Smet, the blackrobe who liked Indians and defended them against sickness and the Yankee soldiers and government.

"What will he be like?" she asked, dreading the answer. Would there be a terrible gulf between his Indian mothers and the educated boy?

"If he comes. Who's to say?" he asked. He peered into her eyes. "I didn't do it for me. If it was for me, I'd have kept him here, showed him everything I learned here. He could be looking after us now."

"Will he hate you?" she asked, the thing that had been smoldering in her breast for many winters.

"He was too young to rip away from us," he said. "But Bullock was leaving. It was then or never."

She didn't like the brittle tone in his voice; this was something he had been rehearsing and reliving and regretting for all those winters past. And the lack of any more children only deepened Skye's desolation. Skye had sent his only boy away and torn his own small family apart.

He rose abruptly, and Victoria knew she must not ask any more or mention Dirk again. He limped to his horse, his back stiff against her, almost in rebuke for opening this subject. He pushed himself heavily into his saddle, and she slid into hers, and they turned their ponies up the red-rock valley and the distant pass they must surmount.

She rode behind, aware that something valuable had happened there, while they rested themselves and their horses. She never did understand goddamn white men, and she had understood Skye not at all when he had sent North Star away and broken the heart of his two mothers. But it had broken Skye's heart too, and that was what she marveled at now. She had never realized that. He had sent Dirk away for the boy's sake, so the boy could find a good life. And he had suffered for it, every day of his life since then. She didn't know the meaning of all this, but she knew, at last, what had gone through the heart of the man she loved.

They rode uneventfully over the high saddle that would take them toward Mary's people, and descended Muddy Creek, through a quiet afternoon. Skye rested often, mostly to relieve his tormented leg. Victoria was grateful for the rests as well. Once she saw a doe and fawn, and resisted drawing her bow. The Texas foreman had given the Skyes enough meat and biscuit to reach the Wind River Reservation. She watched the doe lead the speckled fawn toward safety, and thought about the drovers and their vast herd of beef, which would all be killed and eaten someday.

She wondered whether white men apologized to the spirit of the animal they had just killed, the way many of her people did. She had a ritual prayer. I am sorry to have taken your life, she would say to the downed animal. And she would wish the spirit a good voyage to the place of spirits. She meant to ask Skye whether white men ever felt sorrow for taking the life of one of their cows or sheep. But somehow she could not bring herself to ask him that.

They reached the banks of the Wind River the middle of the next day, and made their way upstream, toward the towering peaks in the distance, following a well-worn trail along the cold river. This was Mary's home. She would be there with the lodge, and there would soon be a joyous reunion of Skye's family.

Within the hour they reached Fort Washakie, and discovered log buildings, and also a cluster of log homes, along with some traditional lodges. There were even some white clapboard structures that she thought were government buildings. These had fieldstone chimneys, some of which were leaking gray smoke. Plainly, the Eastern Shoshones were acquiring the ways of white men. Their great chief, Washakie, had befriended white men and wanted to teach his own people the ways of these Europeans who were filtering through their country. He was as old as Skye but more vigorous, and had an almost mystical power over his people. He knew English and French, having learned it from the trappers, and this had enabled him to deal with the Yankees and win for his people a great and beautiful homeland along the Wind River.

Now, as she and Skye wandered into this sprawling but tidy settlement, she looked for Mary and the familiar lodge, but she saw neither. Skye reined in his pony, unsure where to go or what to do, and then started a systematic search for his lodge, even as Shoshone children and women, and a few elders, congregated around them. They all knew the Skyes, and they greeted the Skye family joyously—except for one thing.

"Where is our Blue Dawn?" a woman asked.

Skye knew enough of the tongue to understand. "Isn't she here?" he replied.

They stared at one another. Mary, it seemed, had not come to Fort Washakie at all, and no one had seen her for many moons.

An unease built in Victoria. Surely Mary would have sent word. But it was plain that Skye's younger wife had never arrived, no Skye lodge had been raised here, and the Shoshones had no knowledge of her whereabouts.

Victoria was well aware of all the troubles that could befall a lone Indian woman traversing a vast land. Bears, storms, hail, sickness, injury, a broken leg, a lamed pony, death at the hands of hostile tribes, and something more. White men. Had that ugly bunch with Yardley Dogwood caught her, saw how vulnerable and beautiful she was, used her, and then killed her as they would kill some camp dog?

The thought must have crossed Skye's mind too, because she found herself staring into his worried eyes. Those savages from Texas knew no boundaries.

About then Mary's brother, The Runner, gray at the temples now, pushed through the throng.

"It is thee," he said. "Art thou here for a visit?"

Skye had always loved The Runner's Elizabethan English, gotten from studying the Bible and Shakespeare given to him by a white teacher long before.

"We are. It's good to see you, my brother. And where is Blue Dawn?"

"Thou hast asked a question I cannot answer."

"She came ahead of us. Victoria left her on the Yellowstone. She was coming here."

But The Runner could only stare, sadly. "Brother and sister, come to my house. We will await Blue Dawn there. See my house? It is built the way of white men."

Skye nodded reluctantly. "Has there been any word of trouble? Are there hunting bands from other tribes in the area?"

"No, only the sweetness of spring doth fill the air . . . But yes, word hath come that some white men with many cattle are upon the Big Horn River."

Skye's dread was palpable to Victoria. She thought that she and Skye might soon retrace their steps, this time looking for a hasty grave.

twenty-five

Mary found herself at a place where the iron horse ran on silvery rails. For a day or two, she had heard the wail of whistles and the distant clatter of the steam cars, but she had never seen a railroad or a train. Now she halted her horses at the sight of a graveled road running along the Platte Valley, and on this road were wooden cross ties, and metal rails, stretching mysteriously east and west. An iron horse would not alarm her. She had seen the fireboats on the Big River, the fires making steam, which pushed a piston, which drove the paddlewheels.

Surely the iron horse would make as much noise and be as ferocious as the fireboats. Sometimes the fireboats had scared the ponies, and she didn't doubt that these horses, given her by the Choctaw Kid, would take alarm too. Still, for reasons she could not fathom, she abandoned the Big Road, which ran closer to the Platte River, for this arrow-straight iron road, and led her horses eastward along it. No iron horse came for a long time, and when she reached a place where there was a big tank of some sort on stilts, she stopped. It didn't take any effort to see that this was a place where they ran water into the iron horse, to make steam.

She stood there, contemplating these wonders, when she did hear the distant chuff of a train, this one behind her, going east. There was the same chuff as the boats, but there was also an odd roar or rattle. She steered her horses back to a grove of box elders nearby, and waited, curious about this thing. She dismounted, for fear that the horse would buck or become unmanageable, and simply waited. Off a way she saw a plume of smoke, and then the iron engine rounded a gentle bend, and behind it was a string of boxcars. She knew at once this train carried freight, not people, and she was grateful because it was white strangers she feared most, especially here. She thought maybe she should not be here, and faded deeper into the grove of box elders.

The chuffing engine, belching smoke, slowed and then she heard a great squealing and didn't know what that was about, but the train was grinding to a stop. The nervous horses yanked at the reins she held in her hand, but didn't balk or bolt. They had seen the iron beast before, she thought, and didn't panic.

The engine halted directly under the tank on stilts, and then seemed to die, or sag into a temporary death. It sat on four big iron wheels, and four smaller wheels in front, and smoke issued from a conical chimney at the front. An iron grille at the front was plainly intended to sweep aside anything in the path of the iron horse.

A man in blue coveralls emerged from the cab on the engine, climbed upward, swung the chute of the water tank to a place on the little car behind the engine, and opened a hatch there. Then he spun an iron wheel, and she knew water was flowing from the big dark tank into the little car behind the engine. Other men climbed to the ground. One lit a cigar. Another turned toward the track and urinated on it. A third, walking along the cars, seemed to study the wheels of each one. The cars looked to be empty, their doors open to the wind.

Her horse snorted, and they saw her then. For a moment they did nothing, but finally two of them headed her way. She did not flee, but held her ground. In fact, she chose to push forward to meet them, so they would know she was not afraid.

"Damned squaw," he said, eyeing her. "Where the hell did she come from?"

She responded at once. "I speak your tongue. My husband taught it to me. I am Mary, of the Snake people. I have never seen the iron horse."

"Snakes, lady, you're a long way from home. Where's your man, eh?"

"I go to St. Louis to see our son. He is in the blackrobe school."

"That's a long way. He couldn't buy you a ticket?"

She didn't know how to respond to that, so she kept silent.

"That's a long way you got to go, lady," said the other, this one with a trim dark beard and kind eyes.

"I wish to see my son. His name is Dirk, but I call him another name."

"Dirk? That's a rare one."

"My man is from this place called England."

"Well, I'm Will Mahoney and I never saw an Englishman I liked."

She didn't like the tenor of this, and started to wheel away but Mahoney stayed her.

"You want a ride? We ain't going to St. Louis, we're going to Omaha, but you just go down the Big Mo from there."

She was confused.

"These are deadheads, empties," he said. "I'll take you if you want."

"I have no money."

"Naw, free ride, unless the railroad dicks chase you off."

"Omaha?"

"Upriver some from St. Louis. You git off, the Omaha yards, and I reckon you can go on down the river road to wherever your boy is."

"Why you doing this, eh? What do I pay you?"

She wanted it plain. There were things she would not do, and white men supposed that they could do them with any Indian woman.

He shrugged. "Deadheads. Most of our freight goes west. Might as well help a lady out."

The one working the water chute had finished, and was cranking a wheel closed. They would go soon.

"I don't know how to feed or water my horses in there."

"I know a car with some hay in it. That suit you?"

"How do I put my horses in one?"

He pointed at something, a wooden structure near the tank. There was a pen there too.

"How do I get them out when I leave?"

He grinned. "Trust us."

The other one, the cigar smoker, yawned.

"I will," she said.

"Beats riding them nags five hundred miles," he said.

They led her to the pen, and showed her the chute that her horses could climb to enter the car.

"Wait here," one said.

A moment later the engine crawled forward until eleven cars had passed, and then stopped when the bearded young man swung a lantern. The car door was open wide, and inside was abundant scattered hay.

It took a sharp rap on the rump to drive each horse up and in, but in moments she was in the car with the gaping door.

"Easy, ain't it?" the bearded one said. "I'm the brakeman. Will Mahoney. I'll keep an eye on you."

She wondered how foolish she had been, but saw only a cheery smile behind that beard.

"My man, Barnaby Skye, would be very pleased with you."

"Maybe I'll make an exception," he said.

He vanished from the door, and a moment later she felt a soft jolt and a thump and the car began to roll east. The nervous horses circled around, but she unsaddled them and tied their bridle rein and halter rope to a rail on the wall. They tugged at the lines, and then settled down, even as the train gathered speed and Mary began to see the trees and meadows whirl by, faster than anything she had ever seen before. She made a soft place in the hay for herself to sit, and then let one horse at a time dig his snout into the hay while she held the line.

Sometimes the boxcar lurched violently. Other times it rolled so smoothly she marveled at it. Sometimes they rocked between woodlands, where the road cut through forestland. Other times the Platte River vanished from view. She could scarcely imagine her good fortune. From her doorway she saw running deer, alarmed crows bursting into the sky, a coyote paralyzed at the sight of the huffing train. And once she saw a wagon on the Big Road, its oxen plodding west.

Still, she realized she was now a prisoner. She could not jump down, and neither could her ponies. They could take her wherever they wished, do whatever they wished, and she could not escape them. She eyed the roadbed passing in a blur before her eyes, and knew that if she tossed herself onto that gravel, she would break bones and abrade her flesh. But trains didn't always go fast. They slowed now and then. They would stop for more water, or more of the black rock that burned.

She resigned herself to a long wait, and settled on a bed of hay she swept together. Then she watched the prairie go by, and the river bottoms pass from view. This iron horse was taking her where she wished to go, and that was all that mattered.

A long time later, the train slowed and then ground to a halt. Some whitewashed buildings stood in an orderly square, but the place looked deserted. She peered out the door, and discovered Will Mahoney approaching.

"Stopping here, if you have needs," he said. "This is Fort Kearny. Used to be a big place when the Oregon Trail was the way west, but now they're fixing to close it. One company's all that's left."

"Soldiers? Will I be safe?"

"Long as you don't scalp someone."

She slid over the edge of the car and dropped to the ground. "It is good to stand and walk," she said.

"I should tell you, this here's where you should get off if you want to ride direct to Independence and St. Louis. From here on the train goes to Omaha."

She had no idea what to do, but he sensed her confusion. "If I was you, I'd just stay on. In the Omaha yards, I'll get you off and you just ride down the river three, four days to where you're going."

"I will do that, then."

"Tell me. Is this son of yours a hellcat?"

She stared, frightened. "I do not know . . ."

"Oh, hellcat. Is he wild as a catamount?"

Mary retreated into silence.

"Reason is, I got me a Pawnee woman. I fetched her out of a cathouse and now we've got a boy, half wild Pawnee, half wild Irish, so I'm wondering if he's going to be like your boy."

"My boy—I haven't seen him for a long time."

Mahoney grinned. "Got rid of the little devil, eh? Well, I figure I'm raising a wild little beast. There's no law, no rule I don't want to bust, and my woman, she never heard of God. I just got the notion my little tiger, he's like your little tiger, he's half civilized, half savage."

She started laughing. "Mister Mahoney, I like you," she said. "But you must understand. In my marriage, my man, Barnaby Skye, he's the savage, and I'm the civilized."

Will Mahoney stared, bright-eyed. "By God, next time I lift a mug, I'll salute you."

She didn't know what all that was about, either, but it didn't matter. They both had mixed-blood boys, and that was what bonded them.

Soon they were rolling again, and night fell over the car, and she could see almost nothing, and lay quietly in the hay through the strange night. But not long after dawn she saw an occasional building, and planted fields, and once a man riding a buggy, and then more buildings, mostly whitewashed places, and finally the train pulled to a halt in the place called Omaha, where there were many tracks side by side, and many buildings glowing in the early sunlight.

Then the train started to crawl slowly, and she heard

voices, and then it stopped. Directly out of her door was one of those ramps leading down to pens. She could unload her horses here.

Mahoney appeared. "I had 'em pull up a bit so you could get these nags out," he said.

In moments, she had unloaded her ponies into the pen, while he collected her saddles and gear.

Now she was in a strange place, with many rails, and many buildings, and she felt utterly helpless.

"You go see your hellcat," he said.

"But, sir, I don't know . . ."

He saw her fear.

"Hey, I'm done. I got to go to that building over there, and then I'll take you down to the river and put you on the road. Whatever you do, stick with the river and go downstream. You'll go through a bunch of towns like St. Joseph and Kansas City, but you keep on going to the biggest one, where the Missouri meets the Mississippi."

"Many days?"

"It's a way, lass. A week or more, I reckon."

She went with him to the building, and soon he was leading her through the city, with its broad streets and shops and ornate houses, larger than she had ever seen. People stared at her, seeing an Indian woman in quilled leather. She lifted her head and sat proudly. She would let them see she was a Shoshone, and proud, and nothing would frighten her.

Mahoney led her down a steep grade, past more handsome houses, and finally to a worn dirt road that ran alongside the great river.

"I guess this is it," he said. "Good luck. Me, I got two hellcats to visit. Pawnee women, Jesus, Mary, and Joseph. It's more than I can handle."

But he laughed infectiously, and Mary decided that a three-hellcat family was probably a good one.

She watched him trudge up the hill, plainly weary after his long hours as a brakeman. Something in her loved him.

twenty-six

Cold rain soaked Mary, but she endured. She had no other clothing than her blue chambray blouse, red-quilled elk-skin vest, and doeskin skirts. It had rained constantly, usually in afternoon thundershowers, but there was nothing she could do, and rarely did she find shelter. The moist climate had bred mosquitoes and flies, which often swarmed her, but there was little she could do about those, either. So she endured. The sun dried her clothing and the clouds soaked it with their tears. Sometimes she thought it was a way of keeping clean.

St. Louis frightened her. Now, as she plunged deeper into its outskirts, she brimmed with anxiety. What if North Star didn't wish to see her? Or was no longer there? Or was so changed by life with the blackrobes that they could only stare at each other across some chasm? Finding him would not be easy. She had only two names. The school was St. Ignatius, named after the founder of the blackrobes. And she knew Colonel Bullock had retired in that place, after years at Fort Laramie.

So she endured the rain, endured the curious stares of people on the river road, endured the occasional boys who raced along beside her, shouting "Injun! Injun!" She knew about boys. Many a time when Skye and his wives entered a strange village, the boys clotted around them, sending mock arrows at them, raising a hubbub. White boys were no different.

The vast valley of the Missouri proved to be a good place to feed herself, with all its berries now in season. She lived on the bountiful raspberries and blackberries, on wild asparagus and green apples, and familiar roots. The land was not so settled or farmed that she failed to find safe havens at night, well hidden from the people nearby.

Soon she would see her son. She would see how he looked as a young man, adult by her standards, almost so by Skye's. Fifteen winters he would have now, and he would have his full height, and broad shoulders, and a man's gait.

Would he even recognize her? Worse, would he care?

Of course he would. She heartened herself with that belief, and continued to travel the river road, now running east toward St. Louis. Now things crowded her senses. She passed farmsteads, with plowed fields and laundry flapping on lines. She passed tall freight wagons drawn by ox teams, driven by profane teamsters, hauling mountains of white-man things to the outlying settlements. Some of those men eyed her with something more than curiosity, and she hurried past them.

She formulated a plan of action. First she would try to find this school herself. She would resort to Colonel Bullock only if she could not find it. She had enough English to ask directions. Where were the Jesuits? Where was this St. Ignatius school that took in Indian boys? She feared that if she went to Colonel Bullock first, he would dissuade her, or even forbid her to see her son. She didn't know why. White men were mysterious to her. But what if the Jesuits refused her? Would they keep her son from his mother? She dreaded that, dreaded not even having a glimpse of him, locked behind stone walls and iron grilles, hidden from her hungering eyes.

The road took her along the waterfront, an area of grim brick buildings and rough wooden structures side by side. A bluff separated this part of St. Louis from the rest, and above she could see homes shaded by stately trees, and women strolling. Occasionally steep roads connected the rest of the city with this waterfront. Some of the buildings had signs she could not read, but plainly one was a saloon. Before it a wagon stood, its big draft horses quiet in their harness, while burly sweating men in grimy aprons unloaded big wooden casks and carried or rolled them into the dark building. Downriver, she saw steamboats docked at the riverbank, tied in place by great hawsers wound around wooden pilings. Some were being loaded; others sat idle, no fire in their bellies.

This did not look like a place where the blackrobes might have a school.

She saw not one woman here, but men of all descriptions, a few in black suits, but most in rough workmen's clothing, such as those unloading the kegs. She trusted workingmen more than men in suits so she edged closer to one burly man in a filthy apron, with cinnamon chin whiskers and watery blue eyes. He paused, eyed her up and down, and grinned toothlessly.

"I am looking for help," she began. "I want to know where the Jesuits are."

"A squaw that talks English. I'll be goddamned. And a couple of dandy horses too," he said, his eyes surveying Mary and her two good animals.

He simply grabbed her bridle. "Looks like maybe I can tell you," he said.

His freckled hand held the bridle, and she knew she was trapped.

"I am visiting my son. The blackrobes at St. Ignatius are teaching him. Please tell me how to go there."

"Got me a pretty squaw," he said, his toothless grin widening. "Got me a couple of nice horses too. What say you come visit me? I live in there. I'll show you how to get around the city. You can pay me any way you want." He was leering now. She understood the leer, which crossed all peoples and cultures, and was very plain.

He had her horse. No one paid the slightest attention. And she knew no one would heed anything an Indian said. If it came to an argument, his word would win. He would accuse her of stealing his horses, and he was just getting them back. Something like that, anyway.

She didn't intend to give up her horses to this man, even if he weighed twice as much as she did. But she was not without a few ploys, some of which Skye had taught her. She dismounted, sliding off the horse, which lifted her skirts a little as she settled on the brown paving blocks that surfaced the street.

"Hey, you want a good time?" she asked, drawing close. "I'll give you a good time. You want a squaw? You'll get a squaw."

He grinned, and nodded toward the building. He was still holding the bridle.

She stood before him, alluring and tall and slender, and she smiled.

"Go on in there, squaw, and I'll be right along," he said.

"What's your name?" she asked.

"Oh, you'll find out," he said.

She edged close to him, smiling, until she was practically in his arms, which he enjoyed. But he was still holding the bridle. She brushed against him, closer now, eyeing him carefully because she would have only one chance, and if she failed he would probably beat her senseless.

She caught his eye. "You big man?" she asked, even as she lifted her knee smoothly, fiercely, and with deadly aim, into his groin.

"Yooww," he bawled, his arms flailing outward and then down to his crotch. He folded like an accordion, holding himself and wheezing. He was gasping, red, his mouth a big Oh, his lips drooling saliva. She dodged back, recovered the rein of her skittering horse, threw herself upward and over, before the bearded man recovered enough to roar and spring toward her. But he missed, and she was clear, her packhorse too.

She hastened away, but he stood there watching, and strangely laughing. It was all in a day's work for him.

But she had other ideas. She would never seek directions from a man again.

The city was strange, a world utterly amazing, and she wondered what to do. Mostly from instinct, she took one of the steep roads that led away from the muddy river, and when she topped the slope she found herself in a different world, a place where people lived in buildings unlike any she had ever seen. Some were made of brick, and had tall glass windows and wooden porches. Others were made of wood. Great trees cast shade over emerald lawns. She wandered aimlessly, past stores that displayed goods in their windows, or had signs swinging in the morning breezes. Some buildings seemed beyond her fathoming, and she had no idea what happened inside of them.

Horse-drawn buggies rattled past, and big freight wagons drawn by massive horses rumbled by, or paused at a store to deliver crates and cartons. She wondered where the horses were fed because she saw no pasture anywhere. She wondered where she would feed her pack and saddle horses. Pasture would be a long way away, and her horses would be very hungry soon.

She saw young women carrying empty baskets she thought were intended to carry their purchases, while others wheeled small carriages with babies or children in them, and she marveled. The women wore long, full dresses and covered their arms, even in the moist summer heat, and wore bonnets or hats. The men usually wore black suits and white shirts, but the workingmen dressed in rougher clothing, but were just as covered as the women. She could not fathom it. In any camp of her people, on a moist, hot day like this, the men would wear very little, maybe just a breechclout, and the women would be sleeveless at the least. She eyed these people, thinking how much they had to suffer through the fierce heat. She could not imagine why anyone would live with such discomfort.

She herself endured the rain and heat, but the moist air was not pleasant. It made her flesh oily and she yearned to return to the mountains. She discovered that St. Louis seemed to have districts, some with old, narrow streets and ancient houses, and some newer. She occasionally attracted attention, especially from children, who swarmed around her until she feared her horses would kick at them, while they studied her angled face and strong cheekbones and the clothing that told them that she was from one of the tribes. She smiled, and they tentatively smiled back.

But this was an urbane city, and it largely ignored her as

she wandered her helpless way through it. She had utterly no idea where this place of the blackrobes might be, or where she might find North Star in a city that contained more people in it than all of the Shoshone, east and west, every branch.

A carriage sailed by, pulled by a pair of high-stepping white horses, reined by a man in a shiny black silk hat rather like Skye's, and beside him was a red-haired woman in gauzy white, with sleeves that were almost transparent. Mary thought it might be a chief and his woman, because she could wear something more pleasant on this sopping hot day. The air was so heavy and moist that she felt suffocated, and every instinct in her cried to flee to the country where there was real air.

Some great bells began to bong, and for a moment she was paralyzed with fear. Would the noise signal soldiers? But no one on the cobbled streets paid heed, and she realized that these bells were ringing in the towers of a great stone edifice nearby, one with endless steps climbing upward, and crosses topping the towers. The crosses she recognized. Ah, now she knew where the blackrobes would be, so she turned her horses that direction, up a mild slope toward this great and frightening building, taller than four or five buildings piled on top of one another.

Father Sun had climbed as high as he would go this day, and burned down from above, making the heat all the worse. She knew one thing: she would never, not in a thousand winters, choose to live here. It was so hot that not even the flies lingered in the sunlight, and very few buzzed about her horses.

Then she saw a blackrobe walking down the steps of this great building, and she rejoiced. She steered her horses to the foot of the wide stairs and waited, and when he approached, she spoke.

"Sir, could you direct me?"

He peered up at her, and she marveled. He was gowned head to toe in black, but he showed not a drop of sweat in his face. His gaze took in her native dress, and he frowned slightly, as if not approving of her.

"Madam?" he asked.

"I wish to go to the place of the Jesuit blackrobes called St. Ignatius."

"I'm not a Jesuit," he said.

Her heart sank. This one looked like the blackrobes she had seen among her people.

"But yes, I can direct you. And why do you ask?"

"I have come to see my son."

"Ah," he said. "Yes, they school some red boys there." He eyed her doubtfully. "It's four blocks that way, two more, over the bridge, and then back one."

He was waving his black-encased arm this way and that.

"What is a block?" she asked.

"I see," he said. He eyed her amiably. "Follow me," he said.

He strode away from the river, his pace fast, his robes flapping, and she followed behind, past streets and people and houses and a small green park given to trees, and she soon didn't know which direction she was going, but he never paused until at last he came to another building with towers with crosses, and a high brick wall surrounding whatever structures lay within.

"There," he said, pointing to a narrow grilled gate.

She nodded her thanks, but he had already wheeled away, his black skirts flapping, and soon was gone.

Here was the place she had sought months earlier, the place where her own North Star lived, where her flesh and blood slept and ate and learned. She thought of all the days and moons she had traveled, the perils and starvation she had endured, the gifts of those who had helped her, and the hope that had inspired her. If only she could see her boy. If only she could gaze upon him for a while. She tied her horses at a hitching post with an iron ring in it, turned toward the grilled gate, found a cord, and pulled it.

twenty-seven

Mary struggled with an instinct to flee but forced herself to stand quietly. When a man appeared, it was not a person in black robes, but a man wearing the suit of the white men, and wire-rimmed glasses perched far out upon a bulbous nose. He peered at her.

"I have come to see my boy," she said.

He looked doubtful. "But it is class time . . ."

"I have come from the mountains to see my son," she said.

The mountains meant something to him, and he softened. "You are?"

"I am Mary, the woman of Barnaby Skye, and Dirk Skye is my son."

"Oh, Dirk," he said, warming a little.

He opened the grilled gate and she entered a serene courtyard, with somber buildings surrounding it. Somewhere, somewhere near, would be the Star That Never Moves. Her pulse lifted. In truth, she hadn't the faintest idea what she would do when she saw him. But that was all she wanted. She had come all this distance, all these moons, to see him.

He led her to an austere reception room, white plastered walls, a crucifix, some chairs, a small window opening on the yard. He nodded her toward a wooden chair and vanished through a door.

She felt utter confusion then. Why had she come here? What did she expect? Who was she, that she had abandoned her husband to come here? What would her son look like? Would he accept her? Would he smile? Would he turn his back to her?

It took a long time, and she resisted an impulse to flee to the safety of the street, collect her horses, which she had tied to a hitching post, and escape.

But then she heard noises, the door opened, and she beheld a thin young man in white men's clothing with warm flesh, medium height, dark hair, the strong cheekbones of her people—and blue eyes.

She gave a small cry. It was North Star. She uttered his name in Shoshone, but he looked puzzled.

"You are Mary of the Shoshones?" he asked in English.

"Oh, my child."

"Are you my mother?" he asked, his own bewilderment as large as her own.

"Seven winters, seven winters," she said, a river of anguish flowing through her now. "Seven winters ago."

He stood quietly. "That was what Papa wished for me," he said.

But she could not speak.

"Ah, I'll leave you to your reunion," the man said. "Dirk, you'll not want to miss chapel."

The young man nodded. The graying man in the dark suit vanished, and then Mary was alone in the austere room with her only child.

"I have only a few minutes," he said.

"What are minutes?"

"Ah, little bits of time."

"Then you must go?"

"We cannot miss chapel, not ever."

"Sit here," she said, motioning him toward the other chair.

They sat, staring at each other. She could not fathom him. Everything had vanished behind his white man's mask. She understood even without words that the years with the black-robes had driven his Shoshone nature from him. He looked uncomfortable.

"Can you speak the tongue of the People?" she asked softly.

He stared, and finally shook his head. "The words might come back, but offhand I don't remember them," he said.

"Then we will talk in Mister Skye's tongue," she said.

He nodded. "I am wondering—why you came now. Is my father here too?"

"No, I came alone."

"Is he—dead?"

"He and Victoria are old but they are well enough. He is very stiff, and his eyes trouble him."

"He never came here to see me," he said.

She knew this was painful ground, for her son and for her.

"I know. It was because . . . it would hurt too much."

"Does he want me now? Is this why you came? To take me back?"

She carefully chose her words. "No. He is old and proud, and won't say that he needs you, even if he does. I came to see you by myself."

"All alone, across the plains? To see me?"

She nodded.

He smiled suddenly. "You came to see me!"

"It is my way. I wanted to see you now, with fifteen years upon you."

"I am doing well. I get high marks. They say maybe I will be like a white man. Tell Papa that I get good grades." But then his bravado faded. "I wish I knew Papa. It's like . . . I am an orphan. Year after year, I waited for him to come visit me here."

She didn't want to hear that. He had ached for Skye and her to come see him, spent the months and years waiting and hoping. And Skye had let him down.

There was another pregnant pause, and finally she broke it. "Are you happy?"

"I am treated well. They tell me I can be a clerk or a teacher someday. The good fathers are kind to me. They say that a mixed-blood can do as well as a full-blood."

"Is that good?"

"I suppose it's better than living in a buffalo-hide lodge, freezing all winter, wondering where the next meal will come from." He eyed her uncertainly. "I am very fortunate. They tell me hardly anyone from the western tribes has the good luck that I have."

Her son was staring at her, absorbing her, his gaze missing nothing. No doubt comparing her to the white people in this city.

Sunshine and shadow crossed his face as he wrestled with strange and conflicting feelings. "I don't know your world, or my father's anymore. My memories don't go back that far. My life really began when I came here. So it's not easy, seeing you, knowing you are my mother, you raised me in a lodge, and my father hunted and kept us alive." He brightened. "You are all that I dreamed you would be," he said. "I had no mother. I lived with other boys, but you were only a memory. And the full-bloods . . ." His voice trailed off.

She understood at once. Mixed-bloods were not respected. "Do the blackrobes treat you well?"

He shrugged. "I don't know what that is. I don't know what being treated badly is, either. They have always been kind to me."

"Do they favor other boys, North Star?"

He nodded, slowly. "They are very kind to the Lakota boys."

The Sioux. "Do they let you have your Shoshone name?"

"North Star? No, the blackrobes call me Dirk Skye."

"Would you rather be North Star?"

"Please don't ask me!"

She sensed she had transgressed.

"We were free," she said. "We went where we wished. Now they have put us on a reservation, with lines around it we cannot see, but we are forbidden to cross them. Things will be different now. Chief Washakie is helping this to happen."

The youth stared dreamily out the window, which opened on the lushly planted courtyard. "I dream sometimes," he said. "Of you and my Crow mother and my father, and a world where we could go anywhere, anytime we wished." He smiled slowly. "But it is gone."

"I have two horses," she said.

He stared at her. Not until she said it did she admit to herself that the entire purpose of this trip was to bring him back to his people, and his family. Skye and Victoria needed him. She needed him. She suddenly grew aware of something that had burned in her bosom all those days of travel.

"Your father, he needs you. Your Crow mother, she needs you," she said.

"Are they failing? Dying?"

"It is hard to live when you hurt. He hurts. She hurts worse but doesn't show it to anyone. We cannot help him. Before I came here, he left us to find a place where he could build a white man's house, with a bed in it and a chair in it and a stove and a fireplace in it, and a porch where he could watch the clouds skim across the peaks."

"Where would this be?"

"The upper Yellowstone."

"That is a good place to grow old," Dirk said.

"For him and Victoria," she said, leaving herself out of it.

"They tell me I am bright and there isn't much more they can teach me," he said. "They want to teach many boys with Indian blood, so that the boys will go back and teach the tribes."

"Teach what?"

"All about God. Farming. Cattle raising, plowing, black-smithing, living the way white men live."

"And how do they live?"

He smiled. "I wouldn't know. I have scarcely left here, but once in a while they take us to the cathedral."

"You cannot leave?"

"A little. They watch over us."

"You see no one? Just the students and the blackrobes?"

"Once in a while Colonel Bullock came. He sat there where you sit, and he would ask me how I was doing, and whether I wanted anything, and what should he tell my father? And then two years ago he stopped coming. I learned he had died. He grew old and his lungs would not take air. I haven't seen anyone from outside since then."

"No girls?"

"Especially no girls." His face clouded. She saw a

melancholy in him so deep she could barely fathom it. She saw all the spirits standing above him, sighing in the quietness. It was more than melancholy; she saw anger and frustration and loneliness too.

"There are full-bloods here, and there are breeds like me," he said. "The full-bloods, Blackfeet, Pawnee, Assiniboine, the Jesuit fathers like them and treat them like chiefs."

"And those born of two bloods?"

"Born in sin," he said.

She found courage to ask one of the big questions. "Was it hard—going away?" she asked.

"Not at first. I sat with Colonel Bullock in the stagecoach. It was an adventure. I looked at everything through the windows. It was only here, when I was given a narrow iron bed and a small locker in a dark room with other boys, that it was hard. Then my sunny world stopped. Do you know what I missed? Sunshine, open country, with you and my father bathed in sunlight. My new world was dark; dark walls, small windows, dark classrooms, teachers in black, darkness everywhere. That is the world of these Europeans."

"Is it still hard?"

He looked away. "I am a white man now. I take my solace in work. They tell me none do better. I make the time go by with work. The suns and moons and winters of time, I make them go past me. I read the classics. I know French. I do algebra and geometry. I have learned their history. I know their authors, the storytellers. I can compose a letter or a pleading or an index. They have even made me a mechanic. I know about iron and wood and the tools to shape them. I know about farming, even though I've never farmed." He smiled. "See? I am a white man now."

She scarcely knew what he was talking about, strange

words, strange studies. Did he know anything of his own people? Had he sat with the elders and learned? No, and he couldn't remember the tongue of his childhood. He was as mysterious and difficult as any white man, and strange as Mister Skye.

She remembered how hard it had been for her to fathom her man, once the blush of her marriage had faded and she found herself trying to learn his ways. Now this son was like his father. That had been Skye's intent. Send North Star here so he might become a white man, and not one of the People.

"Star That Never Moves," she said in her tongue.

"It has been a long time since I heard that," he said.

"We gave you two names, and now you have chosen."

"No, I never chose it, my mama."

"The blackrobes, they chose it, then."

"No, they didn't choose it either. It just happened. When I was a boy, I called myself North Star, and it was lost."

The words ceased then, and they gazed at one another, and she felt him slipping away, and she wondered why she had come. She knew it would end like this. She would look at him and be glad, and then he would slip away, and she would sorrow. Now there was a gulf between her and him. He would call her a savage, and tell them he had a savage for a mother, and she would carry this in her heart.

A low, mournful bell tolled.

He smiled. "Vespers," he said.

"What is it?"

"It is a small service late in the day, offered to God."

"Do you follow the same path as Skye?"

He paused, hesitantly. "No," he said.

The door opened and a blackrobe swept in, this one young and dark, with almond eyes.

"Vespers, Dirk," he said.

The boy bolted upright out of his chair. "I must go, Mama. It is time for chapel. Good-bye. I am glad you came."

The father stood amiably in the door, waiting. He smiled at her. "Ironclad duty," he said to her.

"Give my respect to my father," he said.

North Star followed the blackrobe through the door, and she saw the door close behind them. She sat in the small silence of the waiting room, with a heavy heart.

Was this it, then? Had she come across the mountains and plains and rivers, through these nearby woods, across great rivers, for this moment, now passed? She had. She always told herself she only wanted to see him, just to see him, and now she had seen him, and had feasted on him, this slender, serious, two-bloods boy with blue eyes and strong cheekbones and warm flesh.

The soft bonging of the bell ceased, and faint on the air came the sounds of solemn song, boys' voices, many voices, singing something that sounded a little like the songs sung at a Shoshone campfire by old men, to the sharp syncopation of the drums.

She could not bring herself to leave, not with North Star so close that she could hear the singing, so close that one of those male voices must be his. So she sat in the starchy room, listening, until at last the song ended, and she imagined he was going to his bed. She rose, stiffly, glad that she had seen her son, glad that he was alive, and he was very bright and pleased the blackrobes. She looked around, uncertain how to navigate to the ponies tied outside, but she found her way out the door, into the yard, and she saw no one. Maybe they were all at this vespers. She found the grilled gate to the street, and saw how to open it, and stood one last moment, knowing she would never see North Star again, knowing that her journey was complete. She saw birds flocking in the lush trees, trees of a sort she didn't know, and then she stepped through the iron grille and closed it gently behind her, and stood staring at the moss-covered wall, which was crowned with vines, which grew in profusion from the moisture and heat.

The horses stood quietly, their tails lashing at the clouds of flies. She felt sticky from the heat and wet. Beside her, the great edifice of St. Ignatius rose silently, its walls a reproof to this world of the street.

She slowly undid the rein, and also the lead line of the packhorse, and climbed onto her saddle horse, and turned to leave.

The gate clanged, and she turned to see him there. "Mama, wait," he said.

twenty-eight

*S*kye had known loss all his life, and now that familiar and ancient grief flooded through him. Mary had vanished. No one in the village had seen her. She should have been there long ago. Victoria stood stiffly, her loss as large as his, her lips taut.

Mary's brothers and clan could offer nothing. Skye found himself cataloguing all the ways that people died in the wilderness. Snake bites, grizzlies, sickness, broken bones, a tumble down a cliff, getting bucked off a horse or stepped on by one, a runaway horse plunging into forest, a poisoned spring. And that was only a beginning. A lone, beautiful Indian woman in her middle years was prey. She might be a slave of the Arapaho or Sioux or Cheyenne. Or still worse, she might have become the plaything of those Texans in the Big Horn Valley, someone to use and abandon.

The bleak catalog scrolling through his mind could embrace only a few of the possibilities. He probably would never see Mary again, nor would he discover her fate, and as the days and weeks and months rolled by, all hope would fade and there would be only loss.

He had first known loss when a press gang had plucked him off the streets of London and he found himself a powder monkey in the Royal Navy. He never saw his mother or father or sister again, nor any of his cousins or other relatives. That had been the greatest of all his losses, but he had lost friends, horses, clients, and colleagues over the decades in the North American wilds, each loss vivid and mysterious.

Now his younger wife.

"We'll go look for her," he said to Victoria.

But she seemed afraid. It had been all he could manage to ride here to the Wind River Reservation. Her odd expression told him that she doubted he would have the strength to go look. And it seemed a futile enterprise anyway. Look where? There were many thousands of square miles to search, and each one contained its secrets.

He and Victoria would be welcome with any of Mary's clan or brothers, but somehow without Mary it wouldn't seem right. He thought maybe after he had rested they should return to the Crows and wait. And wait. And wait. But even as he contemplated this, a youth arrived, and the lad spoke a surpassing English he had gotten somewhere.

"Sir and madam," the bronzed boy began, "our good chief, leader of all the Eastern Shoshone, wishes the honor of your presence."

Skye nodded. "Tell Chief Washakie we will be along directly, and thank him for inviting us," Skye said.

The slim boy smiled slightly, and trotted toward a white clapboard cottage, one of the first at the Indian agency.

Skye and Victoria excused themselves from Mary's clan,

and led their horses across a green sward toward the cottage where the great chief awaited them on his porch. He wore a denim shirt and black britches and a flat-crowned felt hat, but kept his jet hair in tight braids, in the style of his people.

"Ah, it is you, Mister and Mistress Skye," he said, waving them up the wooden steps to his broad roofed porch.

"Shall we go in? I live like a white man now. Come and see," the chief said.

And indeed, Skye discovered an interior furnished very like the homes of white people, with a rocking chair, Morris chairs, stuffed horsehair couch, a dining table and chairs, a well-equipped kitchen and two bedrooms, each with a brass bed frame. His women stood shyly, in gingham dresses.

"Tea for the Skyes," Washakie said, steering his guests to the parlor.

Victoria perched primly on a seat. This was big medicine to her, and she looked to be ill at ease.

"Your beautiful wife is missing," Washakie said.

Skye nodded.

"I have received the news. Anytime someone comes to the agency, I hear everything. So our own Blue Dawn was due here long ago, coming down from the Yellowstone, and she is not here. Have you any understanding, Mister Skye?"

"No, sir, we learned of this only a while ago, and neither Victoria nor I can offer the slightest reason. But all trips have their peril."

"And Texans flood into our lands with their cattle. And these are a particularly—shall I say undesirable?—lot of men."

"They worry me more than anything else, sir."

"Yes, that is my worry, as well. Your Shoshone wife is famous for her skills at travel, her powers over the spirits, and her courage. She can subdue a brown bear with a smile. She can quiet a horse made mad by a rattlesnake. But I am not sure she would be a match for some of those men who herd the cattle onto our lands."

Skye glanced at Victoria, who was keeping quiet. The Absarokas claimed the Big Horn Valley too, and probably had a better claim to it. Some of the tribe wintered there year after year.

"We will go look for her, Chief."

The Shoshone paused, gently. "You look worn, Mister and Mistress Skye. You have traveled far. Even if you should return over the trail from the Yellowstone, you would be covering a vast land, with great mountains, rushing rivers, grasslands as far as the eye can see, thick dark forests, snowfields, strange places where the spirits gather, places where ancient peoples have built rock cairns for their own purposes. Who can find one small, lone woman in all of that?"

"We will go look, sir. Mary is my wife, and beloved spirit sister of Victoria, and the mother of my son, and the woman to whom I have pledged my love and life."

"Well said, Mister Skye. But you are worn, and even as you sit you favor that leg, which hurts so much you cannot let it rest." He paused. "You have come a great distance, longer than old people should have to travel. And if you leave us, looking for this beloved woman in this country we call our home, I will understand, and will make sure you carry some pemmican with you." He smiled slightly. "And your chances would be poor indeed. I have a better idea. It is our home. My young men know it and keep its secrets. I will send them out, all that will go, to look for Blue Dawn. They will cast a wide net, clear up to the Yellowstone, and before long you will have a good understanding of Mary's fate. They have sharp eyes. Young eyes. They see the distant eagle on the wing, and the field mouse at their feet. They see the moving dot on the hillside. If they find Blue Dawn, her heart will be freshened by her tribal brothers. And they will heal her and help her . . . in any case, you will have news. So come, stay here with Mary's clan; I welcome you as honored guests of the People."

Skye choked back his sorrows and nodded. It felt strange, surrendering the fate of his wife to others. All of his days, he had acted on his own, done whatever needed doing, no matter what the risk or the hardship. But now younger men would fan out along Mary's path. He would be grateful to them. Old Washakie had said it gently: they would search with young eyes, sharp eyes, eyes that saw the moving dot on the hillside.

One of Washakie's many women, this one in blue gingham, appeared with a tea tray and poured tea for Skye and Victoria. Skye took it gratefully. He missed tea, which he received only rarely, and which not only tasted fine to him but wrought nostalgia for his ancestral home. And here was a great chief of the Indians serving it to him.

Skye eyed the steaming cup. "This is home, home for me. Please thank the young lady."

"She is my daughter, Wantabbe."

"You are teaching her new ways."

"It is good," he said. "I am following the new road given us by the fathers in Washington. It is not easy. Many of my people resist and say the old ways are good. But the old ways meant we starved when game was scarce, and we had no berries and roots if there was drought, and our lodges didn't protect us from bitter cold. We need to scratch the earth and plant our food, and herd cattle for our meat. I have seen it is good. And we will have houses too, houses like this. And we will be safe from our enemies, and have a great land given us forever, and we cannot be driven off of it. The other Peoples will have their own lands, and they will be protected too, and that is good. The new ways are better than the old. I say it and believe it."

"I hope you're right," Skye said.

The chief stared. "I hope I am too," he said. "It is a hard road."

The chief was nobody's fool, Skye thought. The Yank government made treaties with the tribes, only to break them whenever the Yanks felt like it.

This tea was bitter and harsh, and it suited Skye just fine. He let it cleanse his mouth before swallowing it.

"But my friend Mister Skye, you must tell me about the boy, Blue Dawn's boy, of our blood. How does he do?"

"I believe he is well. I haven't heard otherwise."

"Ah, I remember his name. The Star That Never Moves, what you call North Star, and at the time of eight winters, you sent him to the blackrobes."

"I did, Chief. You remember Father de Smet? He came west many times and visited your people. He offered to school the boy. He wanted to teach Indian boys so they could return to their people and teach them."

"I remember de Smet. He is a great and good man, who brought us the Book."

"But it took Colonel Bullock, at Fort Laramie, to make it possible, Chief. He offered to take my son east and look after him. So I sent the boy to St. Louis, and he's there now. He'll have a chance at life, a chance that was taken from me."

Washakie stared. "A chance? There was no chance for your son among the People? You chose not to bring him to our elders for schooling. You chose not to show him our Ways, or teach him how we govern ourselves, and how we live." Washakie nodded. "This I understand. To give your boy a chance, you sent him to the white men."

Skye found himself deeply discomforted, and scarcely knew how to respond. But Washakie rescued him, with a smile.

"You did the right thing, Mister Skye. Our ways will fade. The ways of the white man will settle upon the breast of the Mother, at least for now. Before white men came, we did not know about wheels, or guns, or metals. We made our tools of stone and bone. We did not know the secrets in the holy book, and the one God of all the world, and all the other worlds, and all the skies and all that is under the world. Maybe someday the white men's ways will be overcome by the ways of someone else. But you saw that the ways of the Snake people are not good ways for your son, and so you did what a good father would do, you gave your son something better."

"I never thought—your Shoshone ways are greatly to be honored, Chief Washakie."

"Have more tea, Mister Skye."

"If Dirk returns, we'll make sure he learns your ways, sir. That's his inheritance."

"If he returns?"

"I don't hear from him, sir. The letters stopped coming to Fort Laramie."

Through the window, Skye saw Shoshone youths preparing to leave. They were saddling their horses, collecting gear, and waiting for the laggards to join them. In a moment, they would ride away, looking for Skye's missing wife.

twenty-nine

*H*er son stood at the gate. She turned toward him, her legs going weak under her. He looked agitated and she feared he might be in trouble.

"Shoshone woman. I am glad you are still there. Stay for a little while. I'm going with you," he said.

"To the mountains?"

"To the People, and my family."

"Dirk . . ."

"I am North Star." He stood uncertainly, and then came to some decision. "I'll get my things and tell them."

He vanished into the schoolyard, and she stood beside her fly-plagued horses on the quiet street. She felt tense. He was gone a long time, and she wondered whether she had imagined what had happened, or whether Coyote had played a cruel trick.

But at last he appeared at the grilled gate, carrying a canvas sack. A young bearded blackrobe followed him.

"Are you sure this is the thing to do, Master Skye?"

"I am needed."

"So close to finishing? One more term. Just one."

"You have taught me well, Father."

The Jesuit turned to her. "Is this the wish of his parents?"

"I am his mother."

The blackrobe surrendered. "We hope you'll take what you've learned to your people," he said to the youth. "Remember the Lord who watches over you in all things."

North Star smiled. "Please thank the fathers. I've been given many things."

The Jesuit nodded, a small tight smile, and he turned into his school. The grilled gate creaked shut, and Mary beheld her son, freed from this blackrobe world, and somehow a man, even if sallow from the lack of sunlight.

"Star That Never Moves," she said. "I must tell you this. I came without the blessing of your father. I came because I wanted to and the need came into me."

"Then we are together in this, Shoshone mother. I am leaving the school without his blessing or knowledge. Aiee! He shall not like this. He shall ask why I threw away the gift he gave me. He shall send me back here. But I shall go to the mountains. I have made my choice. I shall make my own life. Maybe he shall not welcome me but I shall welcome him. I was a boy and now I am myself."

"Yourself, Star That Never Moves?"

"I have two bloods, Mama. I am not the same as you. I am not the same as my father. I am not the same as the Jesuits. Not the same as the full-blood boys in that school. I've learned the ways of the white men and I am glad I did and proud of it. But I am not of that blood. Now I wish to learn your ways too. I'm coming with you, Mama."

"My own son. I need to tell you I have no food. I have no

saddle for you. Only that packsaddle, and nothing much good in the packs."

"Then we shall go to the mountains on faith. They were always talking about faith, about trust in the unseen God. Well, I learned my lesson. We shall go where we are led."

"I don't even know how to go to the road from here."

He smiled. "Then we'll find out."

He lifted his duffel onto the packsaddle and anchored it. "There's not much. A few spare clothes. A few small things. A blanket."

He led her confidently through the great city, and she marveled that he knew where to go. Plainly he had not been confined to that quiet schoolyard. The giant city vaguely alarmed her; yet they had no trouble, and people were not even curious about a youth and an Indian woman leading horses. There were so many of these white people, more than the stars above.

But eventually the city folded away, and they walked along a dirt lane between plowed fields and farmsteads and woods. The river was nowhere in sight and she kept craning her head to find it. She had followed it closely en route to the great city, making her own road but never straying far because the flowing water would take her to her son. But now her son was following the white man's road.

"This is the pike," he said. "It will take us to Independence."

She smiled at him, marveling that he knew so much. This was heavily forested country, and these farms had been cut out of the woodlands and planted with wheat and barley and maize and squash and things she didn't recognize. But her son seemed to know all these things.

She didn't mind walking, even if the afternoon was hot and moist, for she had her son beside her to lead the way, and she had her horse too if she grew weary. They stopped now and then, especially at berry patches, where thick bushes crowded the road, lush with blackberries. She found a place where asparagus grew, and harvested many stalks for their supper. And everywhere they looked, thick timothy grass grew, fodder for the horses.

They talked little. That would come later. For now, this son was a mystery and she was content to let him remain one. When he chose to tell her things, she would listen. But she watched him, letting him walk ahead so she could see her son. They continued into the evening, and finally she chose a place to alight for the night, a woods where they might make a fire and boil the asparagus for their supper. But the mosquitoes were bad so they hiked to a hilltop and found a hollow there that would hide them from owls and night spirits.

North Star knew all there was to know about caring for the horses, and soon had them watered and picketed on good grass. He eyed the skies, noting that clouds were building and it might rain, as it often did here. He dug into his duffel and pulled out a piece of duck cloth and began fashioning a lean-to.

"The fathers have these for their travels," he said. "We were taught many things, and not just from books."

He soon had a decent three-sided shelter erected from the limbs of Osage orange trees with an open side facing the cook fire she was building. She had never seen such a thing.

The storm held off until the middle of the night, and then it rained hard, but her son had chosen good ground, and the water drained away and did not soak her blanket. But the wind rattled her shelter, blew bitter rain into her seamed face, so she sat and endured, listening to the distant rumble of thunder.

This was a good thing. Her son would be a good warrior, at home in a strange world. This day she had learned much about him. He was a stubborn man, as stubborn as any she had known, more stubborn than his father. There would be sparks flying when he returned to the mountains. Sparks and thunder and anger, and then she would see how much of a man was this youth.

The next days passed peaceably. She had no trouble finding food. As they progressed along the pike, she collected wild blackberries, wild strawberries, blueberries, wild onion, and the tuberous roots of arrowleaf plants, which might be boiled into something very like potatoes. Whenever they discovered water lilies, she joyously harvested the large tubers that could be as fine a meal as a sweet potato, while the young leaves of the lily made a good spinach. She continued to collect the knobby white roots of ordinary cattails, which could be pounded and boiled into a white paste that sustained life. There were various types of wild tomato, and berries she didn't know, and sampled gingerly until she was sure they were edible. She and her son yearned for meat, but didn't lack for things to fill their stomachs and keep them going. That was fine for the moment, but in a little while, when summer waned, things would be very different. Soon there would be acorns and nuts in abundance to sustain them, and once they reached the plains, there would be prairie turnips. But as they passed through this moist land, they did not want.

North Star observed her closely, until he, too, was skilled at gathering a meal as they walked along the pike.

"They didn't teach me this at St. Ignatius," he said after

she had collected a heavy load of water lily tubers that would sustain them for days. "I learned other things."

The pike took them to a large town that North Star called Jefferson City, a handsome place with broad streets, shade trees, and noble buildings, as well as great edifices that were plainly important, though they puzzled her.

"This is the state capital. It's where the chief of Missouri lives, and those who govern the people."

"Is this the place of the great father in Washington?"

"No, that's the United States government there, far to the east. This is where Missouri is governed."

The division of the lands by invisible lines mystified her. How could anyone know where the lines ran? They had put invisible lines around her Wind River homeland, and no one knew when they were on the allotted land or off of it.

"These lines, I don't understand them," she said.

"They have a way of measuring the surface of the earth," he said. "They have instruments that tell them where they are, and they measure all things. The boundaries of the nation are measured. So are the states, and in the states, the counties, and in the counties, the cities and towns."

"Aiee! It is beyond me," she said.

They trod unmolested through the gracious capital, while North Star quietly educated her. He told her what each building contained, and what the signs said. She marveled at this world she had scarcely imagined. No wonder her man, Mister Skye, had sent North Star here to learn these things. These were beyond her, but her son knew them all, and was at ease, while she felt taut and worried that trouble might come.

At long last they passed through the city and struck open country again, relentlessly undulating and still largely forested in spite of the many farmsteads dotting the hills.

They found safe places to camp, choosing places away from the pike, where they might build a fire and boil the day's harvest of tubers. Rain came so frequently that she found herself glad to live in the mountains, where the air was dry and sweet and she didn't feel soggy clothing on her flesh.

The horses fattened on the summer grass, and grew sleek and handsome. Mostly Mary walked, but sometimes when her legs wearied, she boarded a horse and rode, while North Star walked beside her, leading the packhorse. It was good. Her moccasins were wearing out, but somehow she would get along.

As they approached the town her son called Sedalia, they grew aware that railroads were nearby. On the hazy horizons, they spotted plumes of smoke and heard the wail of whistles, and sometimes even the clatter of cars rattling along some distant track. And when they did at last penetrate the outskirts, they found a railroad yard, with tracks side by side and various empty cars idled there. She had never imagined there could be so many cars in the whole world. Some were flat, nothing but a floor on wheels, while others had low sides and were open on top, and some were boxcars of the sort she had ridden, while many others had slats in the sides and were obviously used to transport animals. Now and then little engines, stubby and fierce, pushed or pulled the cars around.

This, too, was a white man's wonder.

"M, K and T," her son said. "The Katy. Missouri, Kansas and Texas Railroad."

She nodded, not quite knowing what that was all about.

"They bring cattle up from Texas," he said.

Sedalia proved to be a bustling town, with buggies on the streets, and many pedestrians, and delivery wagons pulled by giant drays. The pike took them near a great edifice in the center of the town.

"County courthouse," North Star said. "This is a county seat."

"What is that?" she asked.

"A smaller government. The cities have governments too."

"Aiee!" she said.

A lean man in a black suit stepped into the cobbled street and stopped them with a wave of the arm. She saw he had some sort of shining device on his coat, and was armed.

He walked across the paving stones, past horse manure, and looked them over, his gaze resting at last on the horses.

"Those sure ain't Indian ponies," he said. "Where you from?"

North Star responded. "I'm Dirk Skye. We're going to the mountains. This is my mother, Blue Dawn of the Shoshone People."

The names didn't interest this man in black. Mary thought he might be a man of authority because of the way he behaved, and that shining device on his coat.

"Indian ponies, they're broomtails, with ewe necks and flop-ears and two, three colors. These here horses, they're showing good blood, nice build, clean sorrel and buckskin. They sure ain't horses two redskins should own. Where'd they come from?"

"Constable, my father is Barnaby Skye, an Englishman, living in the Northwest, sir. He has been a trapper and guide. I'm returning from St. Louis, where I was schooled by the Jesuits at St. Ignatius."

"Sonnyboy, I didn't ask you who you are, I asked you how come you got two shiny well-bred horses that no Indian can afford."

"They are mine," Mary said proudly. "I have the papers."

She walked to the pannier on the packhorse and pulled out the papers that had been given her. She handed them to her son, who eyed them, and handed them to the thin, mean-looking man in black.

"Worthless bunch of scribbling," the man said. "Don't prove a thing. Who you take them from, eh?"

Mary's anger built. "I took them from no man."

"I'm thinking maybe this runt of a boy, all dressed like a white man, he took them, eh?"

"They are mine," Mary said.

The man in black, who gazed at her from smirky eyes, merely smiled, tore up the bills of sale, and tossed them to the cobbled street.

"I know the red kind of human better than you know yourselves, and I know these ain't yours, so I'm confiscating them and getting them to their rightful owners."

"Would you treat my father this way?" North Star asked.

"No, sonny, I wouldn't. Not at all. You ain't your father. She ain't white neither. I would not treat any red-blood the same as the folks here. Now, from the looks of you, you're vagrants. You got any means of support?"

This bewildered her, so she left it to her son.

"My father supports us," he said. "Always has."

"Your father, your father. I ain't seeing any father around here. You got means or not? Show me the purse."

Her son did not reply.

"Vagrants. I thought so. It's illegal to be a vagrant here, and that goes double for wandering redskins. I'm fining you whatever's in the packs. So git. It's over. Vamoose from town, hear me?"

"Those have our bedrolls, our camping gear, our clothes."

"You heard me. You got fined for vagrancy, hear? Do I have to lock you up?"

"Yes, lock us up. At least we'd be fed and have a bed," North Star said.

The skinny man laughed easily, yanked the reins and lead rope from Mary's hands, and grinned. "Git, before there's an accidental shooting."

Mary's heart sank, as this man took away her horses and her packs and left them standing there in the street.

"I'm taking these nags to the livery. If I see you again, your backs are gonna bleed when the whip lands."

North Star choked back whatever he was about to yell, and sagged. Mary shrank into herself. Several people were watching. Off a way, a train whistle moaned. The smirky-eyed man in black cheerfully walked away with everything.

thirty

*M*ary's spirits sagged. They were far from home and had nothing. North Star watched the constable lead the horses away, and then quietly began collecting the scraps of paper lying in the manure of the street. He let none escape, and eventually had every piece in hand.

"We will go there," he said, pointing toward the large building called the county courthouse. "Let me talk."

She wanted only to escape this bleak place and its bleak people, but she reluctantly followed her son, wondering what a youth of fifteen winters could do. He paused, and finally decided where he was going, which was a corner street-level office.

She did not know what lay within, but the gold lettering on the glass seemed to inform him. They entered a small anteroom with wooden chairs. Beyond was an office, and sitting behind a desk was a vast man in an immaculate cream-colored suit, stiff white collar, and floppy black bow tie. His face was as wide as his waist, she thought, and made even wider by those bands of hair down the cheeks that white people called muttonchops. He surveyed them from watery blue eyes, sucked on his cigar, and motioned them in.

"Folks from far away, I imagine," he said. "What can I do for you?"

Mary glanced at North Star, who was steeling himself. "Sheriff, I am Dirk Skye, and this is my mother, whose Shoshone name translates into Blue Dawn, but who is known to my father as Mary."

"Boggs here," the sheriff said. "Is there trouble?"

"We've just had our horses confiscated by your town constable," North Star said. "That and our packs for being vagrants."

Something bright bloomed in Sheriff Boggs's blue eyes. He drew on the cigar until its tip crackled orange, and then exhaled a plume.

"My mother showed your constable her bills of sale, but he said no Indians could have such nice horses. He looked at her bills and ripped them up." North Star placed the shreds on the sheriff's desk. The man eyed them curiously, and then eyed Mary.

"Horses branded?" the sheriff asked.

"No, sir, and not shod, either."

"What'd he do with the horses?"

"Walked off with them a few minutes ago."

"Maginnis Livery Barn," the man said. "What did Constable Barnswallow say?"

"He said we had to leave town fast or he'd whip us."

The sheriff smiled. "People of color never had much traction with Clete. He sure don't even like Italians or Spaniards and he's hard on Greeks."

"I'll help you put those shreds together. You can see for yourself," the youth said.

"Who's your father?"

"Barnaby Skye. Ask anyone at Fort Laramie. He's an Englishman, a guide now. American Fur Company, long ago."

"Yes, Pierre Chouteau's outfit," the sheriff said. "And you?"

"I've been in St. Louis at St. Ignatius, where the Jesuits teach Indian boys."

"Barnswallow, he don't like Catholics, either."

"We've done nothing wrong. We want our horses and packs back. He left us with nothing but the clothing on our backs."

North Star's voice was brave and strong. She looked at her son with wonder. He knew something about dealing with these white men.

Sheriff Boggs arose, revealing a vast girth, immaculate in cream except for a few cigar ashes. "You wait right here, boy. I'll be back in a few minutes. There's chairs out there."

With surprising speed, the wide man swept past them and out the door to the street.

Mary found a seat, but North Star stood rigidly.

"How did you know to do this?" she asked.

He looked broken for a moment, and then said something that astonished her. "My father was trying to protect us when he sent me to school."

A shelf clock ticked steadily behind the sheriff's battered desk. Beyond the office she saw two iron cages, and she knew this man had the power to cage them if he chose, and her fear deepened. Maybe this man would decide they were thieves, and put her and her son inside one of those cages.

It did take time, and the afternoon began to wither away

when she saw the big man in the cream suit leading her mare, and another man leading her buckskin with the packs on it. They tied these horses to a hitching post out front.

"Mistah Skye, it seems the city constable outstretched himself, and I've recovered your nags and your packs. Barnswallow's not my man; he's the city's hire, so there's not much I could do except tell him I'll pound the crap out of him if he stops me, or you."

"Thank you, Sheriff," her son said. "I have a small request. We have no proof of ownership anymore, and—"

"I'll fix it."

The sheriff dipped the nib of a pen into an inkwell and scratched out a document, and blotted it up. He read it slowly.

"'To whom it may concern: this bay mare and buckskin gelding belong to Mrs. Barnaby Skye, known as Mary. I certify it. Amos Boggs, Sheriff, Pettis County, State of Missouri.'"

Mary marveled.

"We'll be going then. Thank you, Sheriff," her son said.

"Oh, you're mighty welcome . . . and by the way. You just set there a moment longer whiles I talk with this hostler."

He barged outside. The hostler listened, nodded, and hastened off.

"Seems to me the city ought to make amends, so I'm adding a sack of oats to your gear. I told the liveryman to bill the city."

In minutes the liveryman returned, shouldering a heavy bag of oats. He laid these before North Star. "I reckon these are yours," he said.

The sheriff had ignited a new cheroot and watched while North Star rebalanced the loads in the panniers to accommodate the oats.

"My old dad, he trapped some, working for the Bents. I

think maybe I've heard the name of Skye once or twice," the sheriff said.

"Then he will remember your father, and will thank you," North Star said.

They escaped town and headed west again, this time with enough food to last a long time. The oats would boil into a tasty gruel. Mary chose to ride, but her son walked ahead, leading the packhorse. She eyed him contemplatively. Had he lived among her people, he would probably be a young warrior now, unless his spirit helpers led him toward something else. He had a warrior's body, lithe and strong, still filling out. But now it was encased in white men's pants and shirt and shoes, the very clothing he wore as a student sitting in quiet rooms all day.

He had not fought the white man who tried to steal the horses. Instead, he had made good use of what he knew about how the headmen ruled, and talked to the man named Boggs, and it had all worked out. If he hadn't been schooled in St. Louis, how would he know such a thing? Just how the whites governed themselves was beyond her. There were too many parts: fathers who ruled over all, and fathers who ruled over smaller parts, and on and on, down to that constable. She gazed at her boy with a new insight: what he knew, locked inside his head, might rescue her people from constant trouble with these white conquerors. For the first time, her bitterness toward Skye softened. He had ripped her boy from her. But now her boy possessed mysterious powers unknown to any other Shoshone. Was that good? It was hard for her to say, but she was proud of North Star, and rejoiced inside of herself.

They walked through Independence and Kansas City virtually unremarked, perhaps because the residents of both of those towns were familiar with plains Indians and thought little of their presence. After that they followed the Kansas River northwest, on the Big Road once again. And soon they were in open country, where the hand of the white men could no longer be seen, and that lifted her heart.

The trip to the mountains proved peaceable enough. They reached Fort Kearny, but no one was counting wagons anymore. They proceeded along the south bank of the Platte River, often without seeing any travelers for an entire day. Now and then the railroad tracks came close, and then they heard the mournful whistles and the clatter of trains. Other times the rails went somewhere else but in the stillness of the nights a distant moan of a whistle reached their ears. The white men went by rail as much as they could, at least those who could afford it.

It was high summer, and the bottoms of the Platte offered her berries and roots in addition to the gruel made of oats, and they got along well enough. Such people as were heading west on the Big Road had passed by in the spring, as always, when the grasses were up and the trail was dry. As always, they started their trip with overburdened wagons, and soon were discarding the heavy items to spare their oxen. She scavenged all she could, acquiring skirts and dresses and shawls and blouses and one pair of brown shoes that fit her, a welcome find after wearing out her moccasins. Several times they discovered worn or wounded livestock, oxen, horses, loose in the bottoms, but these were skittish and hard to catch, and she and North Star had no luck with them. Then one day she found a lamed ewe, abandoned by her herder. It had a broken leg and was wasting away. She slit its throat, and she and North Star gorged on the first meat they had enjoyed in a long time, and kept eating until the meat turned bad. She skinned the pelt and began working on moccasins from it during the evenings.

The air lost its moisture and became more comfortable, in spite of furnace heat each afternoon. Her heart lifted. This was air she knew, air from the great reaches of the High Plains, and the mountains.

They passed immigrant families, and discovered that these white people spoke no English and came from places she didn't know. They were a little different somehow.

"Those were from Sicily," North Star said. "And the ones we passed earlier were from Hungary."

She marveled that he knew these things.

It was only when they were approaching Fort Laramie that he opened the topics that had remained a barrier between them these many days and nights.

"Are you and Father separated?" he asked one afternoon, when she was least expecting it.

"I don't know," she said.

She told him what had been intended. Victoria, Skye's sits-beside-him wife, had directed her to go to the Wind River Reservation and wait for Skye and Victoria. But Blue Dawn had been drawn east by some spirit guide, drawn east in some way beyond her own willpower to resist, as if the wise and frightening owl had compelled her to go.

"I'm not sure where they are now. I think with my people on the Wind River. We will look for them there, because that is where we were to meet."

Then, realizing how little North Star knew of recent times, she narrated the recent past.

"He hurts now, and it is hard for him to lie on a robe and sleep. It is hard for him to get up off the ground, and sometimes he wishes he had a chair, one of those rocking chairs.

The cold comes through the robes on a winter's night and makes him stiff, and then he hurts all the more. Last spring, even before the snows melted, he said he wanted to build a house and have a stove in it and beds and chairs and a fireplace, and the place that would lift his spirits the most would be the great bend of the Yellowstone. He rode away one day, leaving Victoria and me with her people, because he said he wanted to choose the right place. But he didn't return, so Victoria went to get him, sent me away, and more than that I don't know."

"Will he turn his back on me?"

In truth, Mary was not sure of that. "He is torn, Dirk," she said, using that other name for him. "All the while you were gone, he could not talk to me, or Victoria, about you. But you were there in his mind, every moment, every winter, and I think he believed you would need to make your own decision when you left school. To come back, or live there with the white men." She paused. "He knew you could help the Shoshones the most if you learned all the secrets of the white men. But it would be your decision."

"I've already made it," North Star said.

thirty-one

Skye ignored the distant white man with the rakish hat perched jauntily on his head. He patiently hoed a row of potato plants, breaking the soil and chopping away weeds. Each strike of the hoe hurt, but he didn't mind. He was helping raise food for Mary's brothers, and that made him feel useful. There at Fort Washakie, the Shoshones were slowly adapting to white men's ways and raising crops.

But progress in that direction had not been easy. The Shoshone men considered it women's work and refused to labor in the fields. Male Shoshones hunted, made war, and gambled. Women toiled. But there would be potatoes this season, Skye thought. The rains had come and the frosts had held off, and no hail had destroyed the tender plants. Potatoes might not be as satisfying as a haunch of buffalo, but these people had little choice. The Yank government was decreeing how they must live.

So he chopped and weeded and felt a thin sweat dampen his hatband and his shirt, and he counted the time well spent. And maybe the sight of a white man patiently growing food might inspire the younger Shoshone boys to at least try the new life.

The white stranger stared around, looking for something in that pleasant Wind River Valley, and finally strode toward Skye, who imagined it would be another Indian Bureau functionary with new commands or restrictions or rebukes. But this gent was too gaudy and looked more like some dandy from the nearest saloon than a government man. He wore a black waistcoat with a gold fob stretched across it. Gold-plated fob, at any rate. The man studied Skye, made up his mind, and headed down a row of potatoes toward his quarry. The man sported muttonchops and a mustache, and peered at Skye from watery blue eyes that flanked a veined nose that suggested a long acquaintance with spirits.

Skye straightened up slowly to ease the pain in his back and rested on his worn hoe.

"Ah, there you are, Skye!"

"Mister Skye, sir."

"So I've heard. I know more about you than you may think."

"Then you have the advantage of me, sir."

"Buntline here. Ned Buntline at your service." The man seemed to be waiting for something, perhaps recognition, but Skye had never heard of the man.

Skye lifted his hat and let the dry breezes evaporate the sweat on his brow. "A good name, Mister Buntline. I knew that term when I was a boy," he said. "Buntline's the rope along the base of a square sail."

"Ah, we have it in common!" Buntline said. "I was a sailor, and now I'm a scribbler."

"A reporter, maybe?"

"No, no, I spin yarns of the great West, true stories, carefully documented, about the towering border men who opened these lands. I'm going to do a story about Cody, called King of the Border Men, and I want to do you too."

"Do me?"

"You're the one who became king of the mountain men, aren't you? Then king of the guides? Then king of the Indian wars?"

Skye stared, at a loss. "You have the wrong man," he said, and took up his hoeing once again, the strokes of the blade rhythmically opening the soil and vanquishing a creeping vine.

"Ah, a modest man. But I think you're wrong, Mister Skye. There's no man in all the West more honored than you."

"I really need to hoe these potatoes before the weeds take over, sir."

"You're the man, all right. You have not one but two wives, sharing the very same lodge. You've taken scientists and preachers and doctors into the wilderness and got them out safely. You've fought the Blackfeet and Comanches, the deadliest of all tribes, and survived. You've taken white men into forbidden valleys. There's nothing you haven't done. Your name is known from St. Louis to the Pacific. They all say Skye's the man, Mister Skye. Write about him."

Skye leaned heavily upon his hoe. This was heavy work, and his bum leg was rebelling.

"Mister Buntline, how can I say this? I would rather have my privacy. There's nothing I did that dozens of others couldn't do. You want to write about a remarkable man, you just corral Jim Bridger and take down his story."

"Oh, Mister Skye, I don't take down stories, I invent them, always based on truth, of course. I don't really need to know your secrets. The name is enough. Trust me, within a few months yours will be the most celebrated name in every nook and cranny of the Republic."

"I think, sir, I'd like to return to my hoeing."

"And that's a story too. A brave man, giving his last for his wife's people."

Skye smiled. "It's been good to talk with you," he said.

"You're very like you were described, Mister Skye. I got some excellent descriptions of you, but they were wrong on one item. There's no London left in your voice."

That gave Skye his opening. "I'm not a Yank, so don't write about me. Go find a Yankee to write about."

Buntline smiled, his manner apologetic. "You know, Mister Skye, I've talked to people in St. Louis. You worked for American Fur and the Chouteau family, and they told me you were the best man out in the field. I talked to army men at Fort Leavenworth. They told me you're a legend. Whenever the army wanted something, they asked you. They said you'd fought more hostile Indians than any man alive. They said you're the bravest man ever to walk this continent. I stopped in Independence, and learned you're the most trusted guide alive. You got people through."

Skye listened incredulously. This man was inventing things.

"The trouble was, no one knew where to find you. They said you might be with the Crows, you might be with the Shoshones, you might be anywhere. But the best bet was to go to Fort Laramie and ask, so I did, by train and stage, and I asked, and they weren't sure either, but then a young Indian Bureau fellow said he'd heard you'd come to the Wind River agency, and I got a horse and came here. And here you are. I'm hoping you'll hear me out."

The man had crossed a continent for nothing. Skye wasn't

sure how to cope with it. "They probably told you, Mister Buntline, that I wouldn't be very cooperative."

"Oh, they did, but of course that just gets my dander up. I've had trouble lining up Cody, and even more trouble lining up Hickok."

"I suppose I should know who Hickok is, sir, but I don't. What I do know is that I live a quiet and private life and it's going to stay that way."

"Well, I'm not done, not done at all, Mister Skye. There are rewards, compensations, good things in your future."

Skye was feeling more and more testy. "I apologize, sir, for not being civil. You'll excuse me now."

Buntline grinned cheerfully. "I thought maybe you'd like to get rich."

Skye was not averse to the idea, and decided to give the man a few moments before evicting him from the potato patch.

"My backers and I plan to do stage shows, sir. These shows simply pump in cash. We'd like to do one starring yourself, called Trapper Skye, King of the Mountains. We'd have you say a few lines, talk with your two wives, get into a staged battle with some redskins, and discharge your piece now and then—it's marvelously deafening inside a theater. How about a hundred dollars a week, for starters?"

"Mister Buntline, I'm sorry you came all this way. The answer is no."

"You say the word, and we'll pay your way by rail to St. Louis, where we'll organize the show. Yes, bring your wives, and we'll give you a few lines to memorize on the train. The minute you walk onstage, and the audience sees you're the real thing, and the roughest cob that ever came east, they'll sit spellbound, and throw dimes onstage when you're done.

You'll pocket a few dollars of dimes right off the boards every show."

"Are you through, Mister Buntline?"

"Oh, no, not at all. Shipping both ways, one season, bonuses if you pack the house, and plenty of good dime novels about you to spark interest. Do that for a year or two, and you won't be hoeing potatoes. You'll be living like a prince."

"A prince? Me?"

"Onstage for six months, just one season, a hundred dollars a week. You'll have room and board, traveling money, and a bottle anytime you want it. I'll tell you what. If you stick it out, I'll add a bonus after the season, yes, let's add four hundred. That's around three thousand dollars, sir, for one season. Think about it! A home of your own. Something to retire on. Money in the bank. Think on it, Mister Skye. Just for walking onstage and saying a few lines. I promise you, sir, you'll fill up every theater from Kankakee to Pittsburgh."

Skye could barely absorb it.

"How about it?" Buntline asked.

"Mister Buntline, I may have lost my wife Mary. She's gone. I'm awaiting word."

"Well, that's no problem. I know a few Italian actresses who look Indian in front of the gaslights. We'll just dye their faces. In fact, this is even better. We'll give you three or four wives and that will be an even better draw."

Skye roared, swung his hoe at Buntline, missed him, and started after the man. But the impresario was faster and had no limp. Skye lunged again, but too late. Buntline ran over several rows of potatoes and headed for the safety of the clapboard agency buildings. Skye watched him go, his heart hammering, and then settled the venerable hat on his head. The hoe lay two rows away, so he collected it as he watched Buntline vanish inside of one of the buildings.

He hoped Buntline would complain loudly to the Indian agent. That would be the only entertainment the afternoon offered.

He used his hoe as a crutch because he was hurting again, and began to make his way across the potato patch, when Victoria intercepted him.

"What the hell was that about?" she asked.

"Oh, nothing."

She glared at him.

"That man wants to put me in a theater with a bunch of Italian actresses playing my wives, while I run around stage killing Indians."

"Sonofabitch!" she said. "I'll kill him."

"Not a bad idea," he said. "He offered me three thousand dollars."

"He what?"

"To shoot Indians. To cozy up to several wives. That would amuse an audience."

She stared at him.

"I did what I had to do. I've never taken any pride in fighting or killing. When it happened it was because I had no choice. I won't glorify this in a theater. I won't pretend or make believe. I won't turn myself into a hero when I'm an ordinary man. I won't have little boys wishing they could be like me. I won't turn myself into something I'm not and never was. I can't be bought, not for three thousand dollars, Victoria. So I told him my wife was missing and I was waiting to learn of her fate."

"Mary will come back," she said.

He knew better than to ask how she knew that. All his life with her she had visited mysterious insights upon him, and usually was right. But he didn't believe it. Mary was gone. She had crossed the great divide, and nothing would restore her to him. He had been quietly grieving as he hoed the fields each day. Hoeing was the only way he knew to let go of Mary. He hoed one row and then another and another, burying her.

Buntline vanished the next day, but not without leaving an elaborate contract with the agency. An owl-eyed clerk handed him a thick envelope with his name written on it in an elaborate hand. Skye's eyes weren't good, but he managed to decipher the blur by holding the papers at arm's length. Sign right here and you'll be a theatrical star and make enough money to last the rest of your life.

Skye read the amazing document, and carefully stuffed it into the agency stove and watched flames lick it. He had burned Buntline out of his life. The whole thing had left him with an unsated curiosity. Why would some novelist and impresario track him down? There had been nothing unusual in Skye's life. He had survived decades in the wilds, but so had others. He had adopted the ways of the Indians and had become their advocate, but so had others. He had guided a few people, led a few trapping parties, explored a few areas unknown to the outside world. But so had others.

He toiled through another day of heat and dryness, and then the searchers returned. Victoria summoned him from the fields, and as he walked toward the agency buildings, he saw the young warriors collecting at the frame house of Chief Washakie. He saw no paint, which might have signified battle or victory or death, but only bronzed young men, mostly in breechclouts, sinking off their unpainted and unadorned ponies.

The old man appeared at once, and surveyed the quiet young Shoshones as they gathered at his porch.

"I do not see Blue Dawn," he said to Fast Bird, who had led the search.

"Grandfather, she is not anywhere," the young man said. "We looked for her bones and saw none. We looked for her ponies. She has gone to the place of eternal mystery, and we know nothing more."

"How far did you go?" Washakie asked.

"We rode to the Yellowstone, and then we rode along the banks in both directions. The trail would be very old, but we looked. We were thorough. The owls said nothing to us. The coyote did not lead us."

Washakie turned to Skye and Victoria. "Blue Dawn is not among us anymore," he said. "I am sorry. We will not say her name. She will be the One Who Disappeared."

thirty-two

North Star felt some mysterious tug as he and his mother worked their way up the Wind River. Something ancient and powerful was awakening in him. It seemed almost a physical force, though he knew he had scarcely been in this place, and only when he was too young to remember much about it. There was majestic beauty, with snowy peaks rising to the west, but along this trail was greenery and shelter from the winds.

The white man part of him told him it couldn't be familiarity, because he had spent most of his childhood among the Crows of his mother Victoria's people, and he had scarcely been here. But the Shoshone part of him whispered that he had come home, that this very land was the ancient and primal land of his people, and all that he saw was his to possess. His mind had worked like that for years now, a dual way of seeing the world, and he didn't mind. If he was a man of two bloods, then he really wanted to see the world in each way. But just now, he was pure Shoshone, walking beside his

Shoshone mother Blue Dawn, just a little apart from a place he and she had not seen, Fort Washakie.

"I do not know this," she said, the sweep of her hand encompassing planted fields, small log cabins situated well apart from one another, and up ahead, some white frame buildings with a flag flying above them. The new agency, he supposed, given by the Yankees to his people. The thought was a little cynical. The Yankees had forced his people onto a homeland, with borders around it that made it an invisible prison.

Still, this was a good place. He saw smoke curling up from the chimneys of the cabins, and knew life progressed within. He and his mother proceeded into this settled area unnoticed. There was no town crier anymore to herald the arrival of visitors, as there had been when his people lived in lodges and moved camp whenever it was necessary. They saw some women toiling in the fields, patiently using wooden or buffalo-bone hoes to hack down weeds. They saw squash and maize and beans and potatoes and grains, some of it well tended, the rest patchy and in need of hard work.

"This place . . ." Mary said. "We once raised our lodges here. We met with the other bands and had games and feasts. The families arranged marriages, and it was good. Now a plow has torn up the grass."

But the closer they got to the white buildings, the more North Star sank into himself. What would his father be like? When at last, when they stood man to man, would he welcome his son and his wife? What would he think of Blue Dawn after her long absence? Would he and Victoria even be here? Neither he nor his mother were sure.

He could not answer these questions. But this was his home, and he was in a good place and his heart was good.

The sun had dropped to the top of the distant mountains in the west, and now the long light gilded the land, burnished it with gold, so that the cottonwoods were golden, and the grasses too, and the sunlit sides of the log cabins, and the sunlit sides of the agency buildings. And opposite every gilded object was a purple shadow, a shadow that was crawling along the earth as the sun sat for a while right on the distant ridges.

They both saw Skye at the same time. The gold light lit his ancient top hat and turned his white hair bright and caught his ruddy cheeks. He was in a field, hoeing, and there was no mistaking him. Mary cried out suddenly, her hand flying to her face. His own heart tripped, and for a moment he was anxious.

She steered her worn horse toward the distant man, her man, his sire, who hoed in the golden last light, and now they progressed between rows of some plant he thought might be potatoes, and at last Barnaby Skye noticed, and set down his hoe, and lifted his old hat from his head, so the gold light caught all his white hair, and the old man seemed to straighten up, grow taller, as he stood waiting. For it was plain the old man recognized his wife and his son, and now walked toward them, limping slightly, his hoe as his staff.

They reached him and stopped. Mary slid from her horse and went to him. North Star halted, afraid now, seeing the great puzzlement in the old man's face.

"Mary! And you?" his father said, peering first at his wife and then at his son. "You?"

His mother stood stiff and proud, for she was making a presentation. "Yes, Mister Skye. We have come to you. Here is your son."

He didn't speak for a moment, but stood, the breeze riffling his unkempt gray hair. Then, searching for words, he spoke. "I'm glad," he said. "Gladder than I've ever been."

He collected his wife and hugged her, and collected his boy and embraced him, and then stood back to gaze again at these two.

"Now my life is complete," he said. "But don't explain it. Let it be a miracle."

"Mister Skye, we will call it a miracle," North Star's mother said.

Now the sun slid beneath the western peaks, leaving a rim of white fire as the gold faded away into indigo shadows.

North Star had no wish to talk. There was no need for words, and besides, all the feelings within him now were Shoshone, but he had lost his mother tongue and his English seemed poor and inadequate. His father was glad. So it was enough to stand still while his father took the measure of them both, his gaze, which seemed uncertain, absorbing his wife and then examining his son.

"What name shall I call you, son?" Skye asked.

"That name that draws you closest to me, Father."

"Then you are Dirk, lad. And a proud name it is, owned by your grandfather in England.

"And you, my beautiful wife? What shall I call you?"

She grinned. "I'll whisper it in your ear sometime."

He laughed, a rumbling chuckle that wrought memories in North Star. "Let us make the circle complete," Skye said. "Victoria hates cabins and stoves and is probably cussing her way through some cooking." He turned to Mary. "Your brothers gave us a cabin. They are starting another."

They walked through the fields, three people and two horses, in the gathering twilight, and no one noticed them. The first stars emerged, and Dirk looked as always for the

Star That Never Moves, his natal star and one that wrought odd feelings deep within him.

They reached the door, Skye set his old hoe against the logs and pushed the door open. Victoria turned and stared.

"I'll be goddamned," she said.

She set down an iron spoon and examined the youth and the mother, and then she studied Skye, looking for something within him. Whatever it was that Victoria saw in him, she seemed satisfied.

"I am pleased to see you, Mother Victoria," North Star said.

"You are here. You are alive," Victoria said. She turned to Mary. "We stopped saying your name."

Dirk knew all about that. The names of the dead were never spoken.

"There isn't much in the kettle. We don't eat much anymore. You're both thin."

It was true; she had only a few cups of stew boiling on a sheet-metal woodstove. "Eat this," she said. "I'll start some other."

"Let me cook," Mary said.

There was meat boiling slowly in that stew, and the scent seemed heavenly to North Star. They had scarcely enjoyed a mouthful of meat for days on end.

Victoria headed first for the younger wife, and touched her cheek. "It is Mary of the Shoshones," and then she touched North Star's cheek. "What name have you taken, boy?"

"I wish to be Dirk to my father, and North Star to my mothers."

"Aiee, this is good!" Victoria said.

North Star waited for the questions that didn't come. He waited to justify himself. He waited to tell them why he had left school. He waited for them to ask his mother where she had been. About the long trip. About how they connected. About what had inspired her. But Skye and Victoria asked nothing at all of him.

He was ready to tell them that he had done well with his lessons. He was good at arithmetic. He knew some geometry. He could spell. He could write. He could keep accounts. He had read many books written by Englishmen. He had learned the history of the Americans. He had learned theology, and knew the history of the Jesuits. He knew mechanics. He had done some carpentry. He could glaze a window or plane a door.

If he was weak, it was in composing sentences and writing paragraphs and papers. His thoughts were too unruly, and the nib pen too slow in his fingers. And yet, the good fathers had told him he was quick and bright, and they had little left to teach him because he was doing better than most of the other boys. They had told him he could do as well as any white boy. He wondered about that. Could he do as well as any full-blood too? What was it about being a mixed-blood?

But his father didn't ask. His father kept staring at Dirk, staring as if he was trying to puzzle away the gap between the eight-year-old boy he last saw and this youth he was examining now.

So the questions didn't come, and neither did they rain on Mary, and it gradually dawned on Dirk that this was acceptance; that he would not have to justify himself to his father and Victoria, and neither would Mary have to justify what obviously was a long and perilous trip. His father and Crow mother would learn about it in good time, and they were leaving it to him to choose the moment.

So Mary and Dirk spooned the savory stew while

another meal was boiling, the new one without meat because the antelope meat had been the gift of Mary's family, and it was all the meat there was.

The cabin could contain them. It had no furniture in it, but at least it had a straw-covered clay floor with robes scattered about. It was as close to the interior of a lodge as a small structure could get, and it awakened ancient memories in North Star. It was a lodge, but with log walls and a shake roof and a sheet-metal stove.

There was only a small window, and it had no glass, but shutters against the cold. Now, as the last light faded, it grew dusky in the cabin. He could see that Victoria was bent and worn now, as thin as ever but her back had curved and her head rested forward. And Skye had lost weight, and had bent also, but there still was fire in his eyes. Fire in the eyes of both of them.

Someday soon they would know the story. Mary would tell of her impulse to see her son; he would tell of his rushed decision to return with her. She would talk about the long trip on the Big Road, and tell them where her horses came from, and the troubles they had. He would tell them of his honors at school, and what he could do and what he had learned. But not this night, when they paid him and his mother the greater honor of not asking.

"Father and Mother Victoria, I should take care of the horses," he said.

"That's good, Dirk, and I will show you," Skye said.

Together they slipped into the twilight and undid the packs and the packsaddle and the riding saddle and brought them inside. Dirk knew that they would feel very light in Skye's hands. They contained no food at all, and few other things. The trip had consumed whatever small things Mary and he possessed.

Skye gathered the reins. "Good-looking horses. Are they yours?" he asked.

"They are my mother's."

Skye started slowly toward the fields, his limp slowing him. "The herd's off that way. Not many left."

"Stolen?"

"No, eaten. These people don't get the rations they were promised by the government. Either that or the Indian agent skims much of it off. So they're half-starved and living on horse meat until the next shipment of flour and beans comes in."

"I didn't know. I shouldn't have come."

"You can help, son."

They hiked a while more along a lane between planted fields, and then Skye quit.

"My leg's giving out. Here, take these over to that grove of cottonwoods and let them loose. They'll find the herd."

Dirk took the reins, led the horses another quarter of a mile to the trees, slid the bridle and halter off, and let them go. He saw no other horses and wondered if he'd ever see these again.

His father was waiting for him.

"We're living on charity, Dirk," Skye said as they started back. "These people can hardly feed themselves, much less a Crow and a white man. Tomorrow, you get yourself enrolled with the agent. You and Mary. It's worth some flour and beans. Erastus Perkins is his name. Major Perkins. They're all called major, all the Yank Indian agents."

"Where are my uncles?"

"In a lodge upriver, four, five miles. They turned over the

cabin and said they'd live the old way for a time. But no one can leave the reservation without the major's say-so, which means they can't go after buffalo out on the plains, which means that they're worse off than ever. Victoria and I, we're thinking we'd best get back to our Crow people. Wild Indians have it better than tame ones, and we're just robbing them of food, staying here like this."

"It's an outrage, sir."

"It's that. It's slow starvation. They're out hunting rabbits and snatching turtles and trying to kill a few ravens for the kettle."

They reached the little cabin, and Skye paused.

"I'm glad you're here, Dirk. I'd like to help these people but I can't, not with my bloody busted leg, and I get worn-out fast. I hardly know what I'm going to do; everything I try, including hunting, hurts too much."

North Star felt a strange tenderness, and more. He felt that he was destined to return at this very hour. He was standing, man to man, beside his father. They needed him here. The moving finger had written his fate.

thirty-three

*T*he youth wandered aimlessly, wondering what had inspired him to abandon St. Louis. Dirk, or North Star, or whoever he was, drifted day by day, not knowing what to do. His two bloods were at war, but mostly he wasn't sure he cared. These were not the Shoshones he remembered from his childhood, when they were still a proud migrating happy people never far from buffalo or game.

When his mother had suddenly appeared in St. Louis, that ancient memory was kindled in him, and the joy of unfettered freedom, of riding open prairies, of climbing to mountain lakes, of dancing to the drums, of shivering at the sound of an owl's hoot, all trumped everything the Jesuit fathers had instilled in him, and suddenly he had to break free.

But this gaggle of huts being called Fort Washakie was not that place, and it all seemed bleak and unfamiliar. The valley itself was beautiful, but where were the people? They lived now in little cabins far apart, disconnected from one another, their dreams reduced to hoeing and drifting. On his hikes, North Star saw the shanties and the barely scratched plots of land, growing a few scraggly worm-eaten crops that would yield little when harvest came. He saw women alone by the river, rinsing out old clothing, and he remembered how the Shoshone women used to gather together and make their work communal, with gossip and jokes to make the toil pass by easily.

He saw men lounging, smoking, looking unkempt and bored, waiting for the next allotment day, when they would get their few pounds of flour or rice, or beans or sugar and maybe a slab of beef now and then. He wondered what had happened, why these men didn't have fire in their eyes, why they sat passively waiting for whatever would happen to happen. Where had their souls gone?

This wasn't the world of his memories, filled with strong, bronzed men and women in clothing wrought from deer and elk skins or trade cloth, sleeping in buffalo robes, tackling each day with joy. Maybe that world never quite existed, but it seemed real to the seven- or eight-year-old boy who was eventually ripped from it and plunged into another world, in another land. Maybe, had he been older, he would have seen weary, half-starved, diseased people locked in an unending quest to survive. But he did remember laughter, and jokes, and pride, and those who decorated their lodges and clothing and ponies with their own emblems.

North Star had thought there might be rejoicing when he and his mother showed up after her long absence, but there wasn't much, apart from a little curiosity about her. Her brother, The Runner, had come to visit, along with his women, but no one said much. A few people stopped to talk with him, but the Shoshones were spread for miles up and down the Wind River now, and were grimly trying to eke a living from the verdant meadows, and there was little time to rejoice in the prodigal who had returned. Had the heart been torn out of his mother's people?

Chief Washakie had welcomed him warmly, rejoicing in his mother's return. But even he was different. North Star remembered him as a traditional and proud chief living in a large lodge, wearing magnificent ceremonial robes, beaded moccasins, attended by his wives, his lodge a place of power and wisdom. But now Chief Washakie lived in a house with chairs and tables and a stove and a couch and a kitchen, and he wore collarless shirts, with black waistcoats and gray woolen trousers. Only his shining black braids remained as North Star had remembered them. Washakie seemed the only Shoshone on the reservation who still had spirit burning in him, and good cheer always radiated from his face.

"We are glad you have come to us, North Star," he said. "And we are glad that you bring with you the mysteries of the white man, which I hope you will share with the People, so we may be as wise as the Fathers who taught you all they knew."

Washakie blessed Blue Dawn too, and urged her to enroll herself and her son in the tribal ledgers kept by the agent, Major Perkins, in the white clapboard buildings. So Mary and Dirk duly entered the fearsome building, found the major with his boots resting on a cold stove, drinking some amber fluid Dirk thought might be whiskey. The man's beard was unkempt, and his clothing stained.

"Ah, yes, Skye's woman and boy," the major said. "Heard all about it. You should have stayed in St. Louis, boy."

But Gallipoli Sanders, his bespectacled white clerk, enrolled them, writing with a Spencerian hand, and henceforth on each distribution day he and his mother would receive some flour and beans or rice, and occasionally some beef butchered from a few stringy and stumbling cattle delivered by a ranch over in the Big Horn Valley. That meant that the Skye household had three allotments to feed four, because Victoria was an Absaroka woman and not eligible. But Skye himself, as a spouse of Mary, would qualify.

Each day Dirk watched his father crawl from his robes, struggle to his feet, dress and overcome his morning stiffness, and then pick up his ancient hoe and head for the fields, where he would patiently chop weeds away from squash or maize or beans or potatoes until he wearied. Dirk's father had welcomed his son, and yet there had been something unspoken lying between them. Plainly, his father had seen this new world coming, and at great cost to himself, to Mary, and to Victoria too, he had sent Dirk to his freedom and his future. But now Dirk was back, and this reservation was his future, and the youth found himself drifting from sadness to bewilderment, and occasionally to fits of action. He joined groups of boys who went hunting in the old way. He had no weapon and minimal skill with a bow and arrow, but he went anyway, hoping to add food to the larder.

Occasionally he saw his uncle, The Runner, who lived with his family in the traditional way now, having given the cabin to Skye. Mary's brother had been eager to embrace this new world, and had mastered some ancient English, but now he was too busy trying to feed his wives and some clan brothers and sisters. This was not The Runner of yore, either, and that disturbed Dirk. He felt he had walked into some vortex that was sucking him down into a pit. Sometimes the majestic mountains brightened him. Some early September snows had whitened the peaks, making them glow boldly with their promise of liberty. Flee to the mountains, for there is liberty!

Dirk noticed the girls too, quiet Shoshone girls, most of them too thin, some pretty, though he had an odd aversion to the heavy cheekbones he saw in them, and in himself. He thought white women were more delicate, with faces and figures he liked more. And yet occasionally a girl stirred him, and he sometimes talked with one or another, but they took alarm. He had not yet recovered his own tongue, though it was swiftly returning, and the girls shied from him as an odd and maybe dangerous person, who sometimes glowered at them instead of smiling.

Was this all there was to life? He wished he might have books to read now that the whole bright world of knowledge had been opened to him, but there was scarcely a book on the reservation. His uncle, The Runner, had once had a Shakespeare and a Bible, but the pages had been ripped out, one by one, to start fires, and now there were no books, not even in Major Perkins's office and house, except for a Bible, which the agent obviously not only did not read, but rejected.

September was harvesttime, and Dirk helped dig up potatoes, and pluck maize from stalks, and gather squash and stow these in a root cellar dug into a slope. Skye and Victoria and Mary worked steadily, not only harvesting the crops The Runner had planted in his patch of land, but also neighbors' crops, which had suffered from inattention. Few traditional Shoshones cared to garden, and most all of them greatly preferred good meat, even if it was the softer white man's beef, though they all yearned for the rich, textured firmness of buffalo meat.

Dirk sensed that his family was not happy. His mother and Victoria toiled silently, saying little. His father had drawn deep into himself, and seemed to be forcing labor from a body mostly spent and hurting. Dirk heard no complaint; his mothers simply did what had to be done each day and fell into their blankets at night.

The clay-floor cabin itself was not as comfortable as a lodge, and its stove ate firewood, requiring the women to roam farther and farther gathering deadwood. Both Victoria and Mary shouldered heavy packs on their backs, and walked a mile or so back to the cabin with enough wood to keep it warm two or three days. Dirk remembered the lodges, how the tiniest fire would heat the air inside the leather cone, how an insulating layer of robes on the ground would keep the chill off. And yet that was mostly unreliable childhood memory. Each day, as his father struggled just to get up, Dirk knew that a good bedstead would be a treasure for his father. And yet nothing happened. It was as if the whole tribe was waiting, waiting, for something.

There was something else: the silence was terrible. Dirk craved the company of his father and mother and Victoria. There were years of absence, a thousand stories, and a universe of wisdom and anecdote and always the mysteries, the things that had animated his mother's people. This was a cruel world, and was having a cruel effect on his parents.

These people were slumbering through life. The past had vanished, and there seemed to be no future. The agent, Major Perkins, didn't seem to care. He was a time-server, taking his pay from the government, maintaining some sort of minimal existence for his wards, and whiling away his empty hours drinking. And toying with the girls. The agent had two housekeepers, Shoshone girls in their teens, pretty and well fed, and Dirk wondered about them. The girls avoided his eye. One looked pregnant. On distribution days, there never was quite what had been promised, or the food was bad. Wormy flour, spoiled salt pork, bony cattle. Somehow, that never evoked any ire in the agent, though he was responsible for feeding these people and making sure the government was not being cheated by contractors. Dirk began to study the man, not sure what was happening. And the longer Dirk lingered on the reservation, the darker his spirits grew. What had he come west for?

One day, he peered into an empty clapboard building near the agency and discovered an unused schoolhouse, and an unused teacherage next to it. Through the windows he saw a completed school, with desks and a woodstove and a chalkboard. Through the windows of the teacherage he saw empty bedsteads, horsehair furnishings, a table and chairs, a kitchen. All as new and silent as the day they had been completed.

Impulsively he headed for the agency, and found the major more or less drunk.

He stood, hat in hand, because one was required to wait and be invited to speak if one was not a white man. Eventually Major Perkins nodded.

"You, is it? What's the trouble? More bad flour?"

"Sir, I wanted to ask you about that school."

"Oh, that." The agent yawned. "Another bungle. They can't get anything right. Build a school and then there's no budget for teachers or books. Congress won't spend a dime."

"Could we, my father and I, teach, sir?"

"No money, I told you. Not a bloody cent from those skinflints."

"Could we move into the teacher house and teach, sir?"

"What makes you think you can? What are you, fifteen?"

"I was ahead of my class, sir. I can teach the alphabet, spelling, writing, reading, mathematics, some algebra, English literature."

"Oh, now, boy, half the students would be older than you."

"My father was schooled in London and was headed for the university."

"And was pressed at age thirteen, I gather."

"He knows a lot more than the boys here do."

"What's in it for me, young Skye?"

Dirk had no answer to that.

thirty-four

irk Skye fumed his way to the forlorn cabin. Nothing was right on this reservation. And Major Perkins liked it that way. An October chill was a harbinger of what would soon descend on them. The dirt-floored cabin was worse than a lodge, and he knew his father and Crow mother would suffer, and maybe his mother too.

His father wore his age with dignity, not complaining and doing what he could to grow food for them all. But Dirk knew he hurt. His Crow mother Victoria hurt in other ways, torn from her own people and way of life, even as her body lost strength.

He plunged into the cabin just as his mothers were boiling a vegetable stew, there being no meat again. It took the women most of each day just to find firewood, and they were forced to search ever farther away. In the days when the People lived in lodges, they simply moved to a new locale when fuel and grass and wood were exhausted. But now there was no place to go, and few lodges to shelter them.

His mother glanced at him and frowned, well aware of

the fury boiling through him. But she said nothing. They all had turned stoic, their goal to endure one bad thing after another. He wasn't even sure that they had hope of anything better.

They ate the stew eagerly, but it did not fill or satisfy them, because there was no good meat. But they could expect none until the next distribution day, and then it was likely to be a few pounds that must last all four of them the whole month.

Skye, too, was watchful of his son, and when they had all finished their meager meal, he addressed the boy.

"What is it, Dirk?" he asked.

"I despise this place," Dirk shot back.

The women were attentive now.

"Have you looked at the school? And the teacherage?"

"I have," said Skye.

"And what did you see?"

"Empty school, all ready for use, and a house all ready, with furniture and a stove. I went to Major Perkins and asked why it wasn't being used, and he said the Indian Bureau had no money for teachers or books or slates or anything. I said we'd teach, I can teach lots of things, and he asked what was in it for him."

"That's how the man does things here," Skye said.

"We could be teaching. I know my arithmetic and letters and spelling and grammar and a lot of other things. You know a lot more than I do. These people need what we can give them. It's not their world, and no one can help that, but we can help them into the new world."

Dirk saw how attentive they were, and felt heartened. This was the first time in all his days and weeks and months on the Wind River Reservation that he had cried out, that he had been anything but polite and subdued.

"We could be living in that house. It has a floor and bed frames and chairs and a horsehair couch. It has a kitchen and a kitchen wood range and a woodstove in the parlor. We could be there. Every day I see you get up, drive the stiffness out of you that came from lying on cold ground. You never complain." He appealed to them all. "You get up, begin a hard day, no matter that you hurt, no matter that dry firewood is two miles away and you must haul it here on your backs."

Victoria sighed. "A lodge. That's all I want is a lodge. All it needs is a tiny goddamn fire the size of a hand, and it is warm."

"A lodge would be good," Mary said. "This place . . ." She waved at the foul clay floor which soiled their robes, and the gloomy log walls, the one tiny window, scarcely a foot square because glass was precious, the flapping door hung on leather hinges. "It's so hard to live in it."

Skye rose stiffly. "Dirk, we'll talk to the agent."

"About what?"

"About the future."

Dirk's father dusted off his top hat and settled it on his gray hair and brushed his old leathers, making himself presentable.

"What future?" Victoria said.

Skye turned to her. "We don't need to stay here. We can go live with your people."

Victoria's face told Dirk everything he needed to know. For weeks, this ragged family had lived in deep silence, the women bravely enduring a miserable life in a place that was neither a village nor a new home for his mother's people.

Dirk followed his father toward the distant white buildings of the agency, the air sharp against his face.

Skye entered, lifted the top hat, and didn't wait to be summoned by the agent, who it turned out was snoozing, his feet on his desk, his bulk filling a wooden swivel chair. Major Perkins awakened with a snort, eyed Skye and Dirk narrowly, and carefully lowered his grimy boots.

"It's customary to knock," the major said.

"Our apologies," Skye said. "My son and I, we've been thinking about that empty school."

"Think no more. Nothing's going to happen."

"The people here are slowly sinking," Skye said. "We think we could help."

"You were pressed into the Royal Navy at age thirteen, Skye."

"It's Mister Skye, sir. A preference of mine. In the New World, anyone has the right to be a mister, including these good Shoshone people, and my son Dirk. Now, as it happens, something can be done to help them. I was thinking my boy and I could teach a lot more than reading and doing numbers. These people have been pushed into giving up their lodges and building these miserable cabins, but this new life isn't much good, sir. No one has enough firewood, and winter's coming on. It's not like the days when a village could take down their lodges and go to a fresh place with wood and grass. I'm proposing, Major, that we teach these people a little about business. I was a businessman in the fur trade, and as a guide, most of my life. I want to help these people. We need a firewood company, someone with a horse and wagon and a crew with saws and axes. We need a furniture company, someone who can join wood and make chairs and tables and bed frames."

"And earn a lot of coin," Perkins said, amused.

"Barter, sir. We have some potatoes. I'd trade some for

firewood and furniture. What I propose, sir, is that my son and I start up a school. My boy will teach arithmetic and reading and spelling and all that. He knows some mechanics too. I'll teach these people how to organize services and businesses."

"I'm sure you'd draw crowds, Skye."

"I think, with Chief Washakie's help, we would."

"Well, the answer's no. I have no funds for a school."

"There's another thing, Major. This tribe needs its own herd. It needs something to replace the buffalo in the diet, and I'd like to see a few cows and a bull each month set aside from the beef allotment and kept on the reservation."

Major Perkins almost reared back. "I'll not permit it. I've a contract with ranchers to bring in thirty beeves a month, and I won't be undercutting these good folks who supply our beef."

Dirk wanted to yell at the man. What beef? The culls and sick animals driven here each month hardly fed anyone. Just putting them on pasture for a month or two would add plenty to the food supply.

"I will discuss that with Chief Washakie, Major. We all want to see these people properly fed and healthy and on their way to living a better life."

"No, Skye, you won't be competing with my suppliers. This tribe will not grow its own beef."

"Then release them to hunt buffalo," Skye said.

"No, if they feed themselves on buffalo meat, they'll take food out of the mouths of the local ranchers."

"You'd prefer that the tribes remain as they are, Major?"

"Exactly as they are, Skye. It's all orderly and peaceful."

"What about the school?"

"It would just be a magnet of discontent and rebellion. It

would be best if it never opened its doors. In fact, I may have it torn down."

"You don't want them to live as white men do?"

"Well, Skye, that's the policy of the Indian Bureau, but we know what the chances are. These are stone-age people, without the wheel, without metal tools. What good would a school do?"

"I'm sure Chief Washakie would be interested in that viewpoint, Major."

Perkins stared. "You done, Skye? You want to register a complaint? Write my bureau? Stir up the Shoshones? Educate some boys?"

"We have one request: unlock the schoolhouse door."

Perkins looked amused. "I might. What's in it for me?"

"Commendation from the Indian Bureau. Anything you can report to Washington about schooling the Shoshones, making them self-supporting on farms and ranches, would win you advancement."

Perkins yawned. "The position doesn't pay, Skye. What's a thousand dollars, eh? A year of toil and grief and isolation for a thousand dollars? And neither does any other in government service. So what if I rise, and become a supervisor for two thousand a year? What if I reach twenty-five hundred a year, and oversee a dozen Indian agents, eh? What if I dine with congressmen and senators, and bring in a chief now and then and present him to the White House? What then, eh? Why would I want to advance, when everything is fine right here?"

Dirk fumed. This was a world he didn't know about, thanks to all the years he was confined in a quiet compound in St. Louis. But he was learning fast, and it was all he could do to let his father, so weary with age, conduct this exchange.

The agent was absolutely in charge, knew exactly what he did not want changed, while he enriched himself.

Dirk wished he knew just how Perkins was doing it. Each month thirty beeves were supposed to arrive, but only twenty-eight actually came, and those were so miserable that two of them hardly equaled one healthy one. Each month each household got a flour and rice allotment, but it was always short. How did the major rake off a cut? Who got the beef and flour? Who paid whom? And here was the major, resisting a tribal herd, resisting a school, resisting even the teaching of agriculture to Dirk's mother's people.

Dirk's father seemed more accepting of this than he should, and Dirk wondered if age had simply weakened his will or dulled his once-powerful sense of moral outrage. He had swiftly come to understand what age had done to Barnaby Skye. The man never stopped hurting. Dirk, at fifteen, could hardly imagine it, a body that hurt all the time, but his own eyes told him that his father lived with some unimaginable pain, and it was softening and withering him.

The major slowly lifted himself to his feet, smiled benignly, as one does in total victory, or perhaps in total power, and nodded. Dirk saw his father nod stiffly, and slowly limp out the door. But the major's gaze was not on the old man, it was on Dirk, educated by the blackrobes, and that gaze was not friendly.

But outside, where a chill wind whipped through their coats, Skye seemed to transform himself.

"Time to talk to the chief," he said. "We're going to go out on the biggest buffalo hunt ever to leave the reservation."

"But we can't!"

"But we will. And you and I are going to lead it. We're headed clear out to the plains. Out near the old Bozeman

Road. Out in Sioux country, where the buffalo are still thick. And we're going to make meat. And make robes. And make jerky and pemmican and lodge covers."

"But we can't without the major's permission!"

"Exactly," said his father.

Dirk stared at a man who suddenly looked twenty years younger.

thirty-five

hief Washakie met them, as was his custom, on his front porch. He listened closely and came to a swift decision.

"I've been a friend of the whites and will continue. I've guided my people in peace. That is my road. I will not send word to join the hunt." But then he paused, a faint smile on his lips. "But I won't resist it."

That was all Skye needed. He thanked the chief and left.

"Saddle up, Dirk, and spread the word, up the valley first. We'll leave early the day after tomorrow from here."

"Where will we be going?"

"To the plains."

Dirk hastened to collect one of his mother's good horses and saddled it. He would be the messenger of a quiet rebellion, hunters leaving the ancestral home to pursue the buffalo, contrary to the express wish of the agent. It tore at him. He had learned much in St. Louis. He admired the Americans and he knew they held the future in their hands. Even their reservation system was at bottom an effort to give his people and other tribes a safe and productive homeland. His mother's people could only bend, and change, or wither away. But here he was, furtively spreading word of a hunt, in defiance of the Indian agent, a man who was backed by the bluebelly soldiers.

How strange and determined Barnaby Skye seemed in that moment. This was not an old man, but a younger one with a will of steel.

North Star rode up the great valley of the Wind River, his message terse and clear: join Skye in the morning of the second sun for a buffalo hunt. Nothing more needed to be said. There were no remaining buffalo on the Wind River Reservation. The Shoshone hunters would arrive with whatever weapons they could manage, saddle horses, and travois horses. If the weather was good, and the hunting was good, they would bring back frozen quarters of buffalo on those travois. If the weather was warm, they would bring back jerky or pemmican. It would fill bellies during the long winter descending on them.

He found The Runner's lodge and stopped to give word to his uncle, who spoke an odd Elizabethan English derived from his self-study of a collection of Shakespeare's tragedies.

"Prithee what news?" The Runner asked, upon discovering his nephew at his camp.

"My father is organizing a buffalo hunt, and he'll leave the morning of the second sun. All are welcome."

"And where doth he intend to go?"

"The plains."

The Runner pondered that, looking grave. The Shoshones were ancient enemies of the plains tribes. He was not a young man, and his memory stretched back into the hazy past. There was white blood in him because he was a grandson of

Charbonneau, and that was one reason Dirk felt close to him, and to his mother. The mixed-bloods were a people apart.

"It is something to be considered," The Runner said. "A trial fraught with peril."

He was talking about the United States Army, which had a small detachment right there on the reservation, near the agency buildings. It had started up as Camp Brown. "The plains, you say? That which was ceded to the Sioux?"

Dirk nodded. Double the jeopardy, the army and the Sioux.

"Is thy father, the honored Mister Skye, in possession of his senses?"

"He is twenty years younger now than he was yesterday."

"I will think on it," The Runner said.

On a frosty morning a dozen or so Shoshone men of all ages, plus several women, gradually collected at the cabin. They brought riding and travois ponies, and whatever weapons were at hand. Dirk had never hunted before, and now he examined these skilled hunters and warriors with respect. He would help with the skinning, or any other way he could. His schooling had taught him much, but not such as this.

In air as sharp as needles they proceeded toward the Wind River, directly under the eyes of the two platoons of soldiers at the army camp, but they paid no heed. The soldiers were busy erecting a new post, which was the true occupation of most enlisted men on the frontier. The comings and goings of a few Shoshones didn't interest them. Skye wanted it that way; everything out in the open. Dirk rode easily, but not comfortably because the icy wind whipped the heat from him. In time they made the river, far out of sight of the soldiers, and proceeded downstream through the majestic valley, flanked by some of the highest mountains in the Rockies. No one stayed them. Dirk half expected a squad of bluecoats to ride them down and turn them back, but it never happened.

For two days they rode east toward the plains, mostly under cast-iron-gray heavens that threatened to spill snow or icy rain over them. His mother rode comfortably; old Victoria hunched on her pony as if she had lived there all her life, and his father seemed more alive than ever. The Runner and the other Shoshones began to enjoy themselves, and one of them shot a buck that would provide some good camp meat for this large group. These people, Dirk realized, were poor. They could not renew or repair their buffalo-skin clothing because they could not reach the buffalo. They lacked funds to buy wool or cloth, and their allotments scarcely kept them warm. A few had old fusils or smoothbore rifles; only two or three had a modern weapon. Others were well armed with bows and arrows, and a few had lances.

Somewhere or other they crossed the invisible line; Dirk had no idea where it was, and the Shoshones understood it only vaguely. But they were no longer on their reservation, no longer within the "homeland" that the United States government gave them, along with two platoons of soldiers to keep them at home. Just where those lines ran was something Chief Washakie probably knew, but few of these Shoshones knew, and couldn't fathom invisible medicine lines anyway. It was a good home, but it also was a prison without walls, and white men were claiming every inch of land outside of those medicine lines.

The sparkling river took them east, and when it curved north toward the gloomy canyon that guarded the Big Horn River basin, the hunters abandoned the stream and continued toward the plains where the buffalo were thick. They slept out-of-doors, building brush wickiups against the icy nights, and relying on their robes for warmth. Dirk watched Skye and Victoria, fearful that the hardships of the trail would weary them. It was painful to watch his father ride, with his stiff leg poking out, always unbalancing him. His eyes were so bad that Dirk wondered if the old man would hit anything he shot at with an old muzzleloader he had somehow gotten. His birth mother found ways to ease the toil of the elders, but Victoria kept shooing her away, not yet ready to surrender to great age.

The cold weather held, and that was a blessing. Ice skinned the puddles each morning, and rimmed creek banks. Frozen meat would keep. But then one afternoon the thing he dreaded most fell upon them. A patrol of blue-clad cavalry soldiers cantered up and stopped, examining Skye and his cohort. Some of the Shoshones were taut and ready for trouble. The patrol's commander, surprisingly a major with oak leaves on his shoulders, looked dashing, with mustachios and side-burns, and merry blue eyes.

The officer addressed Skye. "Shoshones, I take it."

"Chief Washakie's people," Skye said. "I'm Mister Skye, and these are my wives Victoria and Mary, and my son, Dirk."

"Mister Skye, is it? That name's known, sir, from ocean to ocean. I'm Dedham Graves, sir. Call me Ded."

"Dead Graves?"

"Dedham Morpheus Graves. It runs in the family. My mother is Passionflower Nightshade Graves. My father was Oak Coffin Graves." He eyed the Shoshones and their dozen travois ponies. "Out for a Sunday stroll, are you?"

"It's a good day for a stroll, sir."

"Ah, Mister Skye, I can't let you stroll over to Sioux coun-try. Ever since the Honorable Red Cloud licked the United

States Army, they've been testy about wandering Shoshones and other undesirables sampling their private larder."

"That makes it hard on us, sir. We're some short of meat."

"Short of meat, are you? Don't you get thirty beeves a month?"

"We're supposed to, but it comes out to a regular twenty-eight, and culls at that. Not enough meat on them to feed half these people for one week."

Major Graves eyed him. "How about the other rations?"

"Always short, sir. The agent blames his suppliers."

"Perkins does that, does he? Who supplies the beef?"

"Big Horn Basin people, sir, as far as we know."

"Yardley Dogwood. We've had a few spats with him. He doesn't want any Yank blue-belly soldiers on his rangeland."

"I thought he might be the one, sir."

"He has the contract, all right. I don't know who has the contract for the flour and sugar and all that." Major Graves stared into the cold blue sky. "The army would like to see the Indians well fed and happy on their reserves, and learning to take care of themselves."

"Then you'll let us continue our Sunday stroll."

"I hear tell there's a few buffalo along the foothills of the Big Horn. You might take your Sunday stroll that way, steering well clear of Yardley Dogwood, of course."

"We'll do that, Major."

"I know a place," Mary said. "In our tongue it is mee-teetse, the place of meeting."

"Very good, madam." Major Graves smiled cheerfully. "I must report this, Mister Skye. I'll let my superiors know I had a pleasant visit with you and your family who were out on a picnic."

He wheeled his horse to lead his parade, and then looked back.

"Mister Skye, don't confuse Dogwood's longhorns for wild game. It would cause no end of trouble."

"My eyesight's getting bad, Major. Never know what I'm shooting these days. I can't even tell if it's two-footed or four-footed."

The major laughed and wheeled his patrol west.

Victoria looked irritated. "When white men talk, I don't understand nothing," she said.

"He said he won't report us, and don't get caught."

"Then why didn't the sonofabitch just say it?"

"Politeness, I imagine."

"I'll never understand you crazy people," she muttered.

Skye turned his party north, where he would intercept the Bridger Road and could follow it into the great valley to the north.

"Dirk," he said, "tell our people that all's well. We can hunt, but not where the Sioux are buzzing."

Dirk let the others catch up, and quietly explained that the army didn't mind, and this hunting party would slip north, past the ranch there, and look for buffalo in the hidden draws near the Place of Meeting.

If the conversation with Major Graves had fascinated Victoria, it has fascinated Dirk even more. Here was something his schooling by the Jesuits had not touched upon, an entire visit in which the principal concerns of each party were scarcely addressed. Skye wanted to lead his hunters to the plains but didn't say it. Graves wanted to know why the Shoshones were off the reservation but didn't say it. Skye wanted the major to know that the food allotments were seriously short, but made no accusations. Graves wanted them to know that this state of affairs justified a hunt, with the army's blessing, but didn't say it that way. And the major said he would consider all this a Sunday stroll, and a chance encounter with Skye and his family.

Why hadn't the conversation been direct and open? Dirk grasped that there was a world among white men he knew nothing about, and his father was a master of it, using innuendo and guile, even as the major did.

Skye led them into the Big Horn Basin over the next days, where they cut west, keeping a sharp eye out for Yardley Dogwood's drovers. But it was a vast basin, and they never sighted the Dogwood company, even as they skirted the western foothills until they arrived in the place his mother called meeteetse, or meeting place, and found buffalo hidden in the nearby ravines.

thirty-six

The hunt required only minutes. The butchering took the afternoon. They dined on tender, hot buffalo tongue that night, while the chill wind froze the quarters of three cows and two bulls. Never had meat tasted so fine. Never had they been so happy. They watched sparks fly into the heavens, and sang songs and settled into their robes. The world was good. The next dawn they left for the reservation with as much meat as they could carry or drag, all frozen solid. It would be a bounty for the hungry people on the reservation. People would laugh and smile once again. Two days later, not far from the reservation line, they ran into a patrol from the reservation, led by Captain Orestes Wall.

"The agent's some put-out that you left the reservation without permission, Skye."

"It's Mister Skye, Captain Wall."

"Well, whatever. Major Perkins requested me to confiscate any meat."

"Is it his intent to starve the Shoshones?"

"No, he wishes to teach you a certain lesson."

"There are over four hundred Shoshones on the reservation, sir. They receive twenty-eight culled beeves a month. Most of each month they have no meat. And live on short rations."

"You don't have to explain, Skye. I'll have to take that meat."

Bitterness flared in Skye, but he contained it. "All right then," he said. "We'll leave it here for you."

"No, bring it along."

A sorry parade of Shoshones, their spirits bleak and their hunting triumph ruined, rode wearily toward the Wind River Agency, escorted by soldiers with carbines in their sheaths. The soldiers wore heavy blue overcoats. The People wrapped blankets or old robes about themselves and hunkered deep into them. At some point they crossed the invisible line, a line scarcely understood by these people. The mounted infantry rode to either side, pinning the Shoshones between them, as if they feared that these people, dragging a heavy load of meat and buffalo hides, would escape.

"Bastards," hissed Victoria.

Captain Wall heard her and stared.

Skye eyed her. She was worn from the butchering, and so was Mary. Their dresses were smeared with blood and offal. Dirk stared bitterly at the soldiers, saying nothing, but Skye knew things were brewing in the boy's head. They had worked hard in a cruel wind to gut and skin and quarter the buffalo, wanting it done before the gore froze to their hands. Maybe it was all for nothing.

They rode under a cast-iron sky, past cottonwoods naked of leaf, past reeds and rushes faintly red or orange. Snow lay in patches on the hilltops. That last dozen miles was hard and cold, and worse, it was angry. The hunters fumed, whispered to one another, eyed the soldiers with frank bitterness, and Skye imagined some of them were thinking of causing trouble. He hoped they wouldn't.

At last the whitewashed agency buildings hove into sight. The wind was whipping the chimney fires downward, making the smoke crawl the tawny grasses. The army camp lay a half mile upriver. Major Perkins saw the sorry party coming, and was waiting for Skye on his veranda, dressed in a thick long buffalo coat with a hood.

The hunting party paused before him, and the soldiers spread out, ready for trouble and expecting it.

"Sorry about your meat, Skye, but you took my wards off the reservation."

"There's no game on the reservation, Major. Every last deer's gone. There's no elk or bear or wolves or coyotes or foxes or marmots or beaver, either."

"What is that supposed to mean?"

"There's no beef either, because two are missing each month and the rest are hardly worth slaughtering."

"So?"

"And not much flour or sugar or beans or rice, because not enough reaches here, or maybe enough does but it doesn't reach these people."

"Enough of this." Perkins addressed the captain, "Take the meat to the camp. It's yours."

Slowly, wearily, Skye dismounted, favoring his bum leg. He limped to one of the travois horses and settled himself on the heavy load of meat. The travois bent under him.

"Over my dead body," he said.

Dirk jumped off his horse and threw himself over another travois. "And mine," he shouted.

"Skye," Wall shouted. "Get off of there."

"You heard me."

Victoria staggered off her horse and threw herself over another travois. Mary descended to the ground and swiftly unhaltered a travois horse.

"Skye, I'm warning you," Captain Wall roared. "Get off. Get your family off."

But then The Runner leaped to the ground and threw himself against a packhorse carrying a quarter of a cow. And the rest of the hunting party leaped to guard the remaining meat and hides.

"Over our dead bodies," The Runner said, sonorously, in a voice that oddly carried deep into the afternoon.

Wall turned to his squad. "Withdraw arms. Load and aim."

Reluctantly, the unhappy bluecoats unsheathed their Springfield carbines and leveled them at the hunters, at Skye and Victoria and Mary and Dirk.

"Now get off," Wall snapped.

Skye stared at the black barrels pointing toward him, the dark bores ready to spit flame.

"I suppose my time's come," he said. He did not move.

The Indian agent slid to the side, getting out of the line of fire.

A gust of wind caught the flag, flapping it hard, until it snapped and crackled in the gale. Wall glanced at it, at the Skyes, at the hunters, and at the agent, who looked frightened.

He turned to his men. "Sheath your weapons," he said.

His frightened bluecoats swiftly returned their weapons to their saddle sheaths.

"Take your meat to your people, Skye," Wall said.

"Insubordination!" the agent said.

"Yes, Mr. Perkins, it is that, all right."

Skye waited until every carbine was sheathed, and glared furiously at Dirk who began to stir. Dirk caught the glare and stayed quiet, his body across the buffalo quarter.

"Now, Captain Wall?" Skye asked gently.

"Now, Mister Skye."

Mary addressed her Shoshones and told them they could go, divide the meat, give to the poorest, and sing a song this evening.

Skye listened.

Wall turned again to his men. "We'll ride to the post now and let these people feed themselves and their kin."

The soldiers looked relieved. They knew these Shoshones as friends and neighbors, knew them by name. Slowly, they wheeled their horses about and rode to their encampment.

Skye lifted his old top hat and settled it, an ancient salute. He hurt again. He never stopped hurting.

Perkins retreated to his lair, slamming the door behind him. Skye watched the windows, fearful that something bad might yet befall them, but he saw no sudden menace crowding any window frame.

Victoria, old and gray and worn, walked to Skye and pressed her gnarled hand in his.

"You are a brave man," she said.

"You and Mary and Dirk give me courage," he replied.

She turned to Dirk. "Goddamn, you're a man," she said.

Dirk seemed to straighten and stand taller. He, too, had put his life on the line for his mother's people. Skye eyed his son, who eyed him back, and something fine passed between them.

Mary caught the shoulders of her son and gazed deep into his eyes, and then released the youth. Skye and his wives all knew that at this moment, the youth had passed into manhood. Maybe Dirk understood that too.

They found the cabin numbingly cold, and there was no wood for a fire. Victoria, too weary to go hunt for some, sank to the robes and pulled one over her. Wordlessly, Mary collected a hatchet and started for the door, but Dirk stayed her.

"I'll find some," he said.

Mary gratefully gave him the hatchet. Deadwood was now more than an hour distant, and it would be a long time before Dirk returned with enough for a fire. They had a buffalo tongue to boil, if only they could start up the stove.

Skye peered around the dreary cabin, wishing he had a lodge, where a small flame in the middle of the cone soon spread its delight. He sat down beside Mary, as worn as she, and drew a blanket around him, but it didn't offer much comfort.

At great peril he had won a small victory this afternoon, but it was no victory at all. A darkness hung over the Wind River Reservation, a homeland that was really a prison, where they were starting to starve. Maybe, if he could summon the strength, he could take his family back to the Crows, who still roamed freely in buffalo country. Not that the Crows' freedom would last long, either.

There was no escape from the encircling darkness. He slumped wearily, favoring his bad leg, and waited for Dirk. Even Mary, much younger, gave up her toil and climbed under a robe, trying to ward off the damp, rank cold of the cabin, a cold that reached right to the bones.

What had life come to? For the first time in all his years, giving up life seemed seductive to Skye. He stared at Victoria, and found her staring at him in the gloom, their unspoken thoughts plain to each other.

They were startled by a sharp knock. Mary rose swiftly, while Skye was still struggling, and opened to Captain Wall, who stood there with an orderly behind him.

More trouble, apparently.

"May I have a word?" the captain asked.

This was the man who only a while before had ordered carbines drawn and aimed at all of them. Skye nodded curtly.

Wall stepped in, noted the coldness, and the dead stove.

"No wood?"

"My son is getting some."

Wall turned to his orderly. "Bring these people an armload of firewood, and don't forget some kindling."

"Yes, sir," the private said, and hastened into the gloom.

"We have no chairs, sir," Skye said.

Victoria sat on the ground, her robes around her. She looked gray.

"A lodge would be more comfortable than this, Mister Skye."

"Yes, sir." Skye wondered what this was about. Maybe an apology, though the army never apologized for anything, including massacres of red men.

Captain Wall stood awkwardly, and then slowly settled himself on the cold clay. "You'll have some warmth soon, Mister Skye."

Skye waited, not much caring what might be transpiring.

Wall was an older man, trapped by the army's glacial promotions, and not far from retirement. He had been breveted a colonel during the recent war. Now he was filling time at a lonely post. Skye knew that much about him, and had no wish to know more.

"This isn't right, Mister Skye. Not right at all, and the army is caught in the middle of it."

That faintly surprised Skye.

"Have the Shoshones been getting their full allotments?"

"No, Captain. Not even close."

"Let's start with the meat. The reservation is supposed to receive thirty cattle a month in good flesh."

"That's never happened, sir."

"Right you are, Mister Skye. Twenty-eight, and most of them so poor you'd get more meat off a deer. What about the grains?"

"The people here don't have scales, and many don't know what a pound or a gallon is. They take what's given them by Perkins and his two assistants."

"Badly short?"

"Not what was guaranteed in the treaty."

"How do you know that?"

"I spent much of my life in the fur trade, Captain. I'm familiar with every trading post trick in the books. The thumb on the scale, the finger in the measuring cup, the miscount or misweighing."

The orderly returned, bearing wood, was admitted, and swiftly built a fire and lit it. There would still be a long wait before any heat permeated this chill room.

"Thank you, Corporal, you may return to the post," Wall said.

The mustachioed corporal nodded and retreated into the twilight.

"Now again, Mister Skye, if you'd oblige me with a few more answers. Do you know whether these shipments are short when they get here, or something is held back?"

"They're short when they arrive, Captain. There never are thirty cattle."

"Mr. Perkins's books acknowledge receiving thirty."

"I never see anything shipped out, and I've never seen anything held back in the warehouses, Captain."

"Yes, it's all accomplished elsewhere. The army's looking into a few things, including large increases in his accounts in Washington. Have you or your people anything to add?"

"Yes, goddammit," Victoria said. "There's not a deer or elk or other game left. It's all been hunted away inside the invisible lines."

"We don't even have firewood," Mary said. "Before, we could move our lodges to firewood and game."

That seemed to end the discussion. The captain stood, hat in hand. "I deeply regret what happened today. The army is supposed to heed the directions of the agent in a time of crisis. I came to my senses much too late." He paused, in the midst of the deep silence. "We're looking into Major Perkins."

Skye nodded.

"You've answered the questions we had in mind. Perhaps we can help matters."

"Thanks for the firewood, Captain. Nothing could be more welcome than that wood."

The captain nodded curtly.

The beginnings of warmth began to fill the cabin as the stove popped and the fire within it began to crackle.

Skye was slow to his feet, but Mary showed the captain to the door.

Skye slid back into his robes, grateful for the tender heat.

thirty-seven

$\mathcal{E}$arly snow blanketed the valley and brightened the distant peaks. It grew harder and harder to heat the cabin. Dirk collected the half-starved ponies and threw packsaddles over them, and added an axe. He was forced to travel two miles to wood now; others were competing for the deadwood. His days were filled with little but hiking up slopes to find deadwood, hacking it to pieces, loading it onto his pack frames and tying it down, and returning to the cabin, where the stove ate his wood at a terrifying pace.

This cabin, erected by The Runner, had been located near the agency buildings but far from forest. Mary's brother was better off, living in a lodge the traditional way, able to move his household to fresh woodlots. And it was easy to stay comfortable in a lodge, with only a small fire. Dirk wondered what sort of nightmarish life he had returned to; nothing here resembled what he remembered from his earliest years.

Victoria looked gray, and spent her time in the buffalo robes, lost in deep silence. And Skye seemed old, or at least worn down, and unable to help much. So it befell Dirk and his mother to care for the older ones. Skye talked now and then of going back to the Crow people, and living out on the plains with them. There still were buffalo there, and the army left them alone even if the Sioux didn't. Skye knew now that his lodge had been cached on the Yellowstone, and it would probably still be there. The thought of going north tantalized them, but the weather was not cooperating, and they had too little food. Dirk knew little about hunting, and Skye's eyesight was weakening, and Victoria's strength with her bow was declining. So the whole idea of abandoning this miserable place seemed never to take wing, and they endured from day to day.

For a few days after the hunt they feasted on buffalo tongue, their share of the meat, but it was long gone and they hadn't seen meat since. It was said that the supplier, Yardley Dogwood, had not bothered to show up with animals when they were due December the first, and there would be no meat at all in December.

There were muted things happening at the agency; couriers coming and going, bluecoated military men in and out. But these events did not bear upon the Shoshones, who were struggling to get through a hard winter. Dirk thought that if things didn't improve, they would all soon be eating horses. But there was no fodder for the horses, and they were slowly starving their way toward spring, sometimes gnawing on green cottonwood bark to make a living. What sort of life was this? A life imposed by white men bent on making all this land their own, no matter who had first claimed it.

Then one day half a dozen cavalrymen arrived at the post, along with some freight wagons. Skye watched from a great distance, sometimes standing at the door of the cabin, but rarely venturing into the snow, which he found treacherous with his bad leg. Mary watched a moment also, and returned to her housekeeping. She had learned something of making things from flour, and was making flat, round loaves of Indian bread employing grease and flour, to sustain them all. The gray skies seemed lower, the days shorter, the dark more pervasive, and Dirk took it as a sign. He had come all the way from comfortable St. Louis—to this.

But one morning, the first sunny one in a week, that cavalry officer, Major Dedham Graves, came to call on foot, having negotiated a half mile of snowy turf.

Dirk remembered the man well. His mother admitted Graves, whose glance took in the state of affairs, lack of furnishings, the two older people swathed in buffalo robes as they sat against a gloomy log wall in deep cold. Graves settled on the clay floor near them, his eyes as bright and cheerful as the day they first encountered one another.

"Mister Skye, sir, it's my pleasure to bring some good news. At least the army thinks it's good news."

"I'm glad to hear it," Skye said.

"In a nutshell, we've cashiered Perkins. He was a bad lot, and we were able to catch him in wholesale peculation, and even as we speak he's being ejected from the agency and is being sent packing."

"Say that in words I've heard of," Victoria snapped.

"Perkins is a crook. We've gotten rid of him. He was raking off about thirty percent of everything. That's most of the reason the people here haven't gotten their full share. Others made a few dollars too, Yardley Dogwood was one. And some other scoundrels. So there's change afoot. The reservation is about to have a new agent. He's been appointed, in Washington, if he agrees to a few stipulations."

"If the people get their full measure, and if this is not a prison for them, that's all I care about," Skye said. "The actual agent is of no consequence to me."

"I'm talking about you, Mister Skye."

Skye bolted upright.

"Annual stipend, a thousand dollars."

"Me?"

"We've been burning up the telegraph lines. The Indian Bureau wants you. Army wants you. Some of your fur trade friends were excellent agents for their people. William Bent, Tom Fitzpatrick. So will you be."

Skye clambered to his feet, staggering a little on his bad leg. "I'm a wreck. How can I perform my duties with this?" He jabbed a finger at his leg.

"Broken-Hand Fitzpatrick didn't have any trouble."

Dirk was agog. This thing filled this gloomy little room and threatened to burst outside.

Major Graves played his ace. "Ask your wives, Mister Skye. They rule the nest."

"Rule the nest, do they? I'll send you packing out that door if you . . ."

Victoria was looking smug. "Take it, Skye."

"We're hoping you'll look after these good people, and see that they're properly cared for. The army wants nothing more than some happy Shoshones, working with their great chief, Washakie. We're calling the post Fort Washakie. Only army post in the country named for a chief. You'd better sign up and help these people."

Skye was standing now, his face more grave than Dirk had ever seen it. "It's an obligation," he said. "You might not like what I'll be doing. Your government might not like it."

"That brings up another matter, Skye. Citizenship." He

reached into his portfolio and withdrew some papers. "You'll need to sign here, and I'll administer the oath."

"Citizenship?" Skye said.

"We can't appoint a Briton to be our Shoshone Indian agent, Mister Skye."

A dead silence fell over the room. Dirk knew all about Skye's occasional bitterness toward the Yanks, his habit of cursing Yank folly, his scalding comments about the way Yanks treated Indian people. But there always was more. His father had some difficulties with his own England, with its class and caste system. He always insisted on being called Mister Skye because in the New World any man was entitled to be a mister, a man on the same footing as anyone else.

Graves quietly dipped into his portfolio and withdrew a stoppered ink vial, and a steel-nib pen, and handed them to Skye.

"I can hardly see this thing," Skye muttered.

"You know, sometimes, Skye, the army manages to do things right." Graves withdrew half a dozen wire-rimmed spectacles. "Try 'em."

Skye did, one after the other, found a good one, and slowly his face lit up. "I hardly could see."

"Read it, Mister Skye. You commit yourself to citizenship in the Republic of the United States of America."

Skye looked remarkable, Dirk thought, almost eagle-eyed, his gaze focused on the document, his new spectacles propped on the majestic prow of his nose. He read, stared off into space for a little, and nodded. "Does this make my wives and son citizens too?"

"Your son was born here and already is. Your wives, by virtue of marriage to you, are eligible, and can make that choice anytime."

Dirk had never thought of himself as a citizen before. He had thought of himself as a Londoner's son. It amazed him. He was a Yankee.

Skye unstoppered the ink flask, dipped the nib, and scratched his name.

"I'll witness it, Mister Skye, and congratulations," Major Graves said. The officer added his signature.

"Now, sir, another small matter. This is an employment agreement. You'll agree to uphold the laws and Constitution of the United States, and to proceed under the direction of the Bureau of Indian Affairs. Your annual stipend will be deposited wherever you wish. You will have the use of the agency residence, the agency offices, the agency horses and buggy and wagon, and will also receive expense allowances for lamp oil, firewood, office supplies, and the like. You can move in at once. Perkins is off the reservation, and the staff have prepared your house."

Skye skimmed through the agreement, and signed.

Dirk marveled. Was this commanding man the same one whose old face was etched with fatigue and loss only a while before? Was this old woman, beside him, once so gray and worn, now this eagle? And was his own worn mother, Blue Dawn, so tall and proud ever before?

"I can weather a few years," his father said. "If I can put this place on a sound footing, and help these people find a way to live, and defend them from predators, and give them something to live for, well, Captain, that would be all that a man could ask of his remaining days."

"Mister Skye, half the things you want your superiors will veto. Or Congress won't fund. But you probably know that."

"Will I be able to call on the army, Captain?"

"No, not for much. The army's in worse shape than the Indian Bureau."

"Has Chief Washakie been told of this?"

"We thought to tell you first."

"Will you tell him?"

"He's our next stop. We needed to find out whether you would accept."

"Hey, how did this happen, eh?" Victoria asked.

"We knew Erastus Perkins was . . . pocketing whatever he could. But that's not what you mean, Madam Skye. You mean, how did your man get chosen, I take it. Your husband's a known man, I assure you. He's lived among your people all his adult life. He's fought at your side. He's fought us, sometimes. He's known for, what'll I say? Grace, let's say grace. An odd idea being mouthed from some old soldier, close to retirement. Grace it is. If any man can help your people, madam, he can. He knows us, and he knows you. He knows what to tell us, what's gone wrong, what won't work, what violates your deepest beliefs. There are some in the Indian Bureau who want to turn all of you into white men, but Mister Skye here is going to say no to them, and is going to help find a way of life that fits with who you are and what you believe." Graves paused. "I'm told that no one in Washington dissented. Not one."

Mary said, "Will my people now cross the invisible lines?"

"I think the new agent will allow it, don't you? But, madam, I wish to offer you a somewhat different idea. Those boundary lines are there to keep white men out, not keep you in."

Oddly, Dirk didn't much care for all this. One man, Skye, could not bend the will of the Yankee government. This would only mean no change, but now a man friendly to the

Shoshones, and bound by marriage to them, would be telling them what to do and how to live. Now his old and ailing father would be an instrument of the Indian Bureau. It might all work out, and at least his father and mothers would be comfortable. But what would a mixed-blood man do with his life?

thirty-eight

Within the hour, army teamsters had moved the few possessions of the Skyes into the agency house, even as Mary and Victoria wandered through the small frame building, noting its kitchen, parlor, two bedrooms each with two narrow cast-iron bedsteads, and outhouse out back.

Two young Shoshones appeared, one a deaf-mute girl named Keewa, who understood sign language, and her mate, going by the name of The Walker, a general factotum whose days were largely devoted to cutting firewood for the agency house as well as the agency offices.

Dirk watched his weary father stare at the object of his desire for many months, a bed with a mattress, a haven for his aching body. His mothers, by some agreement, took one of the bedrooms, leaving the other to Skye and Dirk. Skye settled in a chair; his face filled with pleasure. He had scarcely sat in a chair his entire adult life, and often squatted on his heels, in the fashion of the mountains, until age and stiffness kept him from it. But now his father settled in a Morris chair, and then rose to try a horsehair settee, and then a straight-backed dining chair, all with such childlike joy that Dirk realized at last what pain meant to an old man, and how relief from pain could be a life goal and vision all in itself.

Skye even wandered to the two-hole outhouse, and settled on a seat in wonder, and then retreated to the warm agency residence. The mute girl followed anxiously, eager to please, and Dirk thought she might have been abused. Victoria watched her, and employed the ancient sign talk of the plains to tell the girl that she was welcome, all was well, and she was appreciated. She and her man had quarters at the back of the agency building, which they cleaned.

But something was gnawing at Dirk, and it had to do with this sudden luxury, while just beyond these walls his mother's people, his own people, were struggling to stay warm and fed. But after a grateful tour of the premises, Skye asked how much wood there was.

Dirk hastened out to the woodlot, and found what he thought was two cords.

"Tomorrow, early, harness the team, load half of that wood in the agency wagon, and take it to our people."

Somehow, Dirk's anguish eased. This would be Skye's first official act.

The whitewashed house was small, not grand, but it seemed a palace to the Skyes, especially that first night when each of them slept on a cotton-stuffed mattress in a warm house. True to his charge, Dirk arose before dawn, found the agency's barn and harness and draft horses, and soon began loading wood, until he thought he had half of it.

When he returned to the house, he found all his parents were up and cheerful.

"How did you sleep, Papa?"

Skye yawned and smiled. "Maybe I'll go back for another round," he said.

His wives laughed.

"Goddamn white men need soft beds," Victoria said. "So do old Absaroka women."

They looked uncommonly cheerful while Mary brewed some coffee.

Dirk drove into a frosty dawn, crystal-white haze on top of a thin cover of snow, and made his way up the valley, the two draft animals exhaling steam. Dirk knew where to go: the isolated cabins dotting the great valley. But he found no one present at the first place, the stove cold; and the pattern repeated itself as he drove upriver. Then he discovered an encampment next to some woodlands, traditional lodges bleeding white smoke into a white sky, and he knew the people had solved their firewood troubles their own way, by returning to their traditional ways. Some lodges had been cut up to make moccasins and shirts and coats, but enough remained to shelter the Shoshones. He drove to the encampment and made a symbolic gift of a piece of dry wood to each household, including his uncle, The Runner, and in each case he told his people that his father would be their agent and this was his gift to them. This would be a good day, he thought. A very good day. The people, mostly wrapped in blankets or buffalo robes, smiled their greetings, and then set out to share the great news with all the rest. And so the trip to deliver firewood turned out to be an announcement.

His last call that morning was at Chief Washakie's home. The youth carried the gift of wood to the door, but the chief was waiting for him.

"It is a fine morning, North Star. I have heard the good news," Washakie said.

"Grandfather, it is my father's wish that each Shoshone household receive the gift of firewood from him."

"Ah, warmth. It is a fine gift. Warmth, North Star, is more of a gift than any other."

Washakie took the firewood and hefted it, and smiled. "You will come in now," he said.

North Star knew it was a command. He tied the harness lines to a post and entered. The chief motioned him to a seat, and vanished into the kitchen for a moment.

"The ladies will bring us tea," he said.

North Star nodded, wondering what all this was about, as the chief settled himself on the horsehair sofa.

"It is a good thing, our friend Mister Skye becoming our agent. My heart is lifted up."

"Mine too, Grandfather. There will be more food delivered on each allotment day."

Washakie stared into the brightness of the winter's day outside. "I despise allotments, North Star. They make beggars of us. We wait in line for handouts from the Yankee government. Do you know what I am saying?"

North Star did. The monthly dole of food had reduced this proud people to helplessness. Several times, North Star had watched his mother's folk shuffle through the line, be checked off by officious bookkeepers, and then receive a little of this and that, and drift away to live out their lives without purpose.

"The Shoshone People are broken," North Star said.

"I work ceaselessly for the day when there will be no allotments, and nothing is handed to my people," Washakie said. "And I know what must come. We must have our own herds, and plow our own fields, and then we will have food enough. That is how your father's people stay alive through the times when there are no berries and roots to gather, and the times when there are no buffalo or deer or elk to be found."

North Star sensed this was leading somewhere, and it would be best just to let the seamed old chief take the meeting wherever it would be taken. It didn't take long.

"We need more than allotments; we need the wisdom of the white men. They are very wise. They live with grain stored against hunger, wood against the winter, and cattle that can be slaughtered as needed. They have commerce, in which those who have skills produce one thing, and those with different gifts produce another, and they use money to make trades. This is good."

A girl returned bearing a tray with a teapot and cups. She was a beautiful girl, with blueberry eyes and jet hair and golden cheeks. She eyed North Star with demure curiosity, but he caught her glancing at him, and she caught his swift glances that absorbed everything about her. She wore a white velvet ribbon at the end of each of her two braids.

"North Star, this is my youngest daughter, whose name is Mona, and the reason I am keeping you here, even though I am sure you wish to return to your father and mothers, is to ask something of you."

Mona passed steaming tea to each man, and shyly vanished into the rear of the little white house.

The chief lifted the teacup. "I will sip in honor of this day, and of our good fortune, and of the appointment of Mister Skye," he said.

North Star followed the ritual, and smiled.

"It is my wish that all of my people be educated in all the mysteries of the white men. Some things about them are excellent. Some things make me wary, and some things worry me. But they are the future, and they have wonders we did not know, guns and wheels and metal and marks on paper they can turn into words. It is my wish, North Star, that you will tutor us all, and especially my daughter Mona. And if you will set a time early each morning, I will have us all gathered here, in the parlor, and we will receive your instruction. I would like for us to learn something of each of the things you know. Would you do it?"

"Grandfather—"

"We will share some of our allotment with you."

"But, Grandfather, I don't know much. I didn't finish the schooling. The blackrobes still had more to teach me."

Washakie smiled slightly. "I thought you might at least teach what you know. It is more than we know. Mona is very eager to learn everything you might have to show her."

"I would be pleased to teach her, Grandfather."

"Ah, North Star, it is done, then. Now, we will be ready when the sun first shows himself, and we will learn from you. A little while each morning, if that is suitable."

"It is, sir."

The chief rose smoothly, and escorted North Star to the door.

The young man turned at the last, and saw Mona shyly peering from within.

"Grandfather, tell Mona I will be pleased to teach her everything I've been taught."

"I thought you might, North Star."

He untied the harness lines and returned to the agency with an empty wagon, the backs of his dray horses frosted, and after he had cared for the animals he entered their new house. And there, once again, was that Major Graves.

"Ah, young Mister Skye, this is fortunate. I came looking for you."

Dirk stood uneasily, wondering what he had done wrong.

"It was the Quakers, the Society of Friends, that got it done," Graves said.

Dirk had scarcely heard of them. Some sort of Pennsylvania society that was attempting to help western Indians cope with the tide of settlement. Dirk didn't know what to say.

"The school, my boy, the school. Would you like to teach?"

"Teach? Teach who or what? Why do you think I'm qualified?"

"They have it from the Jesuits that you'd do just fine, and could teach the ABCs, writing, composition, arithmetic, including addition, subtraction, multiplication, and division, and you'd be just fine with history, some geography, mechanics, religious instruction, and moral instruction."

"But who?"

"These good people. Here at the agency, in the government schoolhouse."

Dirk felt the weight of his youth on him. "I'm not sure I'm the one, sir."

"Ah, young Mister Skye, do you want to? Would you like to see these people master the skills they'll need in the future?"

Dirk stared out the window. A part of him said that he only wished the government would leave his mother's people alone to continue as they always had. But another part of him knew the world would never be the same.

"Yes, sir, I would."

"The Quakers can't afford much. It's all subscription for them, but they'll pay twenty dollars a month, and of course the government will supply the schoolhouse and teacherage, and handle basic expenses."

"But where are the slates, and primers, and all that?"

"Ah, a sticky business. My officer colleagues at Fort Laramie have rustled up some readers, a few slates and chalk, a few pencils and some paper. Enough to start. The Quakers are working on it, but it won't be until spring before you'll be adequately equipped."

"You think a person my age would be accepted, sir?"

His mother replied at once. "North Star, you are a man."

He had not thought of himself as a man, but now he would be stepping into a man's job. He would need patience and courage and idealism. He would need to persuade young people his own age to come to his class, learn, and make use of what they learned. There would be immediate utility in it: they could make their grievances known. They could make sure whatever agent governed them was acting justly.

"Let's go look at the goddamned place," Victoria said.

They rose at once, wrapped shawls and robes about them, and hiked across a snowy reach to the school, where Skye let them in. This place was a single room, with a potbellied stove, student desks, windows out upon a snowy world, and little else. But it came alive, even as Dirk walked the creaking wood floors. It came alive with Shoshone faces, young and old, with the radiant heat of the stove, with pretty girls and seamed old men, with ponies tied to the hitchrail outside. He would give them what he could. He would try to teach a practical education, so they might operate businesses, raise meat and grains, supply wood, build roads, repair wagons, and all the rest.

"Major Graves, I will do this," he said.

"The teacherage is yours if you want it."

"Maybe someday. Just now, I want to help my parents."

"Yes, helping Major Skye would be a welcome service," Graves said.

"Major? Major?" Skye asked.

"A courtesy rank, sir. Indian agents are commonly called major."

"Not I, Major Graves. I am Mister Skye. I have always been Mister Skye, a man without rank. To the day I die I will be Mister Skye."